IN RIO'S SHADOWS

(Women Of Strength Series Book 1)

Lucy Appadoo

This book is dedicated to the victims of favelas. May

they get justice for their suffering.

Contents

CHAPTER 1
THE CORRIDOR

Wearing only a flimsy nightgown, she crept down a dark, narrow corridor which grew smaller with each step forward. The air was dank, damp, and the floor was cold on her bare feet. A draught made her body and lips quiver.

In the distance was a door. She stopped in her tracks, waiting. For what, she didn't know. The tangy, rich smell of blood filled her nostrils. A murmur of voices made her jerk and turn around. The sound came from behind another door at the other end of the long corridor.

Blanca swallowed. She could not take her eyes from the floor as the corridor filled with blood. Soon it covered her feet. She screamed, holding her head in her hands. She couldn't move her feet. A bullet whizzed past her and penetrated the door ahead. Panting, she stared down at the thick blood, which began to congeal, sticky. She waded forward, the thick matter sticking to her legs, slowing her down.

When she finally reached the door, she found it locked. She turned and ran, blood splashing as she raised her feet over the surface. When she turned the knob on the opposite door, it refused to open. She was stuck in this small, cramped space. Cold penetrated her core.

"Please help me, help me," she begged. "Open the door. Let me out. Please." A bead of sweat slid down the back of her neck. Her body quaked in the chill, dense corridor.

The doorknob turned slowly. Hope rising, she stepped back as the door opened towards her.

From beyond the door, a faceless man with large hands threw bodies into the corridor. They landed close to her feet. Blanca screamed. The young bodies floated in the sticky blood. She pressed her back against the wall to avoid contact.

From beyond the door, she heard voices. *"She knows too much. The boss said not to touch her. Leave her alone."* The faceless man shut the door again.

Blanca froze on the spot, fighting against the smell of death. More blood oozed out of the door. She cried and shook her head in a futile attempt to shut out the scene. Another gunshot cracked as she stared down at her hands. Little hands. Her eyes roamed her body. It was a girl's body, not a woman's. *What the hell!*

The door opened again, to reveal a man about to come out.

She jerked, to find herself in her own adult body again, in her bed, in her dark, familiar bedroom. Her heart pounded and her sweat drenched her whole body.

Just another nightmare. When will they stop?

She shook off the dream, taking deep breaths as she reminded herself of the special day head. She pulled the cover off and got out of bed, promising herself she would make time to reflect on the nightmare later. She got dressed, collected her baggage then headed into the kitchen for breakfast.

CHAPTER 2
LEAVING HOME

Blanca Castellano sank her body into the comfort of her brown leather sofa and sighed. Her baggage evoked so many thoughts. Her eyes roamed around the house. Its ambience calmed her. Her shoulders relaxed.

She moved around her old Moorish-style home with its floral scroll designs. The house had always brought her comfort: the old brick fireplace below a mantelpiece and square mirror, the landscape oil paintings on the pale green walls, and the classic wooden bookshelf which held a range of books on journalism and current affairs.

The roomy house's eighteenth-century Baroque combination of plain and fancy architectural design had led Blanca to choose it several years ago. She loved the old-style grandiosity. The round arches in the foyer gave the house a Roman feel, and the dark antique furniture blended in well with the house's decorative features.

She would miss it, but business called: tight budgets and staff shortages had led to her boss assigning her to fill in for six months at the magazine's office in Brazil. The senior editor position in the Rio de Janeiro office would be a step up from her editor position in Spain's capital, albeit a temporary one. Not only would she have more responsibility—it would be a new if challenging experience to expand her knowledge of the Portuguese language and experience a new culture.

She rose and checked herself in the foyer mirror, smoothing her jet-black hair, which reached all the way down to her shoulder blades and accentuated her height. She looked close to make sure her dark brown eyes weren't puffy, nor that her almond-shaped face betrayed the trouble she had had sleeping.

Turning at the sound of footsteps in the hall that led to the bedrooms, she greeted her friend and housemate. Daniela stood in the hallway in a flimsy nightgown that did nothing to hide her trim, taut figure. Her dark brown hair was tied up high in a bun and her green eyes brightened. "I'm happy to drive you to the airport, Blanca. What time are you leaving?"

"In an hour. And thanks, but no, I'll take a taxi. You have your young ballet students to teach, and it's not like you can get any back-up teachers at this late notice." She ignored the butterflies that had been fluttering in her stomach ever since she'd been offered the new job.

"And what about your parents? Are they still upset about you going back to their native country? I can't understand why they're bothered by it, girl." Daniela headed towards the kitchen and poured herself a cup of coffee from the pot Bianca had prepared earlier.

Blanca shook her head. "I don't know why, either. The last time I was in Brazil, I was ten. Now that I decide to return, they get angry about it. I've never understood why we left so suddenly. I remember my aunt telling me over the phone that she was worried something had happened on our trip back then."

Daniela sipped her coffee and sat at the kitchen table. "I take it they still haven't explained the reason?"

Blanca joined her friend at the table, shaking out her nerves by lifting her shoulders. "I've always wondered. When I asked my dad again, he used work as an excuse. But with the bits and pieces I remember, something shocked him on the day we left."

She didn't know why she shuddered at the thought of returning to a country she'd last travelled to at the age of ten. "For seventeen years, I've never stopped wondering why my parents cut their vacation short. And when I told them about my temporary work transfer to Brazil, they expressed shock and resistance. At twenty-seven, I'm old enough to make up my own mind."

"At least they calmed down when they learned you'll board with your aunt and uncle in Rio," Daniela said. She rose and wrapped her arms around her. "I am so going to miss you, girl. Please let me know as soon as you arrive in Brazil." She pulled away. "Are you still having nightmares?"

Blanca nodded. "Sometimes. I've always had them sporadically, but they're more frequent now than ever." The vivid nightmare she'd had that morning made her flinch. Male voices resounded in her head. Fragments. "*She knows too much. The boss said not to touch her. Leave her alone."* She didn't want to share the nightmare. Why worry her dear friend?

The nightmares gave Blanca a sense of déjà vu, but the only thing she remembered about that vacation at ten was that she'd had nightmares for years after returning home to Madrid. Her parents hadn't believed she needed therapy for the nightmares as a teenager—it was their old-fashioned way—but she'd gone to therapy once after saving her own money. The first session made her anxiety skyrocket, so she'd stopped.

As she grew up, the nightmares had become less frequent. But they had returned, more vividly, since she received the offer of a position in the Brazil office.

Going back to Rio De Janeiro would stir up memories, but she had to find out the truth. She knew her family had long-held secrets and was determined to discover them.

CHAPTER 3
THE JOURNEY

Blanca settled into the window seat on the plane. Threading a hand through her long hair, she watched the baggage-handlers load the luggage hold and wondered about their lives. Did they have secrets, or were their lives open books? Were they as anxious as she was about the plane's smooth take-off and safe landing?

The voice of the pilot jarred her into the present, announcing the flight would take ten hours and thirty-five minutes to reach Rio De Janeiro, Brazil. She shook away her daydreams, clipped on her seatbelt and ignored the passenger beside her whose bag had knocked her feet.

As the aircraft took off, she gazed over the miniature houses, trees, and people below and sighed in relief and dread, wondering how her new life would be in a new country for the next six months. What discoveries would she find?

The back of the seat pressed uncomfortably against her back as she fought back chills while the plane experienced slight turbulence. The female passenger beside her smiled but Blanca turned away with a frown. She hated planes, and always dreaded the take-off and landings. If there was another way to travel, she'd be the first to take it.

When the in-flight meal appeared, Blanca chose the bland fish and rice dish, served with a Brazilian beer called Caracu. Later, she read a few chapters of a romance novel, and failed to sleep. Still, she was not prepared when the pilot announced they were about to land. Her heart beat fast, and she fought back the shakes. Reality suddenly hit her, as she'd never travelled anywhere on her own. This was a new and daunting experience.

After the plane landed roughly, she picked up her bag and rummaged into it for her phone to check the time had changed. Beads of sweat fell across the back of her neck and a tightening of her chest alerted her to her new reality. *It is just a trip.*

***

Blanca took a calming breath as the locals and tourists lined up, slowly departing from the aeroplane to meet the hustle and bustle of Galeao Airport in Rio de Janeiro. Long delays and a string of questions in customs led to further dread towards her new adventure. Heading towards the baggage claim area, Blanca bumped into a young man who wore dark glasses and multiple layers of clothing. "Oh, so sorry."

The man smiled. "No, I'm sorry. Enjoy your day." He headed towards the other side of the airport while Blanca waited for her suitcase, dodging people who more than once stepped on her feet.

Her phone vibrated in her bag: a loving message from Daniela. As she put her phone back inside her bag, her hand brushed a piece of paper. She unfolded it: *Leave the secrets alone* had been typed on it.

She toyed with her fingers, her feet frozen in place. What the hell was this, and where did it come from? It had to be a silly prank. No one but her had access to her bag. She swallowed and remembered the man bumping into her. Did he slip the note in her bag while distracting her with his kind smile? What did this damn note even mean? What secrets?

Blanca almost missed her suitcase on the conveyor belt. She hefted it off and wheeled it towards the exit.

As she stepped outside, the heat hit her in the face. In January, Spain was in the midst of winter, but she'd landed in Brazil's summer.

She hailed a cab and a young driver with dark curls and stubble smiled as he dropped her suitcase into the boot of his car. As they drove to the city, he tried to make small talk. "Are you here on holiday?"

Blanca's chest tightened, not knowing what secrets Brazil held. "I'm here for work, but only temporarily," she tried in her rusty Portuguese.

Blanca gazed in awe as the taxi drove past mountains, broad, white-sand beaches and sky-blue waters under the early morning glare. She had read in a brochure that Ipanema was one of the safest places in Rio de Janeiro; as the second-wealthiest part of Rio, after another district called Leblon, the beach was patrolled by more police officers than other areas.

In the city of Ipanema, Blanca watched cyclists, roller skaters and skateboarders riding alongside the beach, baking in the blinding sunshine. On the fine sand, others played volleyball and other sports. Hills surrounded the Ipanema beach, and hotels, cultural centres, and museums lined the busy streets. She passed designer shops, including Louis Vuitton, Cartier, and Mont Blanc as well as pizzerias, Spanish tapas, and Brazilian restaurants. She saw a shopping strip filled with boutiques, bars, and travel agencies. It was packed with shops—a tourist's dream.

As the cab drove through the most affluent area in the south of Rio de Janeiro, Blanca wondered what it would be like to visit those expensive, posh restaurants.

The taxi stopped at a medium-sized house with a cream-coloured concrete façade. The driver gave Blanca her suitcase, and she rolled it up a paved pathway through a rose-filled front garden.

The house felt both familiar and mysterious. Would she get answers about why her last trip to Rio De Janeiro had been cut short? Her parents had always been tight-lipped about that trip. She knew her family held a secret, one she was determined to uncover. She wondered whether the note she found in her purse was related to her family.

What if she didn't like what she discovered?

CHAPTER 4
PROPOSED PROJECT

Carlos Silva shifted in his seat in the Rio Cafe as he tasted their version of his favourite meal, *feijoada*. The national dish of Brazil was a rich black bean stew with mixed meat.

Carlos flicked his dark hair away from his eye as he looked up at Luiz, his best friend, sitting across the table.

Luiz sipped his beer, set it back on the table and shook his head. "How in hell do you eat that stuff? I can't stomach it, man."

Carlos put down his fork. "That's where you and I are different. I have impeccable taste in fine dining, while you'd rather eat dirt off the ground." His eyes roamed the café. Sunlight streamed through the double glass doors onto the bench of historical statues and landscape murals, making the customers squint as they sat or rose from the floral-backed chairs.

Luiz grunted. His tall, lanky frame was too big for his chair. His size, combined with his handsome face, smiling green eyes, and shoulder-length, frizzy black hair, drew women to him. He could then turn on the charm easily. "Anyway, man. I asked you here today because I need your help with something." He downed the rest of his beer and wiped his mouth with the back of his hand. "Can you check in on Juliana? I visited her recently and she's still struggling with the loss of her daughter, Antonia, after all these years. Another girl's apparently gone missing in the neighbourhood, and it triggered memories of Antonia." He cleared his throat. "You can visit and take new photos for your magazine job to show the infrastructure upgrades in the favelas."

Carlos nodded. "Sure, I'd be happy to visit. But who's this missing girl?"

"She came from the favelas, but got into dealing drugs and had problems with gangs. She'd been caught a few times by police, but she'd never gone missing before. She always came back even if she was selling drugs. Pimps were hanging around her too, I believe."

Carlos shook his head. "Does it ever end, man? The drugs, the prostitution, the territorial gangs?"

"Never in our lifetime, but I'd love it if you could get in touch with Juliana."

"I know there's a new editor coming from Spain. Pedro might get her to investigate business in the favelas. I'll probably be working with her, taking photos for her stories. And I'm sure I'll get to take photos of the favelas while visiting Juliana, too. Those kinds of issues about business profits and expansion sell magazines, and my uncle thrives on making higher profits each year. He has less interest in human interest stories."

The mention of the editor from the Madrid office brought back Carlos' memories of his two years working in Spain as a freelance photographer. But those thoughts led to memories of his girlfriend, Sophia. They had dated for over a year, and Carlos had even planned to move to Spain to marry her—until she died of cancer. The memories of her sweet face were still painful.

The screams of young children brought Carlos back to the restaurant, to the rumble of the espresso machine, and chatty waiters. He finished the last of his stew. "Why does Juliana want to see me, specifically?"

Luiz frowned. "I don't know. I think she had a connection with your mother and wants to get to know her son." He checked his phone. "If I had the time, I would ask. I have a few projects on the go, and they don't include the favelas." He stiffened. "And I cringe going to the favelas sometimes."

Carlos leaned forward. "It's those under-age prostitutes that repel you." His chest tightened and his stomach churned at the thought.

Luiz nodded. "Seeing those old men propositioning young girls makes me sick. But nothing ever gets done about it."

"There is corruption in every corner, exploiting young girls. It's going to take a huge effort against corrupt police and government officials to end it," Carlos said. "The only positive things happening in the favelas are the infrastructure improvements. But that's not enough to give girls an alternative to prostitution for survival." He squared his shoulders. "I sure as hell plan to talk to Pedro about presenting a balanced view of the favelas, at least through my photographs. We need to see the light and the dark. Hopefully the new journalist will agree with me."

"I hear you, Carlos, but good luck if you think you can create much change. You've got the most violent favelas, the drug traffickers, and damn organised crime. Plus, your uncle wants to publish positive stories about business, not human interest."

Carlos nodded. "You're right, but if my photos can bring change for just one of those girls, I'll have made a difference."

CHAPTER 5
DÉJA VU

Blanca held her breath until her Uncle Julio opened the door. His smile was priceless when he saw her. Her heart warmed and opened up to a gentle man who had always been kind to her. He wrapped his strong arms around her.

Blanca removed herself from his squeeze. He had aged a lot in seventeen years. The dark circles under his hazel eyes made him look tired and his broad shoulders sagged a little. While he had luxuriously thick hair seventeen years earlier, he was now completely bald.

"I thought you were coming tomorrow," he said. "I would have picked you up at the airport." He pointed inside the house. "Come in. Maria will be so excited to see you." He took her hand. "But she's still asleep. She hasn't been feeling well. We'll surprise her. In the meantime, I'll show you around the place. I don't know how much you remember from your last visit, but we haven't changed it much."

Julio picked up her suitcase as Blanca stepped over the threshold. "I remember this place, Julio. It still makes me warm and fuzzy inside."

Julio smiled. He brought her suitcase to a guest bedroom, then showed her the small kitchen, study and bathroom. One of her favourite memories of the apartment was the balcony, from which she could see a path from the apartment complex to the beach. It was only a short walk to the Ipanema beach, which meant living here would be expensive.

When Maria called out to Julio, they went to the bedroom. With the curtains drawn against the strong sunlight, the room was dark. A frail figure lay on the bed, her face gaunt and pale. Light suddenly appeared in Maria's eyes as she struggled to sit up. Blanca fell into Maria's arms, struggling to hold back her tears. Maria's hug was weak.

Maria's blue-green eyes shone. "Oh, my darling Blanca, you made it. I am so glad to see you, my precious one." Grey tinged her short brown hair, but her cheeks had a bit of colour. She was an attractive fifty-seven year-old woman, and she displayed a quiet grace and inner strength that made it hard to believe she could ever be sick. Other than the grey in her hair, she hadn't changed much since she was young.

"I'm so excited to be back here. Julio was saying you weren't feeling well. Are you okay?" She couldn't have come at a worse time when her aunt needed rest.

Maria smiled and turned away. "I'm okay, Blanca. A case of the flu, that's all."

Blanca sat at the edge of the bed and held her aunt's hand. "Have you seen a doctor?"

"Of course, dear." She coughed. "It's been a long time since you've been here. I wanted to come to Spain when that bastard Jorge hurt you. I'm sorry I wasn't there for you."

Blanca pushed back the memories of Jorge's fists. "Oh, Maria it's fine. I had support. Besides, you were there in spirit." She fought down the memories of her neighbour rushing her to hospital.

"Well, at least now he's in prison and can't hurt you anymore." Maria pursed her lips, her eyes peering into the distance.

***

Maria's energy returned a few hours later. As Julio washed the lunch dishes, she sat on the couch with Blanca. They flipped through an album of photographs from her last trip to Brazil.

"I remember this day at the beach. I spilled ice cream over your shirt." Seeing her ten year-old, curly-haired self warmed Blanca's heart. She turned the page and saw a picture of her father standing beside a man she only remembered because of the faint scar across his right cheek.

"Ah, yes, that was your father, Miguel's friend. They were close back then."

Blanca tilted her head, studying the friend's strong presence. This man looked much more powerful as he stood close to her father who had broad shoulders, light green eyes and a black crew cut. "And they're not close anymore?"

Maria shook her head. "No, they stopped talking after your last trip. I don't know what happened with Pablo, or whatever his name was."

Blanco stared at the photo, her hands shaking for no good reason. What was it about this man that sent a chill down her spine? And why did her father stop talking to him after their trip? He'd never mentioned Pablo.

"Do you know why we left early from our trip back then?"

Maria shrugged. "Not a clue." She swallowed and looked into her lap. "You and your parents came back to the house after something happened, but they never told me much of anything. All they told me was you were staying with your father's old school friend for a week, and then when you returned here, you left all of a sudden. I believe you did spend a bit of time with Pablo in the beginning."

"Who were the friends we stayed with?"

Maria put out her hands. "I don't know. Something your father never told me."

Blanca was filled with dread, and now she was intrigued to learn more about Pablo. "What did Dad say?"

"Only that he got a call about an urgent matter at work. He was upset about something, but he only said it was about work."

Blanca shifted in her seat and continued to flip pages, looking at photos of the library and exotic restaurants. "And what about Mum?"

"Nothing. She looked worried about something, and you also looked a bit confused, but quiet. Not your usual self."

Blanca excused herself and went to the balcony to look at Ipanema beach. She pondered the mystery of her last vacation and found herself drifting into the past. She wondered why her father had never mentioned his friend, Pablo. She sensed a prickle of unease down her spine about their holiday, but her parents had never spoken about it. She wondered why she didn't remember the last few days of her vacation.

She had a new mission now, in addition to helping reorganize the *Felicidade de Negocios* magazine's offices. She had to find out what happened all those years ago. It was becoming clear to her now that her nightmares had something to do with Brazil. It was her chance to get answers.

CHAPTER 6
THE NEW JOB

Blanca picked up her rental car a few days later, punched in the work address on the GPS system, and drove to the *Felicidade de Negocios* magazine in the centre of Rio De Janeiro. She wore smart business-casual attire with a fitted silk blouse, pleated skirt, and medium-heeled wedges.

A flutter in her stomach spread throughout her body as she parked the car in the staff area. Her heart skipped a beat as she entered the foyer and asked the receptionist for the editor-in-chief, Pedro Silva.

The receptionist was a glamorous-looking woman who appeared to be in her forties. She was slim with bleached-blonde hair and green eyes. Blanca could tell her face had been botoxed. She wore a tailored suit, and the bling on both arms and around her neck could feed a third-world country. "Oh, you must be Blanca. I've heard about you starting here as the new editor today. I'm Elina. Welcome to Brazil."

Blanca smiled awkwardly. "Thank you, Elina. I'm looking forward to the experience."

The receptionist grinned. "The people are great here, and you should enjoy your stay. How was your flight?"

Elina's friendly greeting warmed Blanca. "Long and tiring, but I got here in one piece."

Elina laughed. "I don't know of many people who love flying." She picked up the desk phone. "I'll call Pedro. Please take a seat, Blanca."

Blanca sat on a red suede armchair, taking in the fine decor, the abstract drawings on the walls and the variety of magazines on the opaque glass table. Her stomach tingled, and suddenly she needed a drink to quench her thirst. She had an overwhelming sense to turn back, but talked herself into calming down.

Soon, a towering man approached her. His top shirt button was undone underneath a double-breasted jacket. He had clean, well-manicured nails, but his blue eyes were not smiling. He had a scar across his right cheek. What the hell! Wasn't this guy her father's friend? The one Maria had called Pablo instead of Pedro?

Pedro's eyes stared with curiosity. His face reddened. Did he not recognise her?

"Hello, Ms. Castellano. Welcome to *Felicidade de Negocios*. I am Pedro Silva, the editor-in-chief. I trust you had a good flight?"

She rose from the armchair, cleared her throat, and shook his hand firmly. This wasn't the time to bring up her father, but she'd definitely be speaking to him back home. "Yes, I did. Thank you." She concentrated on steadying her wobbly legs as she followed Pedro past staff sitting in small cubicles, speaking on telephones or staring at computers. Everyone wore professional attire, and the environment was serious and focused, with quiet chatter amongst a few employees.

Pedro touched his throat. "I'll introduce you to the others later, but for now, we'll have a chat before you meet your editorial assistant, Isabela."

He led Blanca into a large oval office with spectacular views of the city. She sat in front of a mahogany desk stacked with papers, file folders, and books about finance and economy.

Pedro sat behind the desk, clasping his large hands in front of him. He pursed his lips and fidgeted, then pushed a pile of documents to her. "If you wouldn't mind filling in those documents tonight and bringing them back to my office before the end of the day, I'd appreciate it, Ms. Castellano."

His cold manner unnerved Blanca. "Of course."

He passed her a magazine. "This is *Felicidade de Negocios'* latest issue. It sold very well, and made the largest sales profit in five years."

Blanca nodded. "That's an interesting cover." It featured two men in business suits on either side of a large building as if they were holding it up with one finger each. The photo demonstrated photography's ability to create powerful illusions.

He fixed his cold gaze on her. "I think so." He made a stack of more magazines. "As you know from your work in the Madrid office, as a part of the state government of Rio de Janeiro, we strive to promote national as well as foreign companies. Every year, we raise public awareness of all these companies that work diligently to improve Rio's economy. The magazine targets the local market."

Blanca nodded. She looked at another magazine from the bottom of the pile. "I am fluent in Portuguese, so I can help with most of the language. Though I can learn more of the technical language."

"That's fine. Your boss in Madrid explained that." He put the magazine back in the cabinet. "What I'd like your help with is to come up with article ideas for both the online and paper versions of the magazine. As you would've done in Madrid, we do interviews with different stakeholders like government officials, business people, and students, to get a range of perspectives on Rio's economy and market. Part of your job will involve a bit more journalism here by doing interviews with stakeholders. I understand you are proficient in both editing and journalism." Blanca nodded. "The magazine also works to promote global investment to boost the economy." Pedro rose. "I'll take you for a tour, then you can meet Isabela, the editorial assistant you'll be working with."

Blanca stood up and realised Pedro would've known who she was, but she wasn't about to say anything. The fact Pedro said nothing about her father troubled her. Even if he didn't recognise her, he would've known her by her full name, but he didn't say anything by way of recognising her from the age of ten. She knew they'd spent a bit of time with Pedro all those years ago, but why didn't he say anything about it?

Her father had a lot of explaining to do about the possibility he might be hiding something from her all these years.

Pedro introduced her to the staff in layout, web editing, fashion, art direction, and photography. She thought they looked serious in well-fitted suits, whispering softly within their small teams.

They finally entered another office with a wide bay window showing a memorable view of the city and river. The walls were covered with paintings of prominent officials. A thick, mint-green carpet covered the floor.

Pedro directed her to her own small desk with a computer and stationery. Sitting at a large mahogany desk with a computer, fax, and phone was a short, petite young woman with black, shoulder-length hair cut into a bob. "Isabela Pereira, this is Blanca Castellano."

Isabela rose from her desk and beamed at Blanca. "Welcome, Blanca. It's good to have you on board." She leaned forward and shook Blanca's hand. The woman had a smile in her eyes and was sweetly beautiful.

"It's great to meet you, Isabela."

Pedro gazed briefly at Blanca. "I will let Isabela get you started." He walked away without a backward glance.

Isabela stepped forward. "So how was your trip over here?"

Blanca drew a hand through her hair. "It was fine. I just need to adapt to the heat. It's cold in Spain now."

Isabela's eyes focused on her. "At least you're coming from the cold to the warmth, instead of the other way around. I personally prefer the sun to the clouds." She handed Blanca a sheet of paper, which turned out to be a schedule of tasks. "These are some of today's tasks we need to get done, involving research and refining articles, but there's no rush. Pedro's giving you at least the day to settle into the role. Even though it's the same magazine you work for in Madrid, we do things differently in each country."

Blanca's hands sweated. "How long have you worked here?"

"I've worked here for the past two years, since I was twenty-seven. I was a Portuguese teacher before this job. It is a great place to work. And..."

A man burst into the room. Blanca hadn't seen him when Pedro had shown her around in the office. He had cute dimples on his cheeks, shiny dark-brown wavy hair, a lean and muscular physique, and striking dark-brown eyes. His smile was broad. She ignored the tingle in her stomach.

"This is Carlos, our notorious and most efficient photojournalist," Isabela said. "Carlos, this is Blanca." His smile was infectious.

Blanca returned the smile and gazed at his friendly demeanour, his eyes lingering. "Nice to meet you, Carlos."

"You must be the temporary transfer from Spain. It's great to meet a new member of the team." They shook hands briefly, and electricity ran through her body.

Carlos fixed his gaze and turned briefly to Isabela. "I have those photos you asked for, Isabela. Is there anything else you need?"

"No, darl. That's it for today. Thanks a bunch."

"I look forward to working with you, Blanca. It's so refreshing to work with a foreigner." Carlos stared at Blanca again, and her face flushed. She could barely meet his gaze.

After he left, Blanca turned on the computer and ignored the stirring of emotion in her chest. She was on a mission in Brazil, and nothing would deter her from that, not even a handsome man.

Not long after, a young man who resembled Pedro entered the office. This must have been Pedro's son, but why hadn't Pedro introduced them earlier?

Like his father, he had strong features, a Roman nose, and a dark complexion. His V-neck black shirt revealed soft hair on his robust chest. His baggy white trousers displayed the muscular outline of his waist, and his rolled-up sleeves showed muscular, bronzed forearms. He flipped back the blonde tips of his hair through dark brown waves.

He approached Blanca with a prominent frown. "Hi, I'm Jose, the web editor and designer. Carlos and I were out, so we didn't get to meet you earlier. Great to welcome you to *Felicidade de Negocios*, Blanca." He shook her hand firmly, but his eyes held a fleeting hint of sadness.

"Good to meet you too, Jose. I look forward to working with you."

"Same here." He smiled at Isabela. "Hey, gorgeous." He winked at her and Isabela blushed. "Pedro's also my father, but he doesn't treat me any differently."

Blanca leaned forward. "I wouldn't expect him too. He appears very committed to this company."

Jose's smile did not reach his eyes. "Anyway, I'll leave you lovely ladies to it. Shout out if you need anything." He walked out with a spring in his step as if he was on a mission.

CHAPTER 7
THE MEETING

After eating dinner with Julio and Maria that evening, Blanca fell straight into bed. She tossed and turned in her sleep. A beautiful dream of a tranquil, sunlit morning changed to a scene of a wide lagoon surrounded by trees and shrubs. A distant shadow beckoned her to follow, but she couldn't move. She stood frozen as an icy feeling took over her body. She entered an old, decrepit home, covered in cobwebs and dirt, which vanished. Another older, dirtier house appeared before her. A window flashed before her. It had a dirty blanket covering it. A packet of cigarettes lay on top of a tall fridge. She cringed at the smell of blood. A tightness in her chest enclosed her. The small space trapped her. Someone had to save her.

With a gasp, Blanca woke up, wide-open eyes staring at the ceiling, body shivering and teeth chattering. She wiped her damp forehead with a tissue and consciously slowed her breathing. Placing a quivering hand over her chest, she closed her eyes and pushed the nightmare aside.

Her dreaming brain drained her. The dreams had become more vivid and real since she had come to Brazil. With her most recent dream, she felt she knew the home in her nightmare, its darkness and coldness. Something had happened to her there. It had to be that place. Something about it had to unlock the emptiness and mystery inside her. Surely, these nightmares would eventually stop.

Blanca showered, ate breakfast before her family woke up, and drove to work with her head pounding.

As she made her way to her office, Elina the receptionist reminded her of the staff meeting. Isabela had mentioned it the day before, but Blanca had forgotten about it. A nervous energy filled her body as she walked to the conference room. She rubbed her hands together as she stepped inside.

The whole staff sat around a long oak table, facing Pedro at the head. He exuded a commanding presence as he held the agenda in his hands. "Take a seat, Ms. Castellano," he said.

She wished he'd called her Blanca, but he obviously wanted to keep things formal. She sat next to Isabela and noticed Carlos peering at her with a shy grin. She ignored her somersaulting stomach and focused on Pedro.

"I want you all to captivate me with ideas for the next issue of the magazine. A show of hands, please."

Hands raised as a few staff members reported ideas showcasing the mining, oil, gas, and auto-manufacturing industries, all of which held a strong presence in the development of Rio de Janeiro.

Isabela raised her hand. "I spoke to a few people in industry about foreigners and Brazilians setting up businesses in Rio de Janeiro. How the economy's grown because of the scope of business development. It'll be a story about the locals and foreigners looking for business opportunities in the heart of Rio de Janeiro."

Pedro held his thumb and finger under his chin. "That's good, Isabela. I like it."

Blanca limply raised her hand. "What about looking at how Rio's developed since 2010—and the concern about crime impacting businesses, particularly in the favelas?"

Pedro hesitated, clearing his throat. "It sounds promising, Blanca. Look into it with Isabela. Interview a few people, and either make it a longer article merging the two ideas or have two separate articles. I trust you can make it work, ladies." He turned away from Blanca and searched the room. "Now, any other suggestions?"

In the middle of their discussions, Blanca noticed Carlos jotting in a notepad. When he looked up, she flicked her eyes away. Oh, damn! He'd seen her staring. She felt warm in the face and thought she must be still adapting to this unfamiliar weather. Or perhaps the air conditioner might not have been functioning well.

Carlos intervened and put up his hand. "I'd like to tell the story of the favelas through my photos, Pedro. We can focus on crime, but also on infrastructure development in the favelas. Is it okay if I work with Blanca?"

Blanca's heart beat faster at his proposition. She wondered what it would be like to work with him. No doubt he was a photographer who could creatively tell the story of poverty, which had improved somewhat in the favelas, the low-income slum areas, neglected by the Brazilian government for many years. She'd written a few articles about the favelas for the Spanish edition of the magazine, but nothing as comprehensive as she would have liked.

Her reverie broke when Pedro replied. "Fine, Carlos, but you have other projects, too; don't neglect those. If you do, I'll have to get Diego to do the photos with Blanca. I want your other work in my inbox by the end of the week."

Carlos nodded. "Sure. Not a problem."

She stared at Pedro, who held such presence and power, and wondered what had happened between him and her father. The more she knew about Pedro, the sooner she could figure out what had happened in Brazil all those years ago. There had to be a reason Pedro no longer kept in touch with him when her father kept in touch with his other old friends.

***

Carlos stood hunched over a group of photos he'd taken showcasing the CEO of a large conglomerate and his new team as they opened their investment firm. He arranged the images to tell a story—in this case, the wealth and materialism of a company that wanted to outshine its competitors. On a deeper level, it showed the real emotions behind the façade. He worked to capture those different perspectives and make a statement—a visual story.

He moved over to his computer, worked with his photo-editing software when his mind turned to Blanca. Her long, jet, black hair that flowed beautifully around her shoulders, her slim curves that made him wonder what she'd feel like in his arms, and her well-toned physique. Her green, soulful eyes bore into his own as if she questioned his own morality, and her well-defined features would make any man look twice at her.

No woman had caught his attention since Sofia had passed.

He shook away those thoughts. He had work to do. He began editing and cropping the images, paying close attention to details that would make each image newsworthy.

Saving and closing the images of the investment firm, he turned to the photos of the favelas, which captured the story of poverty. Decrepit buildings adorned with amateur paintings and graffiti, and debris-strewn streets. A malnourished young boy walked barefoot across the rocky ground, past rusty, corroded gates that were in need of repair.

Carlos remembered the day he got the poor malnourished boy's mother a job that didn't involve selling her body. He'd made a difference to the young boy, and occasionally he visited to check in on mother and son who were both thriving. Warmth filled his chest when he was able to help a few of those residents who were unable to survive financially.

CHAPTER 8
GUARDED

Parking her car in the *Felicidade de Negocios* lot three mornings later, Blanca felt jittery from broken sleep. Nightmares had kept her awake half the night.

As she walked across the parking lot, a noise behind her stopped her in her tracks. She turned, but the lot was deserted except for a few cars. Why was she being paranoid?

In the office, Blanca began to arrange her notes for her latest article as Isabela ambled in. "Listen, Blanca, I thought you'd like to know that Pedro's in a mood," she said, instead of "good morning."

Blanca frowned. "Why's that?"

"You didn't hear this from me, but it's got something to do with his son, Jose."

Blanca fixed her gaze. "His son?

Isabela frowned. "Not sure. Probably too much partying."

"He obviously likes you."

Isabela ignored her comment. "Jose's looking forward to his father's upcoming party. He holds one every year for his staff at his home. A work thing, you know. Schmoozing with the higher-uppers."

Blanca nodded. "I see." She wanted to ask more about Pedro, but stayed silent. She returned to her notes for the article about foreigners and locals setting up businesses in Rio de Janeiro. She'd done three interviews with managers to get a full account of their businesses from different perspectives.

She finished the article and emailed it to Isabela. "I've done the article. Would you mind checking it for errors? My Portuguese is good, but I tend to make proofreading errors."

Isabela gave her a thumbs-up. "Not at all, girl." It was comforting to have a nurturing work partner, but Blanca missed her colleagues and friends in Madrid.

Two hours later, Isabela turned towards Blanca. "This article's really good."

"Thanks. Why don't you take a break and grab a coffee?" Blanca answered.

"You go ahead. You've earned it." Isabela grinned. "I'll take my break once I've finished with these other articles."

Blanca smiled. "Thanks. I'll see you soon."

As she took a mug from the cupboard in the staff room, a voice behind her broke her reverie. She turned around and smiled. Heat warmed her cheeks. It was Carlos.

"It's Blanca, isn't it?" She nodded. "Good to see you're having a break."

Blanca blushed. "I need one. Coffee?"

He reached into the cupboard for a mug, his shoulder brushing hers. A flutter spread down her spine. "Thanks. I have my own in this cupboard, but I will put the kettle on. The hot water tap needs fixing." He turned on the electric kettle while Blanca slowly added sugar and a teaspoon of coffee in her mug. She tapped her fingers on the bench while waiting for the hot water.

A few minutes later, Carlos filled up their mugs and added milk. "Care to join me at the table for a few minutes?"

"Sure." Blanca sat at the round table, opposite him. His gaze unnerved her, and her face warmed again.

He gripped his cup of steaming coffee. "How are you enjoying your work so far?"

Blanca fought back the flood of emotions as his eyes dug into her own. "It's been interesting. I have a lot of story ideas, but I'm excited about the favelas."

"That's great. Isabela and I have worked well as a team, and we sometimes go out together for photos for articles. Sometimes Diego, the other photographer, goes out with her." He sipped his coffee. "I imagine the Madrid office of *Felicidade de Negocios* is the same as this one?"

Blanca nodded. "It's very similar, but there are different procedures—and the market, of course." She averted her eyes, her heart palpitating and sweat lining the back of her neck.

His gaze lingered. "You speak Portuguese well."

Blanca touched her throat. "Thanks, and you? Do you speak other languages?"

He nodded. "A bit of English and fluent Spanish. I lived in Spain for a couple of years, as a freelance photographer, and visited other parts of South America and the United States." His eyes peered into the distance briefly, as if recalling a memory. "I have travelled quite a lot and plan to do a lot more of it. You get to interact with people, and I like to study languages in those countries, too."

Blanca was intrigued, but his strong presence overwhelmed her. Jorge had been like that, too. Charming until he showed his true colours. She rose. "It is interesting to have travelled abroad and be multilingual."

He nodded. "I like capturing different cultures, settings, and moods through photography. It's about seeing through a different lens, and the camera never lies. I'm really passionate about aesthetics and focus on detail. It's amazing how people can easily brush over things. The details are important."

"I agree. I do need the details for my work as an editor and journalist. I can see things which others can't, but when it comes to my own writing, I don't see the errors at all." She swallowed, focusing on his full lips and the light in his eyes.

"It's why you have Isabela to check your work. Besides, Portuguese is not your native language, so you're doing well, considering."

Blanca looked away. "I'd better get back to work. I'll see you next time." She rose from the table.

"Sure. I'll see you soon for the favela news piece. I look forward to working with you." His eyes turned a shade darker, and she wondered if she'd been too abrupt. She wasn't being rude, but she had to make a great impression on Pedro and didn't want to linger in the staff room.

Blanca paused at the door to the staff room to look back at Carlos, and saw him looking at her intently. Her breathing sped up. Why was she nervous around him? She put it down to her lack of sleep.

CHAPTER 9
RIO CARNIVAL

Blanca stood awkwardly in the street of the middle-class area of Rio on Saturday night. Crowds headed towards the venue for the Rio carnival, some of them holding glittery masks and fancy headpieces to honour the main event. She retrieved her phone from her satchel when it chimed an incoming text notice.

It was from Isabela: "Sorry, got called in to a family emergency. Can't make it tonight."

Great! She didn't want to be alone covering this latest piece of news for the magazine events page, and was looking forward to working with her new friend. She sighed, again scanning the crowd ahead.

She walked towards the Sambadrome and turned at the sound of a familiar voice to see Carlos hurrying in her direction, his camera bag slung over one shoulder. She stiffened and felt her pulse and breathing accelerate. "I thought Pedro was sending you to cover the Rio Carnival tomorrow," she said when he reached her side.

"Change of plans. Pedro thought it'd be easier if we work together."

They made their way to the Sambadrome, displayed their press credentials to the staff member, and took their seats. Blanca's parents had told her about the Sambadrome, an arena for watching the samba-school parades during Rio's annual Carnival. Even so, the size of the place and the tiers of seats packed with spectators astounded her.

Screeching voices and resounding samba music assaulted Blanca's ears. In spite of the pressure around the back of her head, the spectacle captivated her: the skimpy costumes, feathered attire and extravagantly fanciful headpieces of the parade members who danced to the powerful Latin rhythms. She immersed herself in the moment and in the shared ecstasy.

"What do you think?" Carlos shouted over the tumult. He took out his camera, clicking away as he moved to capture different angles.

"This is amazing," Blanca shouted back. "It's not like anything we have in Spain, that's for sure." She jotted in her notepad, ignoring Carlos's thigh brushing against her own.

Carlos lowered his camera for a moment. "I don't know if you're interested in the history of the carnival, but the Portuguese settlers brought this festival from Europe, as a formal ball in upper-class homes."

"I'm glad it's for the public now," said Blanca.

Carlos sat back down and fiddled with his camera as he regarded her intensely. "Carnival is known as the world's biggest party, and attracts millions of tourists to the country. It is great for our economy."

Blanca's eyes widened, her body energised by the loud sounds and movements. "It does draw a crowd. I absolutely love it."

Carlos chuckled. "There is more to come. Wait and see."

Blanca sensed a presence in the distance. She turned to see a strange man watching her from a few aisles down. He was skinny and stood in front of a woman whose view he blocked. The woman shook her head. Blanca wondered whether he was staring at her, or at one of the multitude of people around her.

Her hands shook slightly as she closed her eyes and breathed deeply to relieve her stress. The stranger could have been looking at anyone, but she couldn't help thinking about the note in her bag. *Crazy thoughts!* When she opened her eyes again, the stranger had disappeared. *Where did he go?*

Blanca shook the thoughts away and absorbed herself with the excitement and colour of the night. The entire crowd cheered, clapped, and screamed to those in the parade. Music blared and a new string of people in fancy costumes and masks entered as the wild, erotic dancing continued. The noise was deafening, but it got her adrenaline pumping. The Latin and African beats absorbed her. She leaned back in her seat and took in the musky scent of Carlos as their legs kept brushing together. She turned to him, to see his eyes fixated on her as if he wanted to say something.

He turned away and stared out at the crowd, tapping his foot. "I'm surprised Pedro didn't come. He usually comes to this event every year, so he must have had something important."

Blanca and Carlos made their way backstage, where Blanca recorded some interviews and Carlos took photos of backstage preparations.

Then they visited the street carnivals, interviewing people on the street. Latin music inspired Blanca to move in rhythm.

Carlos bought her a Brazilian churro from a street vendor. She took a bite and licked off the chocolate icing. Carlos's lips parted as he watched her eat the remaining churro. His piercing gaze gave her butterflies. She struggled to immerse herself in the samba music with the sounds of percussion instruments while Carlos bit into his own churro, encasing his own lips in chocolate. She wondered what it would feel like to lick the chocolate off his lips. *Stop thinking stupid thoughts*, she scolded herself mentally.

Carlos pulled her out of her reverie. "How about a coffee?" He pointed straight ahead. "There's a café over there." She nodded, and they made their way to the café.

After Carlos ordered coffee, they sat on hard-backed chairs in the dark ambience of the cafe. A few couples stood in line or at tables, and waiters scurried around, carrying trays of food and drinks. Soft jazz music played in the background.

Carlos leaned in. "Are you enjoying work?"

Blanca nodded. "It's more challenging than my work in Spain, so it will hold me in good stead for the future." She cleared her throat. "But Pedro can be quite intense. What's he really like? I mean on a personal level?"

He tilted his head. "He's a perfectionist even in his personal life. I think that's why he forced his son, my cousin, Jose to study information technology at university. Jose wanted to study creative writing, but he does write in his spare time. He writes erotic thrillers, and Pedro hates it."

She nodded. "Right. And Pedro's not married?"

"He's divorced, but a ladies' man like his son. No doubt." He fixed his gaze on Blanca. "Tell me about you. Have you always lived in Spain?"

Blanca nodded. "My parents were born in Brazil, but later they moved to Madrid, and I was born there. My dad's investment work took him to Madrid where he started up and managed a new investment firm. My parents and I vacationed here seventeen years ago." She didn't want to tell Carlos that Pedro and her father had been friends, as it might get back to Pedro.

"Do you remember much of your holiday?"

Blanca shrugged. "Parts of it. The good stuff, I mean."

Carlos stared at her curiously, but said nothing. The waiter brought over their coffee and they sipped in a comfortable silence. "Brazil can be a tourist's dream. But just enjoy the next few months, and do not let Pedro intimidate you at work."

"I won't." They exchanged in small talk until she stifled a yawn fifteen minutes later. Carlos knit his brows. "You look tired. Are you ready to go?"

"I am. My body's still getting used to Brazil time, so I haven't been getting much sleep. I'm sure it'll get better."

As they walked to their cars, they saw a girl of about twelve talking to an older gentleman in a corner of the street. The girl wore a scanty top which had a low neck line, and revealing shorts that left little to the imagination. They looked like a G-string that made her bottom look bare. She wiggled her body and licked her lips as the man grabbed her chin and whispered something in her ear. The girl laughed and caressed his cheek when the man prodded her towards his car.

She whispered to Carlos. "Is this how it is in Brazil with these underage girls? Right out in the open?"

Carlos nodded. "Unfortunately, yes. More needs to be done to stop this."

Blanca fought back the chills; she had to stay strong. "Why doesn't anyone do anything? It's obvious what's happening right under our noses."

"People are scared." He peered at Blanca. "Are you okay? You look pale."

Her hands quaked and a coldness settled on her spine. "I'm fine." She ignored her upset stomach. "I'll see you at work, Carlos."

He tilted his head. "Are you sure you're okay?" Blanca nodded, bile rising in her throat. She had to get out of there.

Carlos shook her hand, ignoring his worried expression. "You take care, Blanca."

When she sat in the driver's seat of her rental car, she closed her eyes. Images flashed before her. Blood on the floor. A large hand reaching for her. A closed door in a small room. She felt a sense of being trapped, that the room was getting smaller and smaller, as if threatening to crush her.

She snapped her eyes open. *What the hell was that! A daydream? A flashback?*

CHAPTER 10
OLD PHOTOS

Carlos squinted into the glare from his open bay window, overlooking a landscaped garden. His mind churned at what Luiz had just told him about the favelas.

"Juliana wants those photos, Carlos." Drinking beer on Carlos's sofa, Luiz drew a hand through his black hair, which was tied up in a low ponytail. His smiling eyes had turned serious.

"But my mother took those photos over seventeen years ago. I have no idea where they are now. Is there any news on the recent missing girl?"

Luiz's eyes darkened. "No, there isn't. But Antonia's been missing for all these years, and now Antonia's father, Tomas wants the photos to search for her, just like his ex-wife. He wonders if she's strayed into a bad group of people. Juliana has no photos of her daughter as they couldn't afford a camera back in the day. She wants to keep her memory alive."

Carlos shook his head. "Like I said, I don't know where those photos are, Luiz." He cleared his throat. "I'll have to look for them at my dad's place."

Luiz nodded. "Tomas is hoping the photos will help in his search. I doubt Antonia's alive, though. The police gave up on finding her years ago. They're not willing to reopen the case, and I don't blame them. Without new evidence, why should they?"

Carlos froze as he thought about all those innocent girls selling their bodies for money. He remembered his mother visiting the favelas many times to take photos of young girls propositioning men. He had accompanied his mother to the favelas once. A man who was ogling a young girl, approached them and smashed his mother's camera. His mother had been more upset about the cost, as the camera was expensive, than afraid of the violence.

On other occasions, she'd given the girls money and food, and taken them to social work clinics for a better life. She'd saved quite a few of the girls after seeing the devastation first-hand.

To get the photos, Carlos would have to make up an excuse to visit his father—preferably when he wasn't home.

"I'll have to look in my dad's storage room, garage, and bedroom. I doubt he'd know where the photos are, as he never took an interest in my mum's work. He thought it was a hobby, but she made a lot of money as a freelance photographer for magazines on the side while working full-time. He didn't respect the art of photography, and he doesn't respect me or my work."

"Does your dad speak to your uncle Pedro now? Has their relationship changed at all?" Luiz asked.

Carlos shook his head. "No, not since their falling-out after my mother died. If he wants something from Pedro, it's all through me."

Luiz nodded. He picked up the remote on the TV and changed the channel to a football game. He lifted up his chest and tucked his calves underneath his body, which was a feat, considering his towering size. "The match is starting."

***

Knowing his father, Nicolas, was at his office later that day, Carlos used his own key to enter his father's house to look through his mother's old camera equipment. His mother had always kept things well-hidden and he hoped he could find the photos.

Closing the front door behind him, he walked over to the storage room along an outer wall and pushed his way between large boxes, old pots and pans, and dusty books. In one swift movement, he removed a few boxes to create more space. In the corner of the room, he found two large boxes of documents and pulled them out into the living room. He began rummaging into the first, finding tax invoices, appliance manuals, and old recipe cards, but no photos of Antonia. He found old family photos and individual shots of his mother, and put them aside. He planned to take these home with him because he didn't have any photos of his mother in his home.

He dug deep into the other box and found more photos of his family, photos his mother had taken of the favelas with people he didn't recognise, bank statements, and tax invoices. He pulled out a few statements, finding large deposits of withdrawals from an account. The receiver appeared to be a corporation with a name he didn't recognise. *Possessao Valioso.* Taking out his phone, he checked the name of the corporation on the internet, but found nothing. Surely, even if the company had closed down, the internet would still have a record of it, he thought. The amount paid was exorbitant; 60,000 Brazilian Real each month in 2006? Was this his father's account or his mother's? If it was from his father, what was he paying for if the company didn't exist? His father's work afforded him a good lifestyle, but this was extraordinary. He had never heard of it, and whose account was this?

Carlos folded the statements and put them in his pocket without knowing why. He put the boxes back into their places and went to the garage, where he searched in cupboards and under a table, but didn't find anything of value. Feeling defeated, he pondered where to look next. His mother's bedroom had to be a likely option, but his father might have got rid of all her belongings.

In the bedroom, he looked under the bed, but found nothing. He searched inside the walk-in closet, and found his mother's clothing still on their hangers. Why hadn't his father given these clothes away after all these years? On the shelf were three shoeboxes he'd never seen before. With a long, breathy stretch, he retrieved them and lay them on the bed. Sitting on the edge of it, he took out more old family photos, bank statements, and pocketbooks. Nothing of Antonia. In the second box, he found old passport photos and his old school reports. He sighed, hoping that the last box would contain what he came for.

He pulled out more family photos until, like hidden treasure, he found three pictures of Antonia. He remembered seeing her face on the news, and this was definitely her. In one, she wore a skimpy top that displayed her cleavage, and her face was heavily made up with eyeliner and mascara. In a corner of the photo, he could see someone's arm, but not the face. Either she was going to a party or she'd succumbed to the prostitution lifestyle.

Another photo showed her crying, while the last picture showed her hugging her mother. Juliana would love these photos, except for the one which showed her made up for a party. He planned to hold on to the first photo he saw.

Underneath the photos were newspaper clippings, articles with headlines like "Child Prostitution in the Favelas," "Teenage Mum at Twelve," "Pregnant Girls," "Sex with Under-Aged Girls," and "Prostitution for Survival."

Carlos wondered why his mother, Ines had kept such sensational newspaper articles. She had been a photographer, not a journalist.

CHAPTER 11
THE NEIGHBOUR

Blanca yawned in bed the next morning, on a Sunday, stretching out her arms as the sun's glare penetrated through the curtains. Her head weighed her down and her heart throbbed from her flashback last night. She winced at the memory of seeing the underage girl propositioning the older man in the street after the carnival.

In the kitchen, she found the table laden with sweet pastries, bread, butter, fruit, and freshly-brewed *cafezinho*, Brazilian-style coffee. Julio bit into a sweet while Maria looked on with saggy eyes and a pale complexion, slowly sipping her coffee. She lifted her head when Blanca sat in front of them and gazed on the breakfast layout.

Maria put aside the newspaper. "Come and eat, darling. I don't have an appetite this morning, but Julio obviously does." She placed a frail hand over her head and briefly closed her eyes.

Blanca wondered what had changed with Maria, as she appeared withdrawn and anxious about something. "Are you not feeling well, Maria?"

Maria gave her a reassuring smile. "Oh, Blanca. I'll be fine."

This strong woman would of course deny she was sick, Blanca thought. "I want you to relax today, Maria. I'll cook us a nice lunch and dinner, and maybe we can take a walk to the park. Or would you prefer to rest today?"

The doorbell rang and Blanca rose to answer the door. She looked curiously at a heavy-set woman with wrinkles around her eyes and a warm smile.

"Oh, Gabriela, come in. Come in," Julio said. He had followed Blanca as far as the front hall, where he could see the front door. "This is our niece, Blanca. She's working here temporarily before returning to Spain."

"Hello, Blanca. Nice to meet you." She angled her head towards Blanca. "You've been here before, haven't you? I remember seeing you."

"Yes, a long time ago now," Blanca said. Gabriela followed Blanca into the kitchen and sat down.

Maria waved. "Great to see you. Come and join us for breakfast."

"I cannot refuse a coffee, Maria. Thank you." Gabriela sat on the chair while Blanca prepared coffee and set it in front of her. "Thank you, dear." She turned to Maria. "Are you ill, Maria? You look pale."

Her eyes turned inward briefly. "It must be something I ate last night, but I'll be fine."

"You can go lie down, Maria," Blanca said. "I can keep Gabriela company."

Julio looked at Maria with concern, stroking her hand. Then he said, "Excuse me, ladies. The garden awaits."

After he left, Maria took Blanca's hand. "This wonderful woman hasn't been here very long, but she's done an amazing job cleaning my house and doing the laundry," she said to Gabriela.

"I'm going to teach you some yoga exercises to help you relax, too," said Blanca.

Gabriela chuckled. "You're quite the lucky lady, Maria to have such a generous niece." She stared at Maria strangely.

What was going on here? Blanca wondered what Gabriela knew about her past. No harm to ask. "So you lived here when my parents and I came down?"

"I've been here for over thirty years, so I got to meet your parents back then. Lovely people, but then the sudden way you left was surprising. Maria said you had planned to stay longer, but you left early for some reason."

"Were you around that day?" Blanca asked.

"I sure was."

Blanca wished she didn't need to play the twenty questions and interrogate her, but she needed answers. Gabriela might have seen something that day. "And did you see my parents or know why we left early?"

Gabriela turned away as if in thought. She closed her eyes momentarily. "I was sitting outside. I like to do that sometimes, just sit outside. Good for the nerves, you know." Blanca nodded. "I noticed your father's expression. He had his fists clenched, and he was shaking his head a lot. He looked very angry. Your mother was quiet, but she was trying her hardest to calm your father down. Maria told me he had to leave because of his work, but I think—"

Gabriela didn't finish her thought. "You think what?" Blanca asked.

"I think there was more to it." Blanca waited. "I noticed your father's nose and part of his face. It looked a bit bruised. And—" Gabriela had that dazed look again. "And your mother carried you into the house and straight back out again."

She winced. "Is there anything else you noticed on the day?"

Gabriela was lost in thought and again closed her eyes briefly. The silence was unnerving for Blanca. "I don't think so, love."

Maria suddenly swayed and her eyes rolled. She looked as if she was about to vomit. Blanca quickly rose and grabbed her by the arms, pushing her towards the bathroom. She held on to her back, prodded her on to her knees and leaned her over the toilet bowl. Within seconds, Maria vomited twice while Blanca rubbed her back and wiped her brow. She grabbed a face cloth from the drawer, wet it with cold water, and wiped her mouth and face.

"I'm okay, Blanca. I might go and rest if you don't mind."

"Of course. I'll help you to your room." She put her arm around Maria's shoulder and helped her to the bedroom.

"Please apologise to Gabriela," Maria whispered.

"She'll be fine. I'll keep her company." Blanca sighed. "I can take you to the doctor." She tucked Maria into the bed, the blankets up high.

"No, I'll be okay."

Blanca kissed her cheek. Her poor aunt was obviously sick, but at least she was here to support her.

She returned to the kitchen and smiled at Gabriela, whose eyes held concern. "Maria's resting in bed. She's not feeling well."

"That poor woman. She's suffered enough with—" Gabriela put a hand over her mouth as if she had slipped up.

Blanca felt a chill. "What do you mean, she's suffered enough? In what way?"

Gabriela rose abruptly. "Anyway, I'm sure you have loads to do. I'll leave you to it, but I'll come back and see Maria. If I remember anything more about that day, I'll let you know."

"No, wait." Blanca followed her to the front door.

"Bye now," Gabriela said as she scurried out the door as if she couldn't leave fast enough.

What is going on with Maria, and what does Gabriela know? Something spooked Maria. Yesterday, she appeared to be her gentle, happy self but this morning she was sick and Julio was especially sweet with her.

Blanca was curious about why her father's nose was bruised that day. Had he been in some kind of accident he didn't want her knowing about? Or had he been in a fight?

She started clearing up the dishes when she noticed the newspaper's front page. The headline read, "Young Girls Who Survived the Favelas." Was this what had spooked Maria? She skimmed through the article, shuddering at the cases of several young girls who'd been taken away from their families to service older men in different parts of Brazil. One of the girl's family had been held at gunpoint, forced to give away their child. Another had been taken while browsing through a market with her mother.

Her body froze and she struggled to breathe as she held on to the edge of the table. *Oh, Christ!* Why did this article bother her so much?

CHAPTER 12
BUSINESS EVENT

On Friday evening, Pedro hosted a poolside party in Copacabana for his staff. Blanca wanted to avoid it in favour of looking after Maria, but her dear aunt had brushed off her illness, telling her it must have been food poisoning. Blanca didn't believe her. Something was going on and she was determined to find out. But she relented when Maria insisted she attend her boss's party.

Blanca arrived at Pedro's house wearing a black designer mini-dress featuring a cream chiffon buttoned jacket with matching earrings and a pearl necklace. The dress had a V-shaped neck and was three-quarter sleeved, and she wondered if she was over-dressed. She steadied her legs in black, wedge sandals. Her hair was pulled up in a bun with wispy strands falling down the sides of her cheeks.

The warm, pleasant breeze feathered her flushed cheeks. Her hands shook as she rang the doorbell. A short, stout woman, with dark, smiling eyes answered, introducing herself as Pedro's housekeeper, and led Blanca through the house.

Blanca entered the festive atmosphere, uneasy, her throat dry at hearing voices from the back of the grand house. Her spine prickled as she took a deep breath and pushed worried thoughts into oblivion. She'd always hated crowds, but she was overwhelmed by the beauty and magnificence of the home's grand foyer and marble floor. A mirrored wall facing the entrance reflected a wooden staircase spiraling upward. The furnishings and decor were ultra-modern, and high ceilings gave the area a sense of space.

The house was too grandiose for her tastes and gave her a cold, icy feeling. There was no warmth. All this space and expensive decor did nothing to make her feel at home.

Latin music blared in the background as she made her way to the back of the house. The garden was as spectacular as the rest of the mansion, with colourful lights surrounding the expansive deck, bouquets of flowers in stand-alone vases, and a buffet table piled with savouries and alcohol. Uniformed servants carried trays of food and drink.

Blanca swallowed, wondering where Isabela was among the scary crowd. She squeezed her hands tight, holding her breath as her eyes scanned the scene. She sighed with relief when she spotted Isabela, Elina and other colleagues close to the buffet table, and rushed towards them.

"Hi, Blanca. I'm glad you came," Isabela kissed her lightly on the cheek. Elina and the other two co-workers greeted her warmly, and soon they were in deep conversation about the state of Rio de Janeiro's economy, and how it had developed over many years.

Elina wore a low-cut, black satin dress that showed a lot of cleavage, an assortment of jewellery around her neck and wrists, and stiletto heels. Her hair was in a chignon with wispy strands. "You look gorgeous, darling. How's work been for you?"

Blanca looked around, searching for Carlos. "Thanks, Elina. Work is going well. Isabela's doing a great job, training me in procedures and improving my work in general. I love it."

"Isabela is the best," Elina said as she eyed a man who was giving her the seductive eye. She licked her lips, staring at the man when she turned to the group. "If I can make your job any easier, don't hesitate to let me know, darling."

Blanca nodded. "Of course." She beamed. "How long have you worked at the magazine, Elina?"

Elina hesitated as her eyes scanned the crowd. "Oh, gosh. My memory's a bit hazy, but about fifteen years or so. Pedro's a strict but fair boss." She turned to the man who ogled her. "Ladies, a man awaits my presence and I plan to not go home alone tonight." She walked towards the man and the two of them moved to a more private space.

Isabela chuckled. "I swear. That woman has had more men than I've had dinners. She is one horny devil."

Blanca clenched her hands, admiring Elina's free spirit. "I didn't see a ring on her finger, so I assume she's not married?"

"No, she's widowed and doesn't have children, but she loves her men."

Blanca nodded, quickly changing the subject. "Is Carlos coming?"

Isabela eyed her suspiciously. "He mentioned he was, but later. He had something else on earlier tonight." Blanca hid her disappointment when a few moments later, Pedro joined the circle of friends.

"Blanca, welcome to my party." He watched her closely, his kind tone not reaching his eyes. "Come with me. I need to speak to you while I get you a drink."

"Excuse me," she said to Isabela and the others.

He fetched her a glass of fruity wine from the nearby table. "Please have something to eat. There's something to suit everyone's palate."

Blanca sipped her wine. "What did you need to speak to me about?"

His eyes darkened and again he searched the room. She wondered what he was looking for. "I haven't had the opportunity to ask how you're managing at work. Are you experiencing any issues with the staff or the work in general?"

Blanca frowned, wondering if someone had complained about her work. "No, it's all fine. Everyone's been great. No complaints."

He rubbed his hands. "Good, good." An awkwardness settled over them in the few seconds of silence. "How are you finding Brazil? Are you enjoying our fine country?"

She nodded, aware of his hands fidgeting as his eyes roved around the space. "It has a lot to offer, but I haven't had a chance for sight-seeing yet. I'll make time, though." He watched her closely, and she turned away with a sense of unease.

"I'm sure you'll find the time to see our beautiful country. You don't doubt your transfer from Spain, do you?"

Blanca wondered if he was fishing for something, but what? What did he really want to know? It had to have something to do with her father, no doubt. "No, not at all. It's an experience, and I plan to make the most of my six months." She smiled. "There are always doubts when you move to a new country, and one I haven't been to in seventeen years. A lot's changed since then." She braved her next words. "You were a friend of my father's, weren't you?"

Pedro pressed his lips together, fixing his gaze on her. "I will take you back to Isabela and the others. They can introduce you to new people."

A voice interrupted them behind her. "Hey, Dad, great party. Where's all the alcohol?" Jose pushed himself in between them, his energy seeming upbeat. He appeared to be drunk.

Pedro was taken aback. "Over there." He knit his brows. "It looks like you've had enough to drink already. Slow it down, Jose."

Jose jutted his chin out. "I'm in perfect control, Dad. Don't you worry." He took a breath, eying Blanca with a neutral expression. "Why don't you go mingle with your friends. I'll keep Blanca company for now."

Pedro's face reddened as if he was about to combust. What was that about? "Fine," he said when a guest approached them.

"Pedro, we need to discuss an important matter." The tall man wore a fitted jacket over a white fitted shirt with a black bow-tie and black pants. He was bald in the middle with thin, black hair and specks of grey on the sides, and a dimple on his chin. He turned to Blanca, staring through his glasses. "And who is this fine young lady?"

Pedro winced, forcing a smile. "I am glad you could make it." He faced Blanca. "This is my new employee from Spain. She's here for the next five or six months on a contract. Blanca, I would like you to meet Fernando Paes, Governor of Rio de Janeiro. He is a great leader of our community and a former judge."

Blanca smiled, ignoring the bile in her throat and ache in her back. She was unnerved without knowing why. "Nice to meet you, Governor."

He put out his hand and shook hers. "A friend and employee of Pedro's is a friend of mine, indeed. I hope you are enjoying this exceptional country of ours. I aim to provide much-needed resources to Rio de Janeiro, given the hardships we have faced." He nodded to Jose. "And Mr. Silva, I am glad you are here when I'm sure you would have preferred to be with a special lady, no doubt."

Jose shrugged. "I am happy to be here, Fernando, supporting my father. He always gives the best parties."

"Indeed," said Fernando. He touched Pedro on the shoulder. "How about you join me in meeting my daughter. She'd very much like to meet you."

"Of course. Where is she?" Pedro asked.

He pointed behind them. "Over by the trees." Turning back to Blanca and Jose, he said, "Great to meet you Blanca, and good to see you too, Jose."

Pedro looked at Blanca, hesitating. "Excuse me a moment." He walked off but looked over his shoulder at her in a curious manner.

Blanca looked for Isabela but couldn't find her, so she finished the few remaining drops of her wine.

"It looks like you need another drink. Let's go over there. I need one, too," Jose suggested, touching the small of her back and steering her towards the alcohol table. He poured her more wine, and she took a sip, her eyes still searching for Isabela. She wondered whether Carlos had arrived yet. "I'm curious as to why you'd transfer to Brazil when Spain appears to be a beautiful place." His eyes bored into hers.

Blanca took another quick sip and then yet another. As if she'd tell a stranger the real reason she had accepted the transfer. "I wanted to broaden my horizons and have a bit of an adventure."

He nodded. "I get that, but Brazil..." He cleared his throat.

She spotted Pedro speaking to Fernando's daughter and several distinguished-looking men. Intermittently, he watched her with curiosity.

Blanca had a sense of unease with Jose, but she didn't understand why. He was confident and pleasant, but appeared troubled by something. He attempted to mask it, but his eyes spoke volumes. "I should get back to Isabela," she said.

He nodded, appearing to be in his own world. "She is beautiful, isn't she?" He faced her again. "Don't expect to see much of my father. When he has a party of this magnitude, he mingles with all the right people. I guess it's how he's made his fortune."

"He's a smart man," replied Blanca.

Jose scoffed. "If you say so." He wandered off and slapped hands with a group of men near the back garden.

Blanca made her way through the crowd searching for Isabela, unsuccessfully. Blanca could not be on her own at a party and had to find her. She'd always felt uneasy with crowds of strangers, but she didn't know why.

She had forgotten being at the party for a minute as she dodged bodies and bumped into strong arms which grabbed her.

Carlos stared curiously at her, his expression unreadable. "Hey, Blanca." His hands around her waist made her gasp as she ignored the shiver down her spine.

CHAPTER 13
TEAMWORK

Blanca winced and hugged herself when Carlos let her go, goose bumps spreading over her arms as they stood close to the back door of the house. She couldn't help but notice Carlos's taut muscles under his white fitted shirt and black pleated pants. His eyes burned into her as she gripped her wine glass tightly with the other. She had to get a top-up of her drink as her throat was parched.

Carlos smiled. "Are you cold?"

Blanca stood awkwardly. Why was Carlos looking at her that way? "No, I'm fine."

Carlos frowned and rubbed the back of his neck while he slightly shuffled his feet. "It's good to see you here. I usually get bored at these events."

Blanca nodded. "I don't know anyone except for a few from work and yourself, so it's good to see a friendly face."

He shifted his posture and clasped his hands loosely. "Why don't we go sit over there, on the couches. I'd like to pick your brain about a few upcoming photo projects. Do you mind?"

She shook her head. "Not at all."

Carlos led Blanca to a bright red sofa in the corner. The warmth spreading over her body made her yearn for his arms around her waist. She wondered how he got his muscles; did he work out in a gym? Her heart raced and she ignored the fluttery sensations in her stomach, telling herself it was only the wine that made her feel these things.

Their shoulders touched as they sat side by side. He dug into his pants pocket and retrieved his phone. "These are photographs of Sugarloaf Mountain." He touched the screen, sliding his finger from one image to the next as Bianca watched, ignoring the heady sensation from the scents of musk and spice. "I wanted to market these to new businesses when they establish themselves in Brazil, particularly close to these attractions."

From what she'd read, the name of the peak in Rio de Janeiro, Brazil, at the mouth of Guanabara Bay, referred to its shape. Carlos's photos captured the light and shade of the clouds and sky in the background. He swiped to another photo, showing a cable car coming out from behind the grassy peak.

"These photos are amazing." She had a sense of déjà vu. Maybe she'd visited this area the last time she had been in Rio. "You have a good eye, Carlos."

He beamed. "Thanks." He cleared his throat. "Do the mountains tell a story of Rio de Janeiro in all its glory?"

Blanca struggled to breathe as his eyes gleamed in the soft light in the room. His spicy scent filled her senses as she stared at his lips. "They show the story of magical realism, and its aesthetically pleasing. Then you've got the gorgeous bay of Rio de Janeiro. Amazing work."

His gaze lingered but Blanca looked away. "I plan to eventually get into freelance work and sell my photography work at a gallery. Isabela has a friend who owns a gallery."

"Does that mean you're planning to leave your job to focus mainly on freelance work?"

"Possibly. I've always loved travelling and I miss Spain, where I stayed before." He looked wistful again as if recalling a memory. "It held special meaning for me, but my father got sick and I had other...personal issues...and came back home. You might be able to show me around Spain when you get back. Only if I decide to travel there again."

Blanca gave a nervous chuckle, her body heat rising. "I'm still here for another five months before I get back."

He glanced at her. "I'm wondering if you enjoyed the Carnival the other night."

Blanca swallowed. "I did, but seeing the underage girl in the street broke my heart. I know our magazine doesn't cover human interest stories, but I wonder if we can have a special edition article about the favelas. Not so much about the businesses helping out with infrastructure, but the under-age prostitution and poverty. Give a balanced view. How close are you with Pedro?"

"We're close enough for me to possibly convince him to research the human side of favelas, but he likes things to be perfect and it drives me insane sometimes. He has his set ideas, but I'll try to convince him to focus on this other angle."

She nodded. "Are you close with his son, Jose?"

Carlos hesitated. "Pedro's my uncle and Jose's my cousin. We get along, and were close once. But that changed when Pedro stopped him from hanging out with me when we were growing up. Jose was a lot of fun back then."

Blanca tilted her head. "Why did he stop you guys from hanging out?"

Carlos shrugged. "I've asked him countless times, but all he said was that Jose had to focus more on his studies and less on going out. It could be why he's a party animal now. Making up for lost time."

A sense of unease settled in her stomach. "Is he the same age as you?"

Carlos fixed his gaze on her own. "He's thirty-four and I'm twenty-nine."

"And when did that stop? You guys hanging out?"

Carlos knit his brows. "What's with all the questions?"

Blanca blushed, clenching her hands. She was interrogating the poor guy. "I'm sorry. Forget I asked anything. I didn't mean to pry."

He gave a reassuring smile. "It's all good." He touched his temple. "I was a teenager back then."

Blanca said nothing, and wondered why she even cared about his past.

CHAPTER 14
PRESSURE

The Monday after Pedro's party, Blanca sat at her desk at work when her phone buzzed with a notification. She pulled out her phone and saw a text message from Isabela, telling her she'd be in late. Setting aside her phone, she skimmed through her writing piece at work, reporting on Brazil as South America's most influential country. Her work article further mentioned the decrease in poverty and economic growth of the country. Brazil had come a long way in some aspects of its way of life.

The fact that favelas still existed proved the great divide between the rich and the poor. They were not going away anytime soon. The country had made strides and was developing as a nation, but favelas and prostitution continued to exist.

Even if this article had to focus on the positive aspects of Rio de Janeiro's economy rather than the grim realities, she wondered if she could ever live in Brazil when Spain's economy was grander. She even wondered whether she could write an article about Brazil's favelas to show the contrast, and how much businesses could help those struggling in poverty.

She put the article aside when Isabela walked in. "Hey, Blanca. Sorry I'm late this morning. I had to take my car to the mechanic and took a taxi here."

"No worries, Isabela." She waited until Isabela settled at her desk. "I finished that article about the latest economic growth figures." She set it on Isabela's desk for her to check for errors.

"Thanks, girl. I'll get to it in a minute." She rummaged into her bag, then shoved it into a cabinet beside her desk, which she locked.

Blanca opened her calendar app and scheduled a meeting with the magazine's website and digital staff. She scanned through freelance articles for new commissioned ideas from writers submitting on spec. She enjoyed the range of perspectives on the business side of Rio de Janeiro, but started to think about moving to a human-interest magazine in the future. She planned to start looking for positions when she returned to Spain.

Isabela finished reading Blanca's article. "Great article. I'm refining it a little, then it'll be finalised." She looked away from her computer. "Oh, by the way, I didn't see you at the party after we met? I looked for you, but couldn't find you."

Blanca swallowed, a sense of guilt washing over her. "Sorry about that. After talking to Pedro, I met up with Jose and then Carlos."

Isabela knit her brows. "Really? Why are you blushing?" She gave her a cheeky grin. "I hope you had a great time with Carlos."

Blanca shrugged, averting her eyes. "I couldn't find you afterwards, and Carlos and I were discussing work. He showed me photos of Brazil on his phone."

"Hmmm," Isabela said. "Did you have a good time?"

Blanca's heart warmed at the image of Carlos in her mind. She shuddered at the way her body responded when he looked at her. "It was fun."

"That's good. Carlos is a great guy."

She ignored her comment. "Oh, by the way. I met the Governor of Rio."

Isabela nodded. "Fernando's a strange man, but he's helped fund a few businesses in the favelas and in the middle-class community. Not to mention, helping out *Felicidade de Negocios* when we were in a tight spot a few years back."

"Hmm. He and Pedro seem to be close."

Isabela cleared her throat. "They've been friends for a long time." She got up. "Anyway, I need to head over to marketing for a minute. Can you hold the fort for about half an hour?"

Blanca nodded. "Not a problem." She returned to reading the freelancers' articles for the next twenty minutes when Jose entered the office.

"Hey, Blanca." He grabbed Isabela's swivel chair and pushed it over near Blanca's chair. He held a grim expression.

Blanca was curious. "Jose. What's going on?"

"I spoke to Carlos. He mentioned your idea on writing about the favelas and the underage girls. I think you should steer clear of that, as we're not that kind of magazine." He turned away, peering through the window behind her.

"I thought we could have a special edition in the magazine. These types of articles can increase readership and lead to a diversified market. It gets the emotions stirring."

"It's too controversial." He pressed his lips together and his eye twitched.

She took a deep breath. "But Carlos mentioned your father will most likely approve it? Has Carlos asked Pedro about this?"

He rubbed his thigh as if he had an itch. "No, he hasn't, and he would not agree to it anyway. You're only here on a temporary basis, so do not stir things up. Controversy can be a bad thing for this magazine."

She shook her head. "What's so bad about a controversial topic?" Jose straightened his posture and stared straight through her. "Jose?"

He glared, leaned in and moved his face within inches of hers. She smelled his musky aftershave. "You need to forget your idea, okay. Do not mention anything to my father about this ludicrous idea. He always does what he wants to do, and I am sure he wouldn't agree to it."

She moved back. "But how do you know unless we ask?"

Jose flinched. "You do this and you'll regret it, Blanca." Was he threatening her? What was his problem with this?

Isabela walked in and Jose's face turned red. "What's going on, Jose?"

He shrugged. "Nothing, Isabela. I was leaving." He turned to Blanca. "Send me over the article about infrastructure within the favelas. I'll do the web version of the article this week. I'll be seeing you." He swaggered to the door without turning back.

A sudden chill filled her bones as she withdrew into herself and focused back on her work. What was it with the favelas? She wanted to make a difference, but Jose wanted to stop her for his own warped reason. He didn't have the last say. Only Pedro did.

CHAPTER 15
AVOIDING TRUTH

Isabela drew a hand through her hair, a questioning look in her eyes as she watched the back of Jose strut out of the office. "What was that about?"

Blanca averted her eyes. "Nothing."

Isabela pressed her lips hard together. "That wasn't nothing. He upset you."

Blanca wanted to get back to work and forget about Jose. "He doesn't want me writing the human-interest story about the favelas."

Isabela's eyes darkened as she sat in front of her computer. "Why not? I thought it was a great idea to have it as a special edition of the magazine."

"I don't know. He mentioned controversy and how we're not that type of magazine, but I think there's more to it."

Isabela nodded. "Jose's always been particular about what we write in the magazine. Yet Pedro might give the go-ahead, so ignore the guy. Have you asked Pedro?"

Blanca's face felt flushed. "No. Besides, I'm here only temporarily, so I have to be careful. I don't want Pedro writing me a bad reference if I clash with his son. I need this job."

Isabela gave her a reassuring grin. "When Jose was told by upper management they wanted to replace the editor on a temporary basis with someone fresh from overseas, he was none too pleased. He thought we needed someone local who understood the culture of the country. He'd seen your work in Madrid and thought you'd been too controversial with your articles. In spite of being the publisher's son, he doesn't control the direction of the magazine, but sometimes he thinks he does. Jose lost against his father and upper management and here you are. But then again, even Pedro wasn't keen on the idea of a foreigner replacing the editor in the beginning. But something changed his mind, and in the end, he agreed to you coming."

Blanca's chest tightened. "I thought someone from a different culture could bring freshness and new perspectives to the magazine." She didn't mention the real reason for wanting to come to Brazil.

Isabela shrugged. "I agree, but Jose has his set views about the magazine."

Blanca suddenly felt exposed and vulnerable. The reason that Jose had not wanted her to come to Brazil was a mystery. Even Pedro didn't want her in the beginning. Given the history between Pedro and her father, she understood why Pedro was against her coming to Brazil. But why Jose?

Light footsteps interrupted them. Elina entered the office, carrying a manila folder. "Hey, Blanca. I've lost some addresses for these rejection letters. I want to send them off today. I also need your signature on a couple of these ones here." She handed her several documents.

Blanca approached. "Sure thing. I'll sign them now." She picked up the papers, signed at the bottom of the letters, and handed them back. Turning back to the computer screen, she found the addresses as Elina recited the names she required.

"Thanks for that, Blanca." Elina smiled, staring. "Did you enjoy Pedro's party Friday night?"

Blanca smiled "I did, but I drank a bit too much. How was your date?"

Elina chuckled. "That's why I like staying single. Variety is the spice of life, and my man sure knew how to touch me in all the right places, if you know what I mean." She gave them a wink.

Isabela moved forward. "Oh, too much information, Elina."

Blanca grinned. "I'm glad you had a great time."

Elina gave her a thumbs-up. "If there's anything you need me to handle, let me know. No job is too big for me, Blanca."

"It's all good, Elina. I'm fine. Thank you," said Blanca.

Elina looked pensive. "I am excited you're working here, Blanca but don't work too hard, okay? You need time to see the country's sights and have fun while you're here."

Blanca nodded. "I won't work too hard, and I do plan to see the sights."

"Good." She left with a nod and closed the door behind her. Blanca's heart warmed at the thought of another supportive person in her corner. Who knew when she might need her? For a woman who appeared to be in her fifties, Elina had a lot of energy and fire. She appeared to be fun to be around.

***

Returning to her temporary home after work, Blanca walked with a deflated posture. She wondered why Jose got angry with her earlier. Why did it bother her so much? It wasn't as if she would die for not writing the article, but a part of her sensed unease and she didn't know why.

Coming to Brazil was strange. Since receiving the note at the airport, she felt as if she was being watched. The note and her nightmares—did they mean something? What secrets was someone trying to keep hidden?

She greeted her aunt and uncle, poured herself ice water and went out onto the balcony, looking out over the beach and scenery. The evening was warm and humid. As she leaned over the rail, a rush of emptiness pervaded her body, but she didn't know why. Something about this place haunted her, and her anxiety grew.

She wandered into her room and phoned her parents for the second time since arriving in Brazil. If she mentioned Pedro, would her father open up about why they'd stopped being friends?

Her mother, Claudia answered. "Hi darling. I'll put you on speaker, so your father can talk, too." Blanca waited until her father, Miguel spoke up. "We haven't heard about your new job yet. How is it over there?"

Blanca swallowed. "I'm actually working with someone you know."

"Oh, who is it?" he asked.

She braced herself. "I'm working with Pedro Silva, your old friend, at the magazine. When I looked at old photos, I remembered how close you two once were." She waited for a reply, but none came. "Mum, Dad. Are you still there? Did you hear what I said?"

"I see. So have you seen much of Brazil?" her father asked.

Blanca's hands shook. "Dad. What happened between you two? I know the day we left you were angry about something. I know you said it was work, but the neighbour, Gabriela,

55

mentioned you'd had a bruise on your nose. As I've asked countless times before, what happened for us to leave earlier than our scheduled time?"

Her mother replied. "As your father said, it was work and from memory, he might've knocked into a wall when he was hurrying to make the flight. Nothing to worry about, darling."

Blanca's hands clenched. "Dad. You still didn't answer my question about Pedro. Why did you two stop being friends?"

"Oh, Blanca. We grew apart as most friends do over the years," her father answered. "Please focus on your work as you're only there for the next five months."

She shook her head. "You didn't even want me to come to Brazil. Why? I know something happened to me, but I don't remember much."

Her mother replied. "Nothing happened, Blanca, and Brazil has its problems, dear. So much poverty and greed. You know that. It doesn't afford you the opportunities Spain does."

Blanca shook off the excuses. She wondered why she thought her parents would open up now when they'd never shared anything with her about their last vacation over the years. Why would things change now? There had to be a reason for their secrecy. She had an unsettled feeling, but was determined to get answers soon.

She ended the conversation and passed the phone to Maria, whose eyes lit up at speaking to her sister. They had been close, and Blanca often wondered why they didn't live close to one another.

CHAPTER 16
A TRIGGER

Carlos stopped by the kerb and waited for Blanca to close the front door of her family's home. She was a vision in her transparent white blouse over a black camisole, and long red shorts that showed off her toned, tanned legs that seemed to go for miles. He tried not to think of the heat in his loins at the thought of sliding his hands over those legs, and smiled at her.

Before Blanca could get into his car, her aunt and uncle stepped out of the house. Blanca introduced them and he shook their hands.

Her uncle stared at Carlos. Was he sizing him up? "Good to meet you, Carlos. Enjoy your day."

"It's been a pleasure to meet you both," said Carlos. "I'll take care of her."

Her aunt Maria leaned forward. "Enjoy yourselves."

Blanca waved goodbye and jumped into the passenger seat. "Thanks for offering to show me around Brazil. I appreciate it."

He touched her on the shoulder. "I'm happy to be your guide. You might as well see as much of Brazil as you can before you leave. But I'm guessing you have another reason for sight-seeing."

Blanca coughed, ignoring his statement. "It is a gorgeous day today." She pressed her shorts down and Carlos couldn't help yearning to touch her. She smelled of fresh lavender, and her hair was still wet. She looked as sexy as hell. He smiled, turned on the motor and drove her out of sight of her aunt and uncle.

The first stop on his itinerary was Sugarloaf Mountain. The parking lot was a short walk to the cable car station that overlooked Guanabara Bay and the mountain. "I hope you're okay with heights. The view's amazing up high."

She nodded. "All good, Carlos."

Carlos took Blanca's hand as they stepped into the glass-topped cable car. He could see her body shaking as she turned to him with an awkward smile. Why hadn't she mentioned being afraid of heights? It was too late to back out now—the cable car rose off the ground, moving towards the mountain. He savoured the spectacular views of the blue sky misted with clouds, and the greenery and bay below.

Blanca swallowed. "The mountain looks like a huge rock. But the view's beautiful in spite of the jerky movement." She squeezed his hand so hard she cut off his circulation, but he ignored the pain. He wanted to wrap his arms around her and make her feel safe, but he admired her brave front.

The cable car stopped at a scenic viewpoint. They walked along the platform, holding on to the steel bar as they gazed at the trees and brush that climbed the mountains around blue Guanabaro Bay.

But Carlos looked at the way the wind tossed Blanca's hair, which she drew out of her eyes. His body had responded when he took her hand in the cable car, but at least she looked more relaxed, now. "We'll have to get back into the cable car, Blanca. Will you be all right?"

She nodded. "Of course. What's after this?" She snapped photos with her phone.

"We're taking the train. You'll see." He wanted to surprise her, enjoying the light in her eyes at the wonder of the sight.

Returning to Carlos's car, they made their way to the Corcovado Railway. The seats filled up with tourists and locals, and he sat by her side. "The train's taking us to the statue called Christ the Redeemer. It's on top of Corcovado Mountain."

Blanca nodded. "I read about the statue representing Christ's sacrifice."

Carlos leaned forward, their shoulders touching as he told his story. "A priest apparently came up with the concept back in the 1800s. He wanted a Christian statue on top of Mount Corcovado and tried to get a princess to fund it. The idea was scrapped, but after World War I, the church groups were worried about the lack of faith in the Brazilian community. They thought that putting a huge statue of Jesus on top of the mountain would restore the Catholic faith. Having the statue on the mountain meant that people could see it from anywhere and everywhere in Rio."

"Interesting," said Blanca.

When the train let them off at Corcovado Mountain, Blanca and Carlos wandered around the platform and climbed towards the Christ the Redeemer statue. They pushed their way through the crowds and gazed over the congested city buildings, mountain peaks, clumps of trees, and sailboats gliding along the smooth blue water of the bay.

"I cannot put in words how beautiful this is." Blanca took more photos, including one of Carlos, blushing when he posed in a way that showed off his biceps.

Half an hour later, they walked inside the Corcovado restaurant with its padded chairs surrounded by marble tables, displays of assorted fruits on rows of shelves, and glass displays of an array of food. They moved to the terrace and sat outside the restaurant with a view of the mountains and sloping trees.

After receiving their food, Carlos bit into a burger and Blanca dug into a chicken and rice dish. Carlos picked up a napkin and dabbed her chin. "You've got a bit of rice around your mouth." His eyes lingered at her lips with a yearning to kiss her.

Blanca blushed. "Thanks." She appeared to be oblivious to her surroundings as she fixed her gaze on him. His body yearned for her touch. He reached out and stroked her cheek while she closed her eyes, and he savoured the soft warmth of her skin.

Opening her eyes suddenly, Blanca rose. "I think we should go."

Carlos hid his disappointment. "But you haven't finished your food."

"I'm full, and you've finished."

Carlos and Blanca returned to his car in an awkward silence. "Where to next, Blanca? Is there anywhere you'd like to go?"

She nodded. "The National Library. Something about it intrigues me."

Carlos drove to the National Library at the centre of Rio de Janeiro, and parked nearby. At the entrance of the massive old building, Carlos turned to Blanca. "The building's been renovated, which is why there's such an imposing architecture. The structure has a Greek-style setting with its huge columns, windows, and flat-topped roof."

"You know your history. I love it."

"I'll follow you," Carlos said. "I haven't been here for a few years."

The strong, chilly wind in the autumn sunshine tossed Blanca's hair again as she climbed the broad steps with Carlos at her side. She beamed at the massive interior spaces with their statues and sculptures and the skylights of coloured glass. His heart warmed at her sense of wonder at the beauty of Brazil with a special woman beside him.

Blanca and Carlos roamed the library, and joined a group of tourists for a guided tour. They admired the works of art in every corner and thematic exhibitions.

They walked down a red-carpeted, marble staircase with a prominent cast-iron railing that looked like black spirals. Alongside the staircase were two female statues with their hands on their heads, upon which they carried many large lights. Continuing to roam the library, Blanca spotted a collection of Brazilian popular music on CDs.

Carlos picked up a CD. "This music is either samba or *sertanejo*." She looked blankly at him. "Sertanejo music was similar to American country music."

Blanca's body jerked at the sound of a passersby's ringtone. It sounded like cymbals, and drums combined with the screeching sound of a girl laughing. Her legs became unsteady and she sat on a chair with her head bowed. The beating of the drums in the tone reverberated in his ears, not enjoying the sounds.

Carlos came to her side in a flash. "Blanca, what's wrong?" He put his hand on the small of her back as she stared at him, without seeing him. "Blanca." He caressed her back and she came to. He bent to her level. "What happened? You look like you're about to vomit."

She took a deep breath. "I'm sorry, Carlos. I have this thumping sound going off in my head as if it's about to explode, but I don't know why."

"You look rattled. Was it the ringtone that spooked you?" He leaned forward and peered into her eyes, but Blanca moved back, turning her head to avoid his penetrating gaze.

Blanca shrugged. "I don't know, Carlos. I must've heard it before." She slowed down her breath and took a seat in front of a computer. "I'm fine."

He knit his brows. "Are you sure?"

"Can we go now?"

He rose with Blanca and together, they made their way to the exit. "How about an early dinner? I think we need to talk."

Blanca nodded, and they strolled to a local Brazilian restaurant, the warm wind appearing to ease her flushed face. She walked cautiously as they stepped onto an outdoor decking area ignoring muffled voices as she pushed her way through to a table. Carlos sat beside her. "Are you okay to talk?"

Blanca managed a smile. "Sure, I'm fine. I probably didn't get enough sleep."

Carlos knew she was lying. Her demeanour had changed with the ringtone, but what did it trigger in her? She was hiding something.

A waiter approached and smiled, handing them menus. As the evening darkened, an outdoor light came on.

Carlos fiddled with his fingers and peered into his lap. "What did the ringtone remind you of, Blanca?"

Blanca ignored his question. "Let's order dinner."

Carlos nodded. He wanted to get to know Blanca, and he hoped she opened up about whatever was bothering her.

CHAPTER 17
A FRIENDLY DINNER

Blanca and Carlos dug into a dinner of a rice stew with chicken. She was grateful they'd steered towards lighter topics as she couldn't explain why the ringtone bothered her. It had something to do with her Brazil vacation. It had to be that.

He wiped his mouth with a napkin and leaned forward, his eyes filled with concern. "So why did you choose to come to Brazil for work?"

Blanca put down her fork. "Isn't it obvious?"

Carlos shrugged. "Apart from the promotion, was there another reason?"

Blanca didn't want to go there because she barely knew Carlos. He seemed nice enough, but men were always nice in the beginning. Their true colours didn't come out until later in a relationship. When it was too late. Not that she was in a relationship with Carlos, but he looked keen. She did admire the way he flicked the hair out of his eyes, the way he licked his bottom lip when he was in deep thought, and his muscular arms tensing in his tight shirt. Even the way he walked showed a gentle grace and sex appeal.

Stop it!

She brushed her thoughts aside and responded to his question in a manner she was comfortable with. "My parents are from Brazil and I was curious about the place. I wanted to get to know my parents' native country."

He nodded. "Do you remember much about Brazil?"

Blanca shook her head. "Only fragments and feelings of déjà vu, but nothing much." She hesitated. "My dad and Pedro were friends, so maybe you knew my dad. His name is Miguel."

Carlos shook his head. "I've never met any of Pedro's old friends."

"They seemed to have had a falling-out and I wondered what happened to their friendship."

"Have you asked Pedro about it?"

Blanca lightly chuckled. "Not yet, but I will. I spoke to my dad the other day. He said they had grown apart, but I get the feeling there's more to it." She had to change the subject as Carlos obviously didn't know anything. "What do you do for fun?"

Carlos gave her a questioning look. "I keep myself busy with stuff I like to do. My mind gets cluttered with books I love reading, photos I take for my freelance work, and woodwork design. I went to the National Library a few years ago, and got my inspiration for photo collections there. Like I said, a collection of pictures can tell a story a lot more than words. They're priceless." His eyes lit up. "What do you like doing, Blanca?"

She kept a cool exterior. "I like yoga and exercise. I love reading, too."

"And you speak both Portuguese and Spanish. Such a talented lady." Blanca swallowed and blushed, her eyes taken in by his own as his gaze lingered. She looked away and fiddled with the tablecloth. Her hand shook as she gripped the glass of wine and took a sip. Her throat was dry and her forehead dripped in sweat.

"You're also multilingual, more than I am. You speak English, as well as Spanish?"

He nodded. "My English is not enough for a proper conversation, but I can always study it further." He put down his beer. "And what books or authors do you like reading?"

She peered into the distance. "I love Isabelle Allende and Gabriel Garcia Marquez's *One Hundred Years of Solitude*."

Carlos leaned forward, his eyes sparkling. "I like Marquez, but Isabelle's work is not to my taste. We should do a book swap. I'll share mine if you share yours."

Blanca chuckled, her face flushed. Why did her mind envision Carlos's naked torso? "I have a few books here with me, actually."

Carlos opened his mouth, then closed it. He shifted in his seat. Her eyes wandered around the patrons coming and going, a feeling of déjà vu filling her senses. She thought her family must have come to this restaurant on their vacation as an image flashed in her mind: Pedro looming larger than life as he argued with someone, money changing hands. Was he giving someone money or was it the other way around? Her revived memory showed Brazilian notes.

Carlos brought her out of her reverie. "Penny for your thoughts, Blanca."

She would keep it to herself until it made better sense. Besides, he was related to the man and she didn't want to make trouble. It wasn't her style. "I'm curious about Pedro. Was he always so ambitious?"

He laughed. "Always. I guess it might've been why he divorced."

Blanca nodded. "That must have affected Jose."

He shrugged. "I think Pedro tried to compensate by bailing him out of trouble more times than I can count. His personality changed from jovial to a guy who *pretends* to be jovial."

Blanca tilted her head. "What do you think happened?"

Carlos pressed a finger into his chin, then cleared his throat. "I wish I knew. Jose's my cousin and I respect him in some ways, but his behaviour is questionable sometimes. And Pedro's too. He's my dad's brother, but they stopped talking years ago, not long after my mother...died." He turned away, so Blanca didn't question him further.

Blanca's stomach churned as she pondered what was going on with Jose and Pedro—a mystery she longed to uncover. She became wistful at the thought of Carlos losing his mother. She couldn't imagine losing her own the way he had.

CHAPTER 18
FISHING FOR ANSWERS

When Blanca stepped into the house that night, Juan and Maria were whispering in the kitchen. Turning towards her abruptly, they looked as if they'd been caught committing a crime.

Her aunt pressed her lips together and rubbed her hands. "How was your sightseeing, dear? You were gone a while."

"Carlos took me to dinner after showing me the sights. I called, but no one answered. I left a message." She stood awkwardly. "What's going on? Did I interrupt something?"

Maria and Juan rose from their chairs and stared at each other, both quiet. Something was going on. *Had* she interrupted something?

Julio cleared his throat. "We got off the phone with your father. He was asking about you. I told him you were out and he was worried."

Blanca's father had always been strict with her when she lived with her parents, and it was part of the reason she moved out. She'd felt stifled by his stern attitude ever since she was a teenager, and after university, at twenty-three, she had moved into her own home.

She shook her head. "I'm not ten years old anymore, Uncle. Did you tell him that at least?" Maria had turned away as if fixated on something else.

Juan nodded. "I did, but you know your father. He worries as if you were still his little girl." He leaned in and kissed her on the cheek. "I'll be going to bed, Blanca. You have a good night."

"Goodnight, Uncle."

Maria broke out of her reverie. "I'll be going, too. Goodnight, Blanca." Her demeanour was flat.

Blanca put up her hand. "Wait up. I need to talk to you, aunty. It's important. You can sleep in tomorrow morning. How about I prepare us an herbal tea?"

Maria smiled. "No, I'll make it, darling. You take a seat." With shaky hands, she took out two cups and prepared the tea. She appeared to be miles away as she stirred the tea. What was going on with her lately?

After setting the hot drinks at the table, her aunt sat opposite. "What's on your mind, Blanca? Is it work?"

Blanca shook her head and took a deep breath. "I need the truth."

Her aunt's eyes darkened before turning away. "What are you talking about, dear? What truth?" Her eyes peered into the distance as if she didn't want to hear the response.

"I need the truth about the past. I've been having these nightmares and they've been getting worse since I got here. I have this feeling something about Brazil is not quite right. I got this uneasy feeling when I heard someone's ringtone today, and I remembered something about Pedro while I was at this seafood restaurant. What happened all those years ago, Aunt Maria? I know you're keeping something from me, and I need to know."

Her aunt tightened her grip on the cup and averted her eyes. She scratched her forehead. "Nothing happened, Blanca, nothing. Your father had work issues as far as I know."

"You can't honestly tell me we left Brazil early because of my father's work. He had authority in his job and could be flexible. Your neighbour shared a few things. She mentioned his nose was bruised, and he was angry about something. Who was he angry with?"

Her aunt sipped her tea but Blanca's was still too hot. Maria got up, washed her cup in the sink, and turned to Blanca. "Your imagination is getting the better of you. Like I said, your father had a work emergency, I believe. How about you finish off your tea and get some sleep? It's been a long day." She kissed her niece on the cheek. "I'll see you in the morning."

She was holding back about something. "Aunt! Why did the newspaper article about the favelas upset you?"

Her face reddened and her body stilled. "I...I...knew someone in the favela and she was exploited, but that is all I'm going to say. It's late and I cannot get into it tonight."

What was she hiding? "Does it have anything to do with us leaving early for Spain or not?"

Maria swallowed. "No, and as I understand it, your parents moved you to Spain as there were more opportunities for you, and your father headed up his investment business there." Her aunt kissed her on the cheek again. "Good night." She gave her a reassuring smile. "I love you, Blanca. Always remember that, no matter what happens." She walked away.

Blanca smiled at her aunt and went to her bedroom. She lay on the bed, drawing her fingers through her hair. Her aunt had always been nurturing, but the way she expressed her endearment was somewhat strange. It was as if something ominous was coming. But if she had known someone in the favela, who was it and what happened to them? Did the person die? She was determined to find out the truth.

CHAPTER 19
A MOMENT

Blanca hugged her knees as she sat on the blanket over the sand, watching the waves lap at the Ipanema beach. Carlos had invited her to the beach for a take-away seafood dinner. What was she doing, meeting with Carlos at the beach when she couldn't get too close to him? Her ex-boyfriend, Jorge, had been pleasant until his true nature had emerged. How did she know Carlos wouldn't turn out to be the same?

A couple stood in the water at waist level with their arms wrapped around one another, kissing. Why didn't they get a room? She turned and watched another couple walking along the shore, and felt a pang of envy. But she wasn't in the right head space for a relationship, even if she had yearned to have Carlos touch her. Relationships didn't work—plus, she would soon be back in Madrid and far away from him.

A gentle touch on her shoulder alerted her to Carlos. He beamed, laying a large plastic bag on the blanket. Their hands brushed as he sat beside her. She ignored the flutter in her stomach. A wave of unexplainable emotion dizzied her. She breathed deeply, trying to focus on the smells of fish, spices and herbs.

Carlos dug into the bag and handed her a plastic container and a fork. Then he took out his own container, flipping open the lid to reveal mixed, battered seafood.

The silence was pleasant as she savoured the tastes and seasoning, while watching the swimmers who braved the waves.

Carlos broke the silence. "What do you think about me taking photos of you?"

Blanca swallowed her fish and turned to him. "I don't know. Why?"

"I always try to find the rawest emotion in things. A perspective others don't see in my photographs." He smiled. "Think about it while we eat."

Blanca cleared her throat and wiped crumbs of batter from her bottom lip. Carlos wiped it with his finger, his lingering gaze drawing her into his deep, dark eyes. Her breath stopped and her throat felt parched. She looked away to fight back her growing attraction. She spotted a flicker of disappointment in his eyes.

He clenched his hands. "I want to apologise for the way Jose spoke to you the other day. He had no right to intimidate you that way, and I had a few words with him."

She shrugged. "I don't know why he's against me writing about the human side of favelas." She exhaled. "I'll leave it for now."

Carlos leaned forward, drawing her hair out of her eyes. "I'll talk to him again. But I for one, won't let Jose stop me from taking photos of the favelas and helping others out when I can. He was born with a silver spoon in his mouth and doesn't like controversy. All he cares about is partying and drinking away his problems. Anyway, let's not talk about him." Several minutes of silence was comforting. "I'm building a collection of photos that I plan to show in a gallery."

Blanca's eyes widened. "Can you do that when it's meant to be for the magazine article I'm writing?"

He nodded. "I'm turning freelance and plan to leave work one day soon. I have big dreams. My friend, Luiz and I might make a partnership of it. Part of the business might involve training others in photography, consulting businesses, and organising online courses. It's huge for those who need creative design for their businesses, particularly entrepreneurs."

Blanca wiped her mouth. "It sounds good. Where would you be based?" She bowed her head, her mind turning to her aunt.

He shrugged. "I'm not sure at the moment. It's only in the planning stages." He sipped water from a chilled bottle. "What's wrong? Your mind seems to be somewhere else today."

Blanca gazed down the beach. A skinny man in the distance walked nearer and stopped to stare at her. What was he doing? "I believe my aunt knows something about why we left early on our vacation here the last time, but she's keeping it to herself. And the other day she looked frazzled when reading an article about the favelas. She has to be hiding something."

Carlos stared out over the sea, ignoring the seagulls surrounding their leftovers. "This transfer to Brazil is more of a mission than wanting an actual experience of Brazil, isn't it?"

Blanca sensed it was right to share this with him. He might be able to shed further light on Pedro and Jose by searching his memory. "I started having nightmares when I left Brazil the first time, as a child, after we left Brazil earlier than scheduled."

Carlos tilted his head. "Why is the past bothering you so much? You were only ten at the time, so how does it impact you now?"

Blanca bowed her head. "Now that I've returned, my nightmares have come back." She could not bring herself to tell him about the note she received, the flashbacks, or the sense that someone was watching her. "I have a strange feeling that something bad happened during my vacation back then, and my dreams are warning me about something in this place." She paused. "Before we left, my parents went to a lunch gathering at Pedro's house. I could talk to Pedro."

Carlos chuckled. "He won't tell you anything. He's a man who likes a perfect life and sweeps things under the carpet. Nothing to ruin his reputation, especially when it comes to Jose and protecting him at all costs." He leaned in, his scent wafting over her. "Do you think your parents are hiding a secret?"

Blanca hesitated. "I believe so, but they deny anything happened."

Carlos leaned forward, inching closer towards her. "Is it possible your family left early because of your dad's work?

She smiled, her heart warming. "I don't think so." Blanca wanted to share more with Carlos, but wasn't ready. She had said enough.

The man in the distance continued to stare in her direction. She was about to mention it to Carlos when he walked away. He must have changed his mind about the beach. But he did look familiar.

Carlos nodded. "How can I help?"

Blanca shrugged. "I'm not sure, but I'll let you know."

He got up. "Can I take photos of you? This is the perfect setting, and I promise it will be quick." She nodded and rose. "Stand over by that tree and give me your best pose." Blanca stood near the tree and smiled. He retrieved his camera bag and clicked photos. "I want a particular pose and your hair has to be a certain style so I can capture you better in the light. Let me show you." He approached and brought her arms to her side and bent down to have her left leg at a right angle. Blanca stopped breathing, the warmth of his touch drawing her into his body as his musky scent permeated her senses. She couldn't think and her mouth was dry with heat in her loins. His fingers drew a hair strand out of her eye, her skin tingling at his tender touch. Oh, God! He was so handsome and yet she had to think about how wrong this was. Her erotic thoughts about him had to stop.

When he moved away and took pictures of her, she got her breath back.

All too soon, Carlos put down his camera, telling he had had enough images. They sat again, staring out over the waves. When her knee brushed against his, a wave of emotion overwhelmed her. Her heart beat fast and her surroundings appeared surreal as Carlos scooted closer to her, stroking her wrist as if to reassure her. His breath was close to her ear and she yearned to face him. Her lips parted as all rational thought left her mind, her physical and emotional need stronger. Her knees loosened and spread slightly while her breath visibly hitched. He took her hand and pressed it against his lips, closing his eyes briefly. The noises of beachgoers fell into the background. In that moment, only Blanca and Carlos existed. Her hands were warm in his as he lay them down on her lap. He turned his body around, his right hand reaching up to caress her cheeks.

In spite of her initial need for him, her rational mind took over. This wouldn't work between them. They were from two different countries and had both suffered with people they loved. No, it was a mistake to kiss him. How could she trust someone she didn't even know?

She abruptly got to her feet. "I have to go." Quickly, she picked up her bag and scurried away from the shore towards her car, parked ten minutes away. She didn't dare turn back to see Carlos, who had fallen silent.

CHAPTER 20
A MEETING

Carlos paid the taxi driver as he got out in the favelas, gripping a large envelope. He walked through the dirt and debris surrounding the dilapidated buildings and the deserted streets. The rough, uneven ground could make anyone trip and hit their head against loose rocks and rubble.

A few steps away to Juliana's home, a boy of about four years walked alone in the street. He was barefoot and bare-chested and wore only loose shorts. His curly hair was long, and he carried a stick.

Carlos approached. "Hello there. Where's your mummy?"

The boy pointed to a building a few metres away. Carlos took his hand and led him back to his brick and cement house. A teenage woman with a cigarette in her mouth and tattered clothing reached for the boy. She was barefoot with a missing front tooth, and looked malnourished. "Mateo, my son. Where have you been?"

"You're his mother?" asked Carlos. She nodded and wrapped her arms around the little boy. She couldn't have been more than sixteen years old and his heart went out to her. He took out his wallet and handed her several Brazilian Reals. "Please take this." He took out a card from his shirt pocket and gave it to the woman. "If you need help, call this number. This is a welfare agency that can help if you're struggling with money or any other problems." He didn't specify what kind of problem, as these neighbourhoods were all about survival, drug trafficking and child exploitation. He hoped she'd take up the offer of help, or she'd be stuck forever in this place, barely surviving.

The girl smiled. "Thank you."

Carlos made his way back to the street, hoping Juliana was home. Each time he came to one of the favelas of Brazil, his heart broke and his mind scrutinised every detail. He'd seen policemen brokering drug deals with well-known pimps, being handed large envelopes and loose cash out in the open. Young girls solicited old, paunchy men, and pregnant teenage girls were beaten in the streets. He had tried to intervene, but each time, the police did nothing. He wasn't surprised to see the poor son of a teenage mother wandering the streets. Who knew whether she had resorted to prostitution for survival. It was all these girls knew. Often, their parents encouraged them to prostitute themselves to get food on the table, and if they fell pregnant, fatherhood ended then. No man wanted to acknowledge he'd got an underage prostitute pregnant.

In spite of prostitution being legal in Brazil, it was still exploitation for girls under seventeen years old. Yet, many of them approached men wearing their skimpy attire, shorts and fitted tops which displayed cleavage and bare stomachs. The men assumed these girls were consenting to be exploited, ignoring the social pressures that continued the cycle of prostitution due to perpetuating poverty. Many of them were homeless, hungry and addicted to drugs.

Underage prostitution was a huge problem in spite of multiple children's rights organisations fighting against it. The Brazilian government spent millions of Reals to fight against child exploitation, but all these efforts hardly appeared to scratch the surface. More had to be done.

Carlos eased his way towards Juliana's house when a prickle of unease rippled down his spine. He heard footsteps and sensed a presence behind him but when he turned around, the street was empty. He shook off his paranoia, stepped to the front of the dilapidated building and knocked on the cracked wooden door. Juliana was surviving better than others, and his mother had often assisted her financially in the past.

A woman in her forties opened up the door. She wore a long, ripped skirt and a white t-shirt which had seen better days. Her tied-up hair appeared unwashed and her eyes looked sad and fatigued. "Carlos, come in. How long has it been since we last met?"

He walked inside with a reassuring smile. "It's been a long time. I'm sorry I haven't come sooner, but I've been busy with work and my freelance projects." He stretched out his arm. "I have photos of Antonia here." He handed over the envelope, but he had left out the photo of Antonia made up and dressed scantily, with a man's arm in a leather jacket, draped over her shoulder. Juliana didn't need to see her daughter made up as if she was prostituting herself.

Her eyes lit up and she took the envelope with quivering hands. As she took out the photographs, his eyes scanned the home, which featured a wardrobe he'd built for her the last time they'd met. The single bed was covered with a stained bedspread, and mould and cracks lined the walls. He'd have to return and get those cracks fixed and the mould removed. "These are beautiful." She sighed. "I wish this poor girl, Leonor in the favela was not missing. It brings up so much about my Antonia. I wish I knew where my Antonia is, but I hope she is happy and safe. It is all I hope for, but the not-knowing kills me every time I'm reminded of her sweet face."

"I hope you find her soon, Juliana. Perhaps get in touch with the police again."

She shook her head. "I have, but they don't care anymore. They're done."

He nodded. "I'm sorry." He waited until she composed herself. "What do you remember about my mother, Juliana? I know I was young when I came once with her here."

She put the photos on the table and offered him a seat on an old crate, while she sat on her bed. He'd need to return with a proper chair the next time. "I only saw her a few times, but she wanted to return and never did."

Carlos knit his brows. "Why didn't she come back?"

"I don't know, but the last time I saw her she had jumped at every sound and kept looking over her shoulder. She refused to take any more photos." She knit her brows. "How is your mother now?"

Carlos's chest tightened. "She died of a heart attack when I was a teenager." He had not mentioned his mother's death the last time he saw Juliana, and had deflected her question about how her mother was back then.

Juliana rose and touched his shoulder. "I am sorry." Her eyes peered into the distance. "She was a beautiful woman with a heart of gold, and helped me with food and money. Such a shame and waste to lose an amazing soul."

Carlos leaned forward. "Do you know why she was scared?"

Juliana remained silent for a minute and averted her eyes. "I don't know, Carlos, but something definitely scared her. I wonder if it was the reason she stopped visiting me, but who knows. I guess we'll never know, now she's gone."

Carlos nodded. "Can I take a few pictures for my collection? I'm having a gallery showing soon, and need more photos to contrast the range of homes here."

She became wistful. "Of course."

He pulled out his camera and snapped photos of the interior of her house. As he stepped outside to take more photographs, he glimpsed someone peeking around the corner, who disappeared almost at once. His spine chilled as he was certain he was being watched.

CHAPTER 21
UNEASE IN THE FAVELAS

Blanca tossed and turned in bed as a hand reached out to cover her mouth. "It's a dream. Only a dream," said the commanding voice. Sweating and gasping for breath, she woke up and wiped her perspiring brow with the back of her hand.

The light from the partially drawn curtain coming into her room calmed her and brought her back to the present. When would these nightmares stop, and what truly demanded her attention in Brazil? She remembered the counselling she had started a few years earlier, which had only accelerated her anxiety as soon as the psychologist dug into her past. Blanca wasn't ready to face her past then, but she was now.

Shifting out of bed, she turned on her phone and ignored the missed calls and messages from Carlos. She did not want to discuss their near-kiss encounter during her moment of weakness. Being in Brazil made her overly emotional. A cup of coffee would wake her up.

In the kitchen, Maria appeared more haggard than usual. "Are you okay, Maria? You don't look well." She poured coffee and sat opposite Maria.

"I have my good days and bad days, dear Blanca, but I'll be fine. A little rest in bed will help me today."

Blanca wondered whether her aunt had a physical illness, or suffered from something else entirely. On numerous occasions she hadn't looked well, but Blanca knew her aunt wasn't ready to discuss it.

Maria hovered around the kitchen while Julio went out to the back of the house. He liked to putter in his garden.

Blanca sipped her coffee, warming her hands around the cup. "I'm visiting the favelas as part of my work today." She winced as her aunt's face turned pale and her hands shook. "I'm interviewing Carlos's friend, Luiz about infrastructure development in Brazil. It's what Pedro wants for the magazine, and I'm looking forward to it."

Maria placed a hand on her chest. "Oh, but why? The favelas are dangerous places for a young woman like you, dear Blanca. Why must you go there for the interview? Can't he come to you at your office?" Her hands continued to visibly shake. Something was going on with her and it obviously had to do with more than the favelas.

Blanca decided not to bring up the reason for Maria's resistance, but she was curious. "What's going on with you, Maria? You're shaking."

Maria got up abruptly, put her cup into the sink and rinsed it. As she was about to lay the cup on the dish rack, she dropped it, scattering ceramic shards across the floor. As she bent down to pick up the pieces, Blanca pushed her aside gently. "You sit down. I'll get the brush and pan." She swept up the pieces and threw them into the kitchen bin. When she looked at the wall clock, she gasped. She was going to be late to meet Carlos at the favela. But could she leave Maria in this state? Whatever the favela triggered in Maria, it was obviously traumatic to the point of making her physically ill. "Are you going to be all right, Maria?"

Maria nodded as colour returned to her cheeks. "Of course, but I still wish you weren't going to that place on your own. Please be careful."

She would question her aunt about her emotional state another time. "I won't be on my own. My colleague, Carlos will be with me. It's all fine." Blanca waved goodbye and headed out in her rental car.

***

Blanca parked her car a fair distance from the favela and walked to meet Carlos and Luiz. She kept her phone in one hand and gripped the shoulder straps of her handbag with the other. Swarms of people passed her until she reached an empty alley. A sign directed her to the way to the main shops, and Blanca hurried her pace.

A sense of déjà vu overwhelmed her. A prickle of unease ran down her spine as she looked behind her. Why was it deserted in this part of the favela, as if all the residents had chosen to remain inside?

Blanca took a calming breath, shaking away her negative thoughts and laughed to herself. She wasn't far from the main shopping area. She knew she was safe, and her crazy thoughts were ridiculous.

A skinny young man with a missing tooth approached her and put out his hand. He looked like the man at the beach. Was he following her?

"You got money?" He gave her a mocking smile, but she shook her head and pressed on without slowing down. Why did this man look familiar? Had she seen him before? The man followed. "Come on, just a few Real. I need the money for my sick mother."

Blanca averted her eyes and rushed forward, her heart pounding as he walked alongside her. He put his hand out.

"I don't have cash on me. Sorry."

The man's eyes squinted as he inched closer. "Bullshit! You got nice stuff and you expect me to believe you got no money."

Blanca shook her head and accelerated her pace, beginning to pant. "My friend's close, so please leave."

He threw his head back and laughed. Instead of leaving, he shoved her to the ground, grazing her knee. He latched onto her bag but Blanca pulled it back and gripped it tightly, shaking her head. "Let it go. I'll call the police."

He scoffed as he continued to pull the bag strap. "I own the police. They don't do nothing. Give me the damn bag."

She lifted up her body and elbowed him in the chest. He cowered, giving her a few seconds to run.

He shouted out, "Don't go poking your nose in the favelas, bitch."

She didn't dare look behind her for fear he was still following her, and ran to the shopping area, only slowing when the surroundings were quiet. She looked behind and didn't see her attacker, but why had he taunted her? Was he targeting her specifically in relation to the favelas and sending her a message?

Her body shook. Luckily, he hadn't been very strong, but she was still trembling and fighting images in her head. Images of a group of men smoking. The back of a large man inside a home. Pictures of a glass filled with dirty water. Was it a flashback? A memory of the past?

CHAPTER 22
INTERVIEW

Carlos watched Blanca with a keen eye. The way her body swayed aroused something in him, and the way she looked shyly towards him was sensual. He wanted her, but when she came near, her demeanour suggested she'd been in a traumatic scuffle. Her hair was messy, her face flushed, her knee had a scrape, and she walked slower than usual. He frowned. "What happened, Blanca? You look like you've been in a battle. How did you graze your knee?"

She shrugged. "A man tried to steal my handbag as I was walking here."

Carlos gasped and looked around. "Oh, God! Are you all right?"

She nodded. "I was tougher than him, and I got away. Don't worry." He wondered if she was putting on a front. Her hand quivered and she avoided his eyes.

Carlos inched his way forward and caressed her cheek. "Your face is red, too. Are you sure you're okay? I can take you home and I'll do the interview. It's fine."

Blanca shook her head. "No, Carlos. Please don't make it bigger than it is. I'm good."

Carlos didn't believe her, but he didn't have the right to pressure her. She wanted to be independent and do her job, and he didn't fault her for that. But if he ever got his hands on the creep who hurt her, he'd put him in hospital. His protective instinct kicked in, but he made an effort to focus on the task ahead.

As Carlos and Blanca climbed the steep alleys, a strong stench filled his nostrils and the hubbub of activity filled his hearing. Brick and cement houses were built close together. Young children rushed and skipped around them. An older man was making a fence out of rubbish while an artist painted the exterior of an art centre soon to open. Several policemen patrolled the streets, possibly to purge drug gangs.

Carlos pulled out his camera. He turned to Blanca, who watched policemen questioning a few of the children. Most likely, asking them about any signs of trouble from the drug-infested gangs. "Don't worry, Blanca. The police presence provides a bit of a scare tactic for these drug gangs here. But it's much worse in Alemao than here. The police try to pacify all the favelas, but you'll always have conflict between the gangs and the police."

She nodded. "Where's your friend, Luiz, who we're supposed to interview?" Her eyes scanned the neighbourhood, and he wanted to sink deep into them. *Stop it!* They had a job to do and Pedro was counting on them to publish an informative article.

"I'm not sure. We'll wait here for a bit." They sat on rubble, Blanca's shoulders stiffening with each footstep and muffled voice she heard. Her eyes roved as if she was expecting trouble. He wanted to reach out to her, but refrained because she obviously wasn't ready for intimacy between them. Not that he was either, after the way his late girlfriend, Sofia had died on him. He lacked trust in relationships, having lost his mother too, and not to mention, a father who had been absent in his life. No, his life was fine the way it was for now.

The putrid air made him cover his mouth and nose, but he pushed through the discomfort. The way Blanca bit her bottom lip made her even more beautiful and vulnerable, and he wondered what had made her anxious around the favelas. It wasn't only her ordeal with the bag snatcher, but something deeper was going on with her. She kept looking over her shoulder, and couldn't seem to relax in spite of the number of people roaming the area. Something obviously happened to her the first time she came here, but what? Did it have something to do with the reason her family left early for Spain? He was as determined as Blanca to find out so she could move forward and no longer have recurrent nightmares.

He saw his friend, Luiz rushing up the street towards them, waving his large hand. His towering height, broad shoulders and lanky build made him noticeable, and his smiling green eyes showed his humanity. He drew a hand through his black, frizzy shoulder-length hair and looked at Blanca with interest. Carlos hoped Blanca wasn't attracted to him, as he'd have a hard time seeing her with anyone else.

"Carlos, my man." Luiz gave him a high-five and turned his blazing eyes towards Blanca. "And who's this gorgeous young lady?" He put his hand over his heart.

Carlos ignored his jealous pangs. "This is Blanca, the editor from Spain I spoke to you about. It was her idea to interview you about what goes on in these favelas, particularly with infrastructure and businesses helping out."

She smiled awkwardly and shifted back when he approached a bit too close. "Nice to meet you, Luiz."

Luiz bowed. "The pleasure is all mine." His eyes turned towards a small internet cafe. "Let's take a seat over there and I'll grab you both a coffee."

Carlos and Blanca moved towards the run-down cafe and sat on dusty chairs outside the building. They stared at one another. "You're a nervous wreck. I'm glad I came with you today. I don't think you should be coming here on your own."

Blanca chuckled. "Someone has to write this article." She searched the area as if on her guard.

Luiz returned with three steaming cups of coffee on a weathered tray and set it on the wobbly table in front of them. After small talk, Luiz clasped his hands together. "Now, what would you lovely people like to know?"

Blanca took out a notepad and pen. "First, can you tell me about the history of these favelas? How they started and what businesses have done to help."

Luiz nodded. "Sure." He sipped his coffee, set it down and crossed his legs. "The favelas started from the time slavery ended in 1888, when poor imported slaves couldn't find any affordable housing. The poor people built their own houses from brick and cement. There were no zoning laws and no public services. They never had government presence, became self-sufficient, and created their own associations. A mini-city and creative survival is what you could call it. Two extremes of society: the favelas known as the 'People of the Hill' and the richer people known as 'The People of the Asphalt.'" He took a breath. "The police come here and to other favelas for these pacification programs to get rid of drug gangs, but at the same time, when they tried to rid the favelas of crime, there were a lot of deaths. The strong police presence has reduced crimes, but it still exists. It's hard to eliminate everything." He picked up his cup and took another sip while waving to passersby. "I take photos of things that are wrong in the favelas and send them to the media, which creates change. A number of people have set up businesses or services like barber shops, tour guide services, domestic maids, moto-taxi drivers, and daycare helpers. Even banks have started up with quite a bit of help from the outside."

Blanca nodded, busily jotting down notes while Carlos took a few shots of the nearby services and people wandering the streets. She drank her coffee and set it aside. "How much has the Brazilian government helped these favelas?"

Luiz smiled. "The Rio government has set up self-help schemes in the favelas so that communities are given the training to improve their houses. They're offered loans so they can make home improvements. They have creative art centres, photography studios, cafes, restaurants, and barbers. Some are poorer than others, and some favelas are more crime-ridden than others. It's a huge space and anything and everything happens here."

Carlos put down his camera. "The girl, Leonor, who's still missing. Have you heard anything? Not to mention, Antonia who went missing all those years ago? I wonder if the police will ever find her."

Luiz knit his brows. "Her mother keeps asking people about her. I try to help when I can and ask around to see if anyone might've seen her. I've shown the photos your mother took of her to a few people, and I sent them to the media, but nothing's come up. It's a mystery, my friend."

Blanca sighed. "That's horrible. I can't imagine how her mother must feel. Losing her daughter and never knowing what happened. Does she have any other family?"

Luiz shook his head. "Her husband left her for another woman, but she has a sister who helps out. I doubt we'll ever find her daughter. It is her dying wish to find her before she dies."

Carlos frowned. "Do you think her daughter's dead?"

Luiz nodded. "After all these years, I doubt she's alive."

Carlos and Blanca asked Luiz a few more questions. Carlos stretched out his arms and watched calmly as Blanca blushed when Luiz leaned forward to kiss her on the cheek.

"Such a pleasure to meet you, Blanca. I hope to see you again before you leave for Spain. Don't be a stranger." He winked.

Carlos wrapped his arms around his friend. He walked away with Blanca while snapping photos of the steep hills, the houses, the narrow alleys, and the shops and cafes. When he put away his camera, he directed his eyes towards Blanca, who was miles away in her own thoughts. "Are you okay?"

She faced him with worried eyes. "The story about the girl is frightening. I can't imagine losing my own child like that."

"I know. The favelas are famous for deaths, gangs, and missing persons. It's the way of life, but slowly they're changing. As Luiz mentioned, you'll never get rid of anything completely. It's the way of life here and in the rest of the world."

He wondered if the favelas were not changing fast enough when so many people continued to perish or go missing.

CHAPTER 23
RIO NIGHT

Carlos and Blanca sat in their seats at a restaurant across from Isabela and her friend, Juan. Isabela had booked a dinner and samba show in the heart of Rio de Janeiro so that Blanca could experience the full Brazilian experience before she returned to Spain.

Carlos ignored the tight feeling in his stomach at the thought of her leaving. He understood it was best this way. He didn't want to get into a relationship with Blanca when her home was in Madrid. Brazil would be a fading memory for her, and he couldn't commit to someone who didn't plan to live here.

He eyed Isabela's friend, Juan, who sported a moustache and beard with strong, piercing eyes and manly presence. He wondered why Juan was staring at Blanca. Was he attracted to her? Had he met her the last time she was here?

He pushed down his pangs of jealousy and turned to his menu.

A young waiter arrived and placed a skewer of meat in the centre of the table. The delicious char-grilled aroma of the meat and spices made Carlos salivate.

Isabela dug into her piece of meat. "Blanca, here you get to taste the Carioca culture, or what's known as the native taste of Rio de Janeiro. This meat here is known as churrascaria or barbecued meat, and it is to die for, girl."

Blanca beamed, her eyes lighting up as if they could light the darkness that filled Carlos's soul whenever he thought of her leaving. "It looks and smells great." She forked her meat and bit into the tenderness. He was getting aroused by the way her mouth moved, and how she licked up the flowing juices. His heart palpitated at the way she devoured the meat. It was the most erotic thing he'd seen in his life, and he yearned to taste those lips and breathe her scent. *Stop!* "This is heaven. It's so tender and juicy, Isabela."

Isabela nodded. "It's the best." She faced her friend, Juan. "You should tell Carlos what you do for a living, my friend."

Juan looked at Carlos as he wiped his mouth with the napkin and put down his cutlery. He sat back in his chair. "I own an art gallery, and I'm looking for a show about creative expression of life's tragedies and life's beauties." He cleared his throat. "I heard you have an amazing collection of photos of Brazil and the favelas." Juan squared his shoulders. "I have a few photographers lined up for my upcoming exhibition, but I have room for one more, if you're interested. Isabela has been promoting your work to me, and it sounds fascinating."

Carlos leaned forward in his seat, his heart warming. This was his dream come true, and a way to showcase his artistic flair. He took a sip of his beer, not wanting to appear too eager. "I've exhibited in galleries before and I loved the experience." He cleared his throat. "I'd be honoured to be a part of your exhibition. I do have a collection of photos, and I can send you samples if you like."

"It'd be great." Juan dug into his pants pocket and pulled out a business card. "Call me and send me your samples. I'm sure I'll like the photos, and later we can arrange for printing costs, framing, and social media marketing to get the word out there about you possibly joining the herd."

Blanca touched Carlos's shoulder. "What an amazing opportunity, Carlos." He pushed down the tingle in his body, and swallowed.

Juan clinked his glass with Isabela and the rest of the group. "To success." All the others repeated the words, then concentrated on finishing their meals and drinks.

After dinner, they made their way to a theatre a short walk away, sitting in a middle-row seat for the samba show. A row of skimpily clad women waltzed across the stage. They wore feathers in their hair, danced on stiletto heels, and waved a Brazilian flag. A group of bare-chested men wearing red pants strutted and danced, their bare feet gliding across the stage.

Carlos sat beside Blanca. When their hands accidentally touched, Blanca moved her hand away. Carlos could not ignore her sweet, fruity perfume as she turned to see him watching her. She blushed and turned back quickly to watch the samba show.

Outside the theatre at the end of the show, Carlos shook Juan's hand. "I will be in touch about the photos, and thank you for the opportunity."

Juan nodded. "No problem. I look forward to it, Carlos, and thank you for the company." He turned to Blanca. "You have true talent for writing, Blanca. I've read your articles and you have a remarkable gift."

"Thank you," said Blanca.

Isabela wrapped her arms around Blanca. "Hey, girl. I had a great time. You are invited to the photography exhibition, so be prepared."

As Blanca and Carlos walked towards his car, he saw an unknown man watching him. The man wore glasses and stood by his car, a few metres away. His heart raced as he entered his car. When he turned back to face the man, he was moving his finger across his neck. What the hell was going on, and who was this man threatening him? First at the favela and now here.

CHAPTER 24
PHOTO GALLERY

Two weeks after her dinner with Isabel and Juan, Blanca smiled at the name Carlos had written in bold and capital letters on the thick, embossed invitation card, as she got ready to attend Carlos's photographic gallery exhibition.

Blanca wore smart-casual attire. She pressed down her black, fitted dress. Stretch cotton flowed down to her knees, succeeded by black lace down to her ankles. Thin straps showed her well-toned arms, and open-toed stiletto shoes, while comfortable enough, added to her height. With a final look in the mirror, she adjusted her jet-black hair and stared at her blood-shot dark brown eyes. She definitely needed more sleep.

She grabbed her black bag, waved goodbye to her aunt and headed out the door. "Wait, darling," Maria called.

Blanca stopped mid-way out the door. "What is it?"

Maria smirked. "Oh, dear! You look beautiful, Blanca. If your friend, Carlos doesn't sweep you off your feet looking like that, I don't know who will."

Blanca felt herself blush. "Oh, stop it. I keep telling you we're only friends. Okay?"

Her aunt waved her away. "Whatever you say, my dear Blanca. But you do blush every time you mention his name."

Blanca waved goodbye and made her way to the car, grateful to have an aunt who could always lift her mood in spite of her worries. She wanted to stop thinking about Carlos, but his image flashed before her day and night. At least in a few months, she'd be back in Spain and would no longer be dealing with his sexy presence.

As Blanca drove to the centre of Rio de Janeiro, her mind turned again and again to Carlos. She would definitely struggle once she returned to Madrid, but for now she would enjoy his company and support his photographic work. If only Isabela didn't have a family event on today, she could've had company, but Pedro and Elina would be at the gallery to support Carlos. His uncle, Pedro had helped to fund his photographic work.

Blanca wondered about Juan, too. Apparently, he and Isabela were only friends and had been close since high school.

She took a breath when she reached the gallery. She had never been to a photography exhibition, but wanted to support Carlos. She'd get out of her comfort zone and push down the trickles of anxiety. She and Carlos were friends and they supported each other. She was honoured to get an exclusive invitation.

Ferns and colossal trees surrounded the grey building, giving the place a tropical ambience. Blanca made her way to a ramp that led to a glass sliding door, where a towering man dressed in a black shirt and white pants greeted her. He directed her to the second floor. There, people dressed in trendy attire crowded the sparkling, white room with its decorative walls, bar stand, and shiny white floor tiles. Photographs of both Spain and Brazil lined the walls as guests held drinks while observing the photos. Waiters roamed the room in a classic style, wearing fitted black shirts lined with a row of gold buttons, and tight cotton pants.

Blanca stared at the scrumptious-looking finger foods on trays. "What are these?"

One of the waiters who towered over her had smiling blue eyes and carried a large tray of assorted snacks. "We have beef empanadas, Brazilian chicken croquettes, cheese bread, and chicken coxinha, which is a croquette that's deep fried with chicken and cheese."

Blanca picked up a croquette and cheese bread. "Thank you." She savoured the softness of the bread and melting texture in her mouth. Delicious.

A sign listed the few photographers from Brazil and showcased their work from a wide range of cities. The loud voices reverberated in her ears as she stood around awkwardly.

What now? Blanca searched until she spotted Carlos chatting with a gorgeous woman. A pulling sensation in her gut and dry throat made her want to leave, but she put her jealousy aside. The woman was flirting with Carlos, but upon further inspection, she realised it was Elina. She headed towards them and bumped into another waiter carrying trays of white wine.

He smiled. "Sorry about that. Care for a drink, Miss?"

Oh, boy! She could use a drink.

Blanca grabbed a glass with a quivering hand. "Thank you." Heart pounding, she downed half the wine, which warmed her dry throat and calmed her breathing. She suddenly wanted to leave, realising she didn't belong in this scene. It was too fancy for her liking.

She walked around the room and peered at the photographs of clubs, Parque del Buon Retiro, favelas of Brazil, restaurants, cafes, portraits of cafe owners, and the sandy beaches. Carlos had said the theme was "Spain and Brazil at their rawest," and it was obvious the gallery portrayed both the popular tourism of Madrid and Brazil, and the poorer parts and wealthier parts, giving a balanced view of the two countries.

A sudden voice made her jerk. "Blanca, over here." Carlos waved her over, his eyes lighting up.

She took another sip of wine before making her way over. Her nerves started to settle as she dodged circles of chatting people. She pushed down her fluttering stomach. In that moment, Carlos seemed to be the only man in the room, oblivious to the surrounding guests. He wore an immaculate tight-fitting black satin shirt that pressed into his abdominal muscles, and grey pleated pants which fit nicely around his waist. She ignored her shiver at his beauty. "Hi, Carlos." She acknowledged Elina who stood with her hand on Carlos's shoulder.

Carlos kissed her on the cheek. "Hi, Blanca. I'm glad you could make it. You look amazing."

Her face flushed. Elina looked beautiful in her low-cut, glittery silver dress that showed off her slim figure and large breasts. Her bright red nail polish shone in the light as she leaned in to kiss Blanca on the cheek. "Hi Blanca. Isn't this exciting?"

Blanca smiled. "It is, and you look gorgeous in that dress."

Elina's fingers touched her chin. "Oh, this old thing. I've worn it before, but thought it fitting for today's occasion." Her eyes roamed briefly. "Carlos here has worked hard for this showing. When he works hard, he works damn hard. He has such a raw talent."

Blanca smiled, her eyes flicking to Carlos. "I love it. You've done a great job."

Juan and Pedro approached, nodding at Blanca. Their looks screamed magnetism, power and success in their fields.

Juan kissed Blanca on the cheek. "Welcome. I'm glad you could make it. Help yourself to a drink and feel free to look around. Carlos's display is in the corner over there. You surely cannot miss it."

"Thanks, Juan."

Pedro eyed Blanca with curiosity. "Who knew my nephew had such a talent to see the true beauty in the smallest of things." He faced Carlos. "Quite the accomplishment."

Elina played with the tips of her red nails, looking bored. "I'll be around, guys. A cute man over there seems to be calling my name. I'll see you later." She walked off as Pedro said, "Oh, you are such an attention-seeker, Elina."

"And that's why you love me, darling."

Pedro blushed, took a sip of his wine, and faced Blanca. "An exaggeration." He waved to them. "I'll go mingle."

Luiz and a few friends of Carlos approached, and he introduced his friends to Juan. "I have to see your photos, man. This is a long time coming." He turned to Blanca and kissed her on the cheek. "Boy, you are hot, Blanca. Sizzling, in fact."

Blanca drew back and cleared her throat. "Okay," was all she could muster.

Carlos shook his head and shoved his friend. "Oh, stop it, Luiz. You're embarrassing her. Get a grip."

Luiz eyed Blanca closely. "I'm sorry. I didn't mean to embarrass you." She smiled nervously. "I'll go see the photos now. Excuse us." Luiz and Carlos's friends made their way to the photo displays.

Blanca stood in front of Carlos, feeling awkward. "I'm eager to see your work more closely, Carlos, to see if it lives up to its reputation." A waiter offered her crackers and cheese. She dipped a cracker into an olive dip and devoured it, pushing down a shred of nerves. The way Carlos was looking at her was sexy, and other men paled in comparison. He shook his head at the snacks and the waiter wandered off.

Carlos prodded her to one part of the room. "Let me show you my pieces over here." As Blanca squeezed between the guests to follow Carlos across the room, she found herself face to face with Elina again. She was chatting with another man until she turned to Blanca with a smile. The woman's body screamed sex to Blanca, and she had no doubt Elina would indulge. She obviously had a voracious sexual appetite. Blanca gazed at Carlos's photographs of Brazil displayed on the wall. The other guests seemed to admire his work, too. There was a photo of Copacabana at night, the green vines in the Botanical Garden of Rio de Janeiro, Ipanema at sunset, and the Cathedral of Brasilia at night. He'd also photographed the favelas and its residents, cafes and their owners, and the exotic array of restaurants. His theme encapsulated the entirety of Brazil and Spain to demonstrate the way of life, social connections, and culture. She moved in closer to stare at the finest details of each photo, but the ones of the favelas made her cringe. She didn't know why.

CHAPTER 25
DARK FEELING

Carlos and Blanca walked through a sliding glass door. He carried a glass of vodka mixed with cranberry, while Blanca had a glass of champagne. Her black dress, which clung to her curves and left little to the imagination, made him breathless. He wanted to wrap his arms around her waist and kiss those inviting lips, but knew she didn't want anything more than friendship. But he sure as hell wondered what it would be like to taste those lips.

Several guests stood on the outside deck. Carlos looked at Blanca, whose eyes wandered across the view from the balcony. The warm, gentle breeze blew her hair over her eyes. For a fleeting moment, he wanted to reach out and draw her hair out of her eyes, but she appeared distant, turning to look through the glass doors into the party room.

He leaned in closer, smelling citrus and the heady scent of musk, yearning to feel her body against him. Fighting off the thoughts, he faced her. "Are you okay? You look miles away."

Blanca gazed intensely at him. Was she feeling it as much as he was? By the look in her eyes, she seemed to care about him too, but possibly not as much as he cared about her. Something was holding her back. "I'm surprised you photographed the favelas. I'm not sure how Jose would feel about it."

"Don't worry about him. He's not in charge of me nor the magazine. I did speak to him about the article on the favelas you wanted to write, but he didn't say much. He only mentioned it would divert from the magazine's target market." Blanca nodded. Heat flooded his body as she bit on her bottom lip when a young woman approached him with a warm smile.

"Hi, Mr. Silva. My name is Teresa. Sorry to interrupt, but I bought one of your pictures, and wondered if we could discuss custom-made photos to decorate my new home. I'm looking for a landscape and beach theme. Could you do that for me?"

He nodded. "I'd be happy to discuss it further with you. I'll get my business card and we can discuss a time to meet."

Teresa's eyes lit up. "Great. I can call you sometime next week."

"Sure." He checked his pockets. "I seem to have run out of business cards, but I have more in my camera bag inside. I'll be right back." He scurried off inside to head to a private room where he had left his personal belongings and promotional materials. He stopped short at the door as he heard familiar voices inside. It sounded like Elina's voice, and a man's he could not identify.

Carlos waited for them to come out, but sudden silence oozed from the room. Wondering what was going on, he inched the door open, to see Pedro pushing Elina against the wall and kissing her with hunger. His hands prodded her between her thighs, and she moaned as he lifted her dress. Not wishing to see more, Carlos quietly closed the door.

Cursing under his breath, he ran outside to his car, opened the passenger door, and retrieved a business card from his glove box. He shook his head, thinking how rude it was for them to carry on like that when it was his special day. Was this a secret tryst? He never knew they were in a relationship, but it wasn't his business, anyway.

Carlos thought nothing more of Elina and Pedro as he returned to the deck, to find his new client chatting with Blanca. He leaned forward. "Sorry to keep you waiting so long."

"No problem. I was talking to this lovely woman about how she works with you. She only had wonderful things to say about you," Teresa said.

He turned to Blanca to see her face turning red. He handed Teresa his business card. "Here you go. Give me a call and we'll set a time to meet."

"Great. Thank you. I'll be in touch soon." The woman walked back into the gallery, leaving Carlos alone with Blanca again. She peered at the deck, silent. She looked sweet and vulnerable, and he wanted to soothe her troubled soul. Whatever was bothering her, he hoped she would confide in him.

Carlos beamed. "What wonderful things did you have to say about me?"

Blanca blushed. "Only that you're a hard worker and always go the extra mile for people. You have a big heart, Carlos. I can see that."

His heart warmed. "Well, thank you."

She cleared her throat. "What took you so long? The famous photographer got caught up in the crowd, no doubt."

He avoided her eyes. "Something like that." He didn't need to disclose what he had seen Elina and Pedro doing.

Juan stepped out onto the deck and waved Carlos over. "Listen, Carlos. Some of the guests want to talk to you about your photos. Do you have a few minutes?"

He nodded. "I'll be right there." He looked at Blanca. "I won't be long. Will you wait for me?" He yearned to see more of her.

Blanca ushered him off. "Of course, Carlos. I'm sorry to take up so much of your time. Don't worry about me. I'll be fine. You go."

Carlos touched her shoulder. "I'll be back soon." Juan gently pushed him towards a group of people inside. He couldn't wait to see Blanca again and discuss what was troubling her. Her mood had changed after looking at his photos, and he wondered if it reminded her of her past.

CHAPTER 26
A PHOTO

Blanca shifted as she listened to the meeting's agenda. She held a pen, her notepad resting in front of her on the long conference table. Pedro tapped the table with a pen, smirking.

"We pride ourselves on being a magazine with a middle-class business demographic, not an elite one. Scrap that fashion idea, Joan. It won't appeal to our readers." His eyes roamed. "Any other brilliant ideas?"

Joan, a reporter with bright green eyes and a bob-style haircut, sighed and stroked out a line on her pad. She peered away from Pedro's roaming eyes.

Blanca leaned forward. She had spoken briefly to Carlos about her idea, and he was fine with it. "I thought we could do a piece on Carlos's photojournalism business profile and how his work represents both the wealthy and poorer areas of Brazil. The angle can be about showcasing how artistic expression gives Brazil a voice for the government to create new programs, and new funding for artistic or creative businesses like art galleries and theatre companies. I could interview a gallery owner named Juan Carneiro about his profile in his work, and I can approach theatre companies that enhance tourism and give Rio De Janeiro a voice in their shows."

Pedro nodded. "Interesting angle, Blanca. Work with Isabela on that one. And before you give it to Jose for the web version, let me approve it. Remember it's about the rise of the Brazilian economy through the arts, as tourism builds our nation's cities."

"Of course," said Blanca. She sighed with relief. Her eyes wandered over to Carlos, who stared into his lap.

Pedro moved around the room and discussed further article ideas and budget restrictions. "Okay, let's quickly discuss the editorial calendar and stick to it religiously. In the last quarter, several staff members had not met deadlines and chosen different angles. That compromised the integrity of what *Felicidade de Negocios* stands for and cost heavily against our budget. See that it doesn't happen again. You are always required to keep our target market in mind. Is that crystal clear?"

With nods and agreement shouted out, the meeting closed a few minutes before twelve. Back at her desk, Blanca called Juan to schedule an interview.

Carlos entered her office as she checked her phone for the time. "How about lunch, Blanca?"

She turned to Isabela. "Is it okay if I go for lunch now, or do you need me to double-check that global investment article first?"

Isabela waved her hand. "Go on, darl. I'll hold the fort for now, but I'll expect you to check the article by close of business or I'll kick your butt, girl."

Blanca chuckled. "Thank you, kindly."

Carlos was holding a yellow manila envelope, but she didn't question it. She followed him outside the building and they took his car to a tapas bar in the centre of Rio de Janeiro. She was grateful for the opportunity to enjoy Spanish food in Brazil. She missed her hometown. Carlos knew how to make her feel at home.

They sat across from each other at a high table. Large windows gave a calming view of a park. Round hanging lights, wooden flooring, and baskets of plants lent the bar a rustic ambience.

"What would you like?" asked a burly waiter.

Blanca stared at the menu board. "I'd like a tortilla Espanola siglo and a sangria." She turned to Carlos. "That's an amazing Spanish omelet to die for."

He nodded. "I know. I've had it, too." He faced the waiter. "I'll have the same, and a glass of water." His eyes glowed as he stared deeply as if seeing into her soul.

"Certainly sir." The waiter, with hands behind his back, left.

Carlos's hands fidgeted. Was he nervous about something? "Speaking of food, I make a mean paella. I might make it for you one night," he said.

Her heart warmed. "You make a mean paella?"

He nodded. "I tried out a recipe when I lived in Spain, and it turned out well. I didn't die, so it must've been okay." His gaze turned serious. "I wanted to talk to you about my mother, Blanca."

She tilted her head. "I am sorry you lost her, Carlos. How old were you?"

A hint of sadness clouded his eyes. "I was a teenager. My father took it hard and grieved for her for a long time. He was absent before her death, but became more absent afterwards."

Blanca nodded. "I can't imagine how hard that must've been. Was Pedro there for you after she died?"

"Surprisingly, yes. He replaced my father for a while, as if he was compensating for something. It was as if he needed to prove he could be supportive when my father wasn't."

The waiter arrived with their orders and refreshing sangrias. He set them down on the table and left with a nod.

They silently dug into their omelets. When finished, Blanca wiped her mouth with a serviette. "You missed a spot," said Carlos. He raised his finger to her mouth and wiped the crumb off.

Blanca hid her arousal, her eyes diving into his. It was the most sensual thing a man had done for her, and her body responded with dreaded sweat.

The moment burst at a loud noise behind them. A man tripped over a chair and rushed out of the bar while staring at Blanca and Carlos.

She returned her focus to her lunch partner. "I think I interrupted you earlier. Was there something specific you wanted to say about your mother?"

He nodded. "I found a few things in a box in my father's house. They belonged to my mother. She took a lot of photos of these young girls who were exploited in the favelas, and helped some of them out too. But she also kept these disturbing newspaper articles in a box. I think she was investigating something close to home. She always told me to protect the girls. She knew I liked to help them out because we'd sometimes head out to the favelas in Rio de Janeiro. I was just a child when she showed me a different way of life. It made my appreciate my own life, and how much I should be grateful for."

Blanca nodded. "She gave you an amazing gift. So how can I help?"

Carlos took a breath and explained what he'd found in his old home. He put the manila envelope that Blanca had seen earlier on the table. "These are the newspaper articles she'd kept in a box. It has to mean something, or why would she keep them?"

Blanca flattened the crumpled pieces of paper on the table. The headlines of the articles included: "Child Prostitution in the Favelas," "Teenage Mum at Twelve," "Pregnant Women," "Sex with Under-aged Girls," and "Prostitution for Survival." She knit her brows. "I see nothing wrong with this if she planned to research these stories to write the same kind of articles. It might have been a way for her to get into journalism."

Carlos shook his head. "No, this has to be connected to Antonia, because she had a photo of her, too dressed up for a young girl, with a man. If she went missing, it had to do with the man in the photo. I can see his arm in this leather jacket, but nothing else."

She peered at the byline. "These articles were written by a journalist named Paolo Almada. I wonder how he got his information."

He shifted in his seat. "I don't know, but I can show you the photo at my place."

"Okay, let's go." She rose and walked out of the restaurant, leaving Carlos scrambling to pay the bill. At his car, she took the passenger seat, ignoring the way his eyes fixated on her legs as her dress moved up. Blanca pushed it down along with her feelings and looked out the window. This wasn't the time to feel things when so many unanswered questions demanded their attention.

***

Blanca stared at the photo on Carlos's kitchen table. "I feel as if I've seen this person in the photo. I know it's only an arm, but the jacket he's wearing looks familiar. I don't know who it is, but I'm sure I've seen it." She put a hand over her heart. "Do you think Antonia was a prostitute? I mean, look at the way she's dressed, and with this man beside her, it doesn't look innocent."

Carlos shrugged. "What if it's her father or an uncle? Who knows at this point, but I plan to keep digging for information."

Blanca's body chilled. "I don't know, Carlos. We don't know what we're dealing with here. You need to be careful."

98

Carlos picked up the photo. "My mother told me to help protect the girls of the favelas, and I owe it to my mother to honour her request. She had these photos of Antonia for a reason. Maybe she knew Antonia was in trouble." He rose and looked out his window. "These articles and photos mean something, Blanca. Even Antonia's mother, Juliana, mentioned my mum being jittery in the favela the last time she saw her."

Blanca swallowed. "What if you're reading too much into this, Carlos?"

"Possibly, but I'll give it some thought." She watched Carlos bend over the sink, and she had the strong urge to wrap her arms around him for comfort. No doubt he was thinking about his poor mother, who had died so young.

CHAPTER 27
SECRETS

Carlos rang the doorbell of his old home a few days later. He hadn't visited his father, Nicolas, in several months, given they were never close, even after his mother had died. He hoped to have a civil conversation but feared they would end up arguing, as usual.

Blooming flowers and trimmed bushes filled the front garden. Even the path to the door had been re-paved. The elder Mr. Silva never spared expenses when it came to maintaining his home. On the other hand, working on his relationship with Carlos took a back seat.

His father opened the door with a surprised expression. His hair looked even greyer over the last few weeks. He towered over Carlos, and his broad shoulders, permanent scowl, and bushy eyebrows lent him a powerful presence. He'd been handsome in his younger days, and looked distinguished now. But since his wife's death, the light had gone out of his eyes. "This is a surprise, Carlos. What brings you by after all this time? No doubt you need something. That seems to be the only time you come here."

Carlos ignored the comment. "Can I come in?"

Nicolas shrugged and opened the door wider. "Who am I to question anything these days?" He watched his son closely as he closed the door behind him.

Carlos calmed his breathing. "I'm not here to fight, Dad." He followed his father into the living room and sat on the brown leather couch. A large-screen television displayed a news program. His father turned the volume down and sat on a matching armchair, hands clasped and eyebrows drawn together. "I have questions about Mum. I found newspaper articles and a photo of this missing girl, Antonia, in a box you kept hidden in the bedroom. I saw a man's arm in the photo, and am sure she got mixed up in prostitution or some kind of escort service."

His father shook his head. "I should've known you'd resort to sneaking in here and searching through my private belongings. What the hell possessed you to do that?"

"Can we please not get off the topic, and get to the heart of my issue?" Carlos took a breath and leaned forward. He could never avoid judgement by his father. "I want to know why Mum kept those newspaper articles about the problems in the favelas. What was it about those articles she had to keep hidden in a box? Did she know something?"

Nicolas looked away. "Your mother had these wild ideas about becoming a journalist and wanted to go back to college to study."

"If she wanted to become a journalist, why didn't she apply to a college for journalism?"

"She had a full-time job as a hospital administrator," his father growled. "Photography for magazines was just something she did on the side."

"That still doesn't explain why she hid those newspaper articles."

Nicolas stood up with his lips pressed firmly together. "This is ridiculous, Carlos. Why rehash the past? Your mother is gone. She had a heart attack. Your mother burned herself out with her silly notion of working two jobs. She never spent enough time at home as a wife and mother should. For her to study, she'd be away from us even more than she was. I couldn't allow it."

Carlos scoffed. "You still haven't answered my question."

Nicolas's face flushed and he peered at the floor. "How the hell should I know? She might've had the crazy notion to write an article for a magazine. She never mentioned them to me."

"But you knew about the articles. You kept them. You didn't look surprised when I asked you about them." He looked past his father. "Didn't you ask her about them? Weren't you curious?"

Nicolas glared at Carlos. "I want you to leave. I will not be interrogated in my own home. I have nothing more to say."

Carlos had another ball to play. "Why did you and Pedro stop talking for all these years? If I recall, it was after you both banned me from hanging out with Jose. We lost all contact until recently."

"We grew apart, that's all. It happens to the best of relationships." Nicolas was walking towards the door.

Carlos changed topics. "At least answer this. Why did you transfer 60,000 Brazilian Real to a company called *Possessao*

Valioso in 2006? A company which doesn't even exist. Were you into something illegal, Dad? I doubt Mum would have been involved in anything shady." His father turned pale and his eye twitched. "Do you have an answer?"

Nicolas shook his head. "I want you to leave, and don't come back unless you want to have a civil conversation about your life rather than turning to the past. The past is the past, and it's done. Nothing good comes out of rehashing things."

Carlos nodded, relenting. He couldn't reason with his father when he was in such a sour mood. He would have to find other ways to get his information. "Fine, I'll leave, but I will get my answers, one way or another."

His father opened the door. "Leave it alone, Carlos. There is nothing to find, so do not waste your time with this. Your mother was curious, that was all."

Walking to his car, Carlos wondered what his father meant by "nothing good comes out of rehashing things." It made him wonder what his father was hiding. He didn't believe his mother wanted to study journalism. As long as he'd known her, she had only had an interest in photography and capturing a story through the lens. She had told him many times how she hoped to become a full-time photographer, and to eventually travel the world.

He also didn't believe she was stressed to the point of triggering a heart attack. He remembered his mother appeared to love life, her family and her work. She had always had good friends.

CHAPTER 28
AN OBSTACLE

Blanca leaned in her seat at a cafe in Ipanema. A row of timber posts led down steps to an outdoor patio. Round wooden tables matched the low-backed chairs. High in one corner, a large TV played a football game. A few patrons at the bar craned their heads to watch and curse each time the Brazilian team failed to get a goal.

The scents of herbs, spices and freshly brewed coffee filled the air. Rhythmic Latin music poured out of the overhead speakers, muffling the sounds of the small groups of patrons who weren't cursing the football team. Blanca found her body swaying to the beat as she savoured the chilled gazpacho.

Isabela watched, amused, as the football fans slapped each other on the shoulders when a Brazilian scored a goal. She turned to Blanca. "You and Carlos seem to be getting cosy. What's going on between you two?"

Blanca shrugged. "We're only friends, Isabela. Nothing more. Why do you ask?"

Isabela sipped a champagne cocktail, then picked out a strawberry from the glass and took a bite. She wiped her mouth with a serviette. "I can tell you guys like each other but seem to be fighting it. Why?"

Blanca swallowed. "I'm going back to Spain in a few months, Isabela, so what's the point of starting something? Besides, I don't actually have a great track record when it comes to relationships. My last two boyfriends were violent, and I still struggle to trust in relationships. I have yet to meet a man I can trust implicitly, apart from my father."

Isabela touched her on the shoulder, her eyes softening. "I hear you, girl, but Carlos is not just any man. He's unique and he cares about you. I'm sure you care about him, too. Don't let an opportunity pass you by."

Blanca loved Isabela like her friends in Madrid, but still, they didn't share much history. If Isabela had known Blanca's full story, she'd understand. "It doesn't matter how we feel about each other. The fact of the matter is we both live on different continents. I don't believe a long-distance relationship could work."

Isabela knit her brows and took a breath. "How do you know unless you try? If it's worth pursuing, you and Carlos will find a way. You have to believe that."

Blanca's heart warmed at the thought of a relationship with Carlos, but it was an impossible situation. How could she be sure he wouldn't hurt her like her past boyfriends? How could they ask each other to move to a different country, leaving their friends and family? There could be no middle ground. "You've been reading way too many romance novels, Isabela. I admire your beliefs but if you knew my history, you'd understand."

Isabela looked away. "You're right. I'm sorry. I know we haven't known each other very long but I respect our friendship, and I hope we can keep in touch once you return to Spain."

Blanca picked up her hand. "Of course, we'll keep in touch. You can come visit Spain and meet my family and friends there. You'd love it."

The waiter arrived with a shared plate of *pastel* and other assorted pastries, and set it in the middle of the table. Blanca stared at it.

Isabela explained. "It's a deep-fried pastry with ground meat, and it's delicious. But you can have other fillings like chicken, cream cheese, mozzarella or shrimp. Try it."

Blanca picked it up and bit into its crispy, meaty texture. Her mouth watered for more. "It is delicious, but it must be fattening."

Isabela scoffed. "You're gorgeous. You have nothing to worry about." She bit into the *pastel* and closed her eyes to savour the taste.

Half an hour later, Isabela put her hand over her stomach. "I am so full, Blanca. Are you ready to go?"

A group of men came in and sat at a table nearby. One knocked into Isabela's chair without an apology. She shook her head at the rudeness. "Some people," she said.

Blanca nodded. "Thanks for lunch. It's good to try the food of Brazil." Isabela made a beeline to the cash register, but Blanca pushed in front of her. "I'm paying this time." When she opened her purse, she saw a note that hadn't been there earlier on top of her wallet. Putting the note to one side, she handed over cash and followed Isabela outside the cafe. "It's fun going out with you."

Isabela smiled and hugged her warmly. "I had a nice time too. See you on Monday." She ambled off in the opposite direction.

Once in her car, Blanca retrieved the note from her purse. In huge scrawl was written, *Don't poke your nose where it's not wanted or you'll be sorry.*

She stiffened as she thought about it. How had it got into her bag? Had the man who knocked into Isabela slipped it into her purse?

Blanca looked over her shoulder, getting the sense that whoever had sent her the note was watching her right now. Fearful of her surroundings, she sped off and ruminated about the note with a tightness in her stomach.

CHAPTER 29
COSTUME PARTY

Carlos stared in the mirror and played with his tie as he waited for guests to arrive for his birthday party. He was dressed as a vampire in a pin-striped grey suit, sporting a long tie with a white-fitted shirt underneath. He had his hair slicked back, and wore a fake moustache. A pale mask covering his face gave him an authentic vampire look.

Luiz arrived early to help him set up. "It's great you're having a Halloween theme on your birthday, when it's not yet Halloween. Crazy, but a great idea, man."

"I wanted something different for my birthday. It makes it memorable when you make it a little elaborate, and it's a good distraction from all these secrets surrounding Blanca, Antonia, and my father."

Luiz knit his brows, shaking his head "I hear you man, but be careful. You don't know what you're going to find. These men exploiting young girls are not to be messed with. It's a war you'll never win."

Carlos sighed. "I only want to help Blanca get answers about her past. And I have this feeling my mother had something to say, but never got the chance. This is personal."

Luiz sipped his cocktail. "I understand, but do not let your feelings for Blanca cloud your judgement. You need to tread carefully. Besides, you might be reading too much into this stuff about your mum. She had an interest in the girls, that's all."

Carlos shook his head. "No, I feel it in my gut. There's more to this than meets the eye, Luiz." He walked over to the kitchen and stared up at the black tinsel with a skeleton on the ceiling. Stuffed spiders and toy pumpkins surrounded the living room. Candelabra rested on long, rectangular tables filled with assorted hot and cold snacks. Two scarecrows sat on creaky, wooden chairs, and a large ceramic pot sat in front of mannequin witches as if they were brewing a potion. A row of white ceramic pumpkins stood on a side table. Smoke—actually, mist from dry ice—billowed out of pots on the outdoor area. A banner hanging over the patio read, "Happy Birthday, Carlos."

Carlos's heart beat faster when he spotted Blanca through the living window, walking down the path with Isabela. He wanted to wrap her in his arms. He hoped they'd find answers before she returned to Spain.

He opened the door and his body responded to the beauty before him. Blanca was dressed as a mermaid in a flowing green skirt which fell down to her ankles. A white sleeveless top with frills lined the front, and a long, red wig ran past her shoulders. A fish pin pulled her hair back and she wore the red lipstick so bright he wanted to taste it. He wanted to taste all of her.

He pushed aside his erotic thoughts to greet her, but when she kissed him on the cheek, his body became aroused. He thought of how amazing closer intimacy would feel.

Blanca broke the spell by handing him a wrapped gift.

"Thanks. Come in, ladies. You both look gorgeous." His eyes lingered on Blanca, who blushed.

Isabela kissed him on the cheek. "You look handsome, Carlos." She wore a red skirt with a black lacy top, red devil ears and holding a pitchfork.

"I take it you're the devil?"

She angled her head. "Gee, what gave it away?"

"Hmm," he said. "Come on in." He led them to the kitchen when Luiz approached, carrying a giant Halloween cake topped with orange icing, spider webs swirling around the cake and a huge spider on top. He placed it on the countertop.

"Hey, Blanca." Luiz leaned down to kiss her on the cheek, then turned to Isabela. "Hello, Isabela. You look amazing and devilish."

Isabela blushed. "Thank you, Luiz. Good to see you again."

Carlos rubbed his hands together. "What's your poison, ladies?"

Isabela's eyes lit up as if alcohol was a dream. "I'll have a dry wine if you have it." Blanca requested a sangria, and Carlos couldn't stop looking at her as he poured their drinks, spilling some of it on the bench. He wiped up the mess then handed them their glasses when the doorbell rang. "Luiz, would you mind getting that?"

The tall man went to the front door while Isabela wandered towards the living room. Blanca sipped her sangria as Carlos stepped closer. "Blanca, you look beautiful as always. I'm glad you came."

Blanca blushed again. "I couldn't miss your birthday, Carlos."

He so wanted to kiss her in this moment, as their eyes remained fixed on each other. Her perfume dizzied him. "Blanca, I...."

Luiz interrupted the moment. "Carlos, your photographer friends are here. And a couple of your old friends from school."

He drew back, the pull of memories bringing him back into the past. "Come and meet my other friends, Blanca. I've told a few of them about you."

Blanca angled her head. "What did you tell them about me, Carlos?"

He squinted. "Never mind what I told them. Now come with me, lady." He took her by the hand and squeezed it tight.

He introduced Blanca to all his friends, then let her join Isabela in the living room. But even while he caught up with his friends and shared old stories, his mind kept going back to Blanca and the way her costume hugged her body in all the right places. He could barely breathe when he thought the way each of them could see what the other wanted. Could they have a future together?

CHAPTER 30
A HIDDEN THREAT

Blanca eased back into the comfort of the sofa while sipping her drink, the sweetness soothing her parched throat. She took in the table of assorted foods. The aromas whetted her appetite. Even though the food had been catered, Luiz and Carlos rushed around, greeting the guests as they dribbled in for over an hour.

Blanca's mind focused on Carlos whose lips she wanted to taste, and whose hand she could still feel. She'd miss him deeply when she returned to Spain. But how could they ever make a relationship work from such a distance? Was it even worth to try when they were thousands of miles apart? What if he hurt her as Jorge had? She'd been deeply in love with Jorge, or so she thought at the time, and he had sent her to hospital with multiple bruises and cuts.

Isabela pointed a manicured nail in her direction. "Penny for your thoughts, girl."

Blanca came out of her reverie. "Sorry. I'm enjoying my drink."

"Hmm. You're thinking about Carlos, aren't you?"

Blanca shrugged. She put down her glass, her eyes scanning the people she didn't know. "Maybe." She spotted a young woman in a print suit and high pigtails with painted whiskers. She must have been Catwoman, and could easily have been a model with her high cheekbones and strong, green eyes. "It's hard fighting against my feelings, Isabela. I don't live here, and soon, I'll be returning to Spain. I might be wasting my time thinking about a relationship with him, don't you think?"

Isabela scooted closer and lay a hand on her shoulder, her eyes softening. "You guys look great together, and I can see you both care about each other. Don't let distance stop you from having a relationship. He could be the one."

Blanca lifted her shoulder. "How can we consider a relationship when I'm not willing to leave my country, and he has his family and friends in Brazil? He won't want to move."

"I know you don't want to stay in Brazil, but you guys will work it out. If it's meant to be, you'll be together. Have faith and be true to yourselves. I've never seen you happier than when you're with him, Blanca. Give it a chance and see where it can go."

She stared into her lap. "I hear you, Isabela. Thanks for the advice."

Isabela combed her hands through her hair. "You mentioned these secrets from your past, Blanca. Do you honestly think there's something to it?"

Blanca nodded. "It has something to do with the favelas. I keep having these memory fragments or flashbacks in my mind. Even the nightmares seem connected."

"Whatever you need, I can help you get answers. I can talk to Pedro or Jose if you like. Or I can do some research."

Blanca shook her head, realising Catwoman was standing nearby, staring in her direction. "No, I don't want you involved, Isabela. Carlos is helping me with the past because his mother might've had secrets, too." She got up. "I'm getting a refill of wine. Do you want anything?" Isabela shook her head. "I'll be back."

As Blanca poured herself more sangria in the kitchen, the young Catwoman walked up and smiled. "Hi, I'm Consuela, an old family friend of Carlos's." She shook hands.

"Blanca." She left her glass on the counter, realising the lady wanted to speak. They made small talk until moving on to careers. "What do you do for a living?"

The woman hesitated as she poured herself a glass of Chardonnay. "I'm a model. I get to travel a lot, but I'm thinking of changing careers. I've got a degree in journalism, and I've done some freelance writing. I would like to get back into some form of journalism. What do you do?"

Blanca leaned against the counter. "I'm a journalist, but currently working as an editor for a business magazine." At that moment, a loud crash echoed from the living room. Blanca's eyes shifted there to see a man she didn't know pick up a glass he'd dropped from a tray. "Sorry, butterfingers. As you were, people," he said.

Blanca turned back to Consuela. "I'd hate to clean that mess with the shards."

Consuela nodded. "If I wanted to work for a magazine, how could I best apply?"

Blanca sipped her drink. "What experience do you have?"

Consuela downed most of her drink. Up close, her eyes were very bright. "I have experience in a book publishing company, but I've never worked for a magazine."

"Right. The concept's the same, but you would fare well if you had a portfolio of books you've helped publish." She continued to explain the types of roles in magazine publishing houses, but Consuela's eyes looked past her into the living room. She was looking at Carlos with interest, sparking pangs of jealousy in Blanca.

"Thanks for the tips," Consuela said. "I'll try that, and see how it goes." She cleared her throat, touching the centre of it. "Why don't we drink to new beginnings and adventures." Gripping her glass, she drank the remaining wine, and Blanca did the same with her sangria.

"I better get back to my friend, Consuela. It was nice meeting you."

Consuela gave her a wide grin. "You too, and thanks again for the tips."

Blanca moved to the living room, but Isabela had disappeared. Roaming the room, she engaged in small talk with a few guests, but excused herself when she began feeling dizzy. Thinking fresh air might help, she walked to a pergola and saw Carlos talking animatedly with a group of people. When she joined him, he made his excuses to the group and they made their way back inside. "Are you okay?" he asked.

She walked on unsteady legs. "I can't find Isabela, and I need to lie down." Her head became heavy and her vision blurred. "I might've had too much wine. A quick lie-down should fix it, then I'll look for Isabela."

Carlos walked her up the stairs, his arm around her. He led her to a bedroom, which spun around her as he gently lay her on the bed. His voice sounded distant and her head throbbed. The sensation of surrealness continued as she smiled up at Carlos, who looked worried. "Do you need a doctor?"

She shook her head. "No, you go back to the party. I'll be fine here. It'll pass."

He hesitated. "Are you sure? I'm happy to stay with you. Or I can take you home." She waved him away and was closing her eyes. "Okay, you rest, but I'll check on you in a bit." The sound of footsteps drifted as she fell into blackness.

***

Blanca woke with a powerful migraine, the room still spinning. She was surprised a short nap hadn't helped her recover from the wine. Her surroundings still seemed surreal.

Attempting to get up, she winced at the drowsiness and the strange sensation in her jaw and lips. Her body had no strength to move, and her dizziness got worse. She lay back on the bed and pressed her finger against her temple to fight the pain. What was going on with her? She never reacted to alcohol in this way.

The door opened and she smiled, thinking it was Carlos. It wasn't. The Joker, wearing a mask, came into the room and sat on the edge of her bed, staring at her.

"Who...are you?"

The Joker leaned close. His hands ran up her throat, touched her lips, and trailed down to the centre of her chest, caressing and massaging her breasts. She flinched and tried to push him away, but she had no strength. "What...are you...doing?" She tried to fight him off, but her eyes were closing. She had no control over the fatigue that made her powerless. He lifted his mask slightly to reveal his mouth, leaned in and pressed his lips hard against hers, penetrating her mouth with his tongue while his hands wandered down her abdomen to her legs. His hands pulled up her long dress as he reached down between her thighs. She pushed against his hands and wiggled her body, but it didn't help. He was too strong. His lips were not friendly, but angry. His hands were not gentle, but rough. He lay on top of her, and when she tried to push him off, he punched her twice in the face, no doubt bruising her. She moaned in pain. "Please stop!" Drowsiness set in and she had no energy to fight him. He was going to rape her and she had no power to stop him.

112

CHAPTER 31
CALL FOR HELP

Carlos waved goodbye to a few of his guests who had to leave early. He wondered how Blanca was feeling, and realised it had been an hour since he had laid her down on his bed. Isabela had disappeared, too, while he had been mingling with the guests. He began to worry, as Isabela wouldn't have left without telling him.

He rushed into the kitchen and poured a glass of water for Blanca. As he walked up the stairs, he worried she hadn't come out of the room yet. He found his bedroom door locked. Why would Blanca lock the door?

He had no way of opening the door from this side, so she would have to open it. But before he called her name, he heard whimpering and the squeaking of the mattress. "No, get away from me. No, please. Please."

Carlos's body flew into fight mode: pulse racing, heart pounding, breath shallow and quick. He put down the cup, backed away from his door and smashed his shoulder hard into it. It didn't budge. He stepped back again, raised his right leg and kicked his heel as hard as he could just above the doorknob. With a loud *crack*, the door swung open.

Blanca was still on the bed, shaking as she attempted to sit up. Her hair was undone, her face was a mess with lines of makeup running down her cheeks, and her dress had been pulled up to her thighs. She froze, looking not at Carlos but at the open window.

He rushed to Blanca and wrapped his arms around her. Someone had hurt her, but who? Oh, god! He would kill the bastard with his own bare hands. He stroked her cheek. "Blanca. Look at me." She sat as if she was in a catatonic state. He hugged her once more and caressed the small of her back, hoping to bring her out of this state.

He noticed the open window. What the hell! Did an intruder come into the room? He shook her gently. "Blanca, you are safe. It's Carlos. Look at me, please."

Blanca came out of her stupor and gasped. "Carlos. Carlos." She wrapped her arms around him and cried. He held her in his arms for several minutes until she pulled away and moved her dress down her legs. She wiped away the wetness on her cheeks and pressed a hand against the side of her head.

"Blanca. What happened?"

It took her a few minutes to respond as she took a few deep breaths and peered at the drawn window. She faced him. "A man...he came in...he tried to rape me. I tried to fight him off. But...but he was too strong."

He sighed in relief. Thank god, she hadn't been raped, but if he had come a few minutes later, it might have been a different story. Oh, god! Why did he wait so long to check on her? He had wanted her to rest, and then had been distracted by his guests. If only he had come a few minutes sooner, this wouldn't have happened.

He fetched the glass of water. "Drink this. It'll make you feel better." Blanca drank the water and looked past him again. "What did he look like?" he asked.

She quivered. "He wore a Joker mask, so I...I couldn't see his face. He came through the door and when you came in, he jumped out the window."

"Was he at the party?"

She shook her head. "I didn't recognise him, Carlos. I'm sorry."

He brought her hand to his lips. "I don't remember seeing anyone with a Joker mask." He looked into the distance. "You have nothing to be sorry about, Blanca. Nothing at all." He saw crumpled paper on the floor and picked it up. His body stiffened as he read the message typed in a large font: *Stay away from the favelas or else.*

Blanca's eyes widened. "Oh, god, Carlos. Who is doing this to us, and why?"

He folded the note and put it into his pocket. "We need to go to the police, Blanca. Have you had any other threats?"

She nodded. "Yes. One recently. It's at home. I also got a note when I first arrived at the airport here."

Carlos clenched his fists. "Why didn't you tell me about the notes? We have to see these as real threats if they've happened more than once."

She bowed her head. "You're right, Carlos. I'm sorry. Let's call the police."

He took his phone from his pocket and called. "The state police are on their way," he said as he put his phone away. "Now, I want you to tell me what happened, from the beginning. Don't leave anything out."

She recounted the incident.

Carlos stroked her cheek, his heart breaking at her body shaking and tears streaming down her cheeks. "You're telling me this woman, Consuela, might've drugged your drink."

She pressed her fingers into her forehead as if fighting off a migraine. "I drank a couple of glasses of sangria and nothing else. I felt bad after I left the kitchen and refilled my drink. She was there and then some guy dropped his glass and I got distracted. She must've put something in my drink when I looked away."

Carlos tasted bile in his throat. "I don't even know a Consuela, but I'll ask around and see if she came with one of my friends. I'm sorry this happened to you, Blanca, but you're safe now." He wondered what the hell was going on. A stranger might have gate-crashed his party unnoticed. But the point was, someone was playing with their lives. "Let's see if we can find Isabela. I can take you home if we don't find her."

"No, I'll look for her."

"I'm ending the party, Blanca. Give me a few minutes."

Neither of them could find Isabela. Blanca called her phone, which went straight to voicemail. She chatted with Carlos's friends as they left, masking her worry.

Once the guests were gone, Carlos started to clean up, but then stopped. He realised the police might want to check fingerprints or DNA. He walked outside into the back yard to see if the man who hurt Blanca was still here. He heard a rustle behind the tree, but saw nothing.

Back in the house, he found Blanca sitting on the couch, staring up at the ceiling. She was obviously still rattled.

He joined her on the couch. "The police are taking their time." Carlos took a breath. "If they can get fingerprints here, they might get a lead and find this bastard." His glare was obvious.

Blanca's shoulders relaxed as if comforted by his company. "I hope you're right.

Carlos's heart palpitated at the thought of their lives being endangered. It was most likely best to leave things to the police. He refused to look into these secrets if it would put Blanca's life at risk.

CHAPTER 32
POLICE INVESTIGATION

Carlos saw the police arrive, but waited for them to ring the doorbell before opening the door. He looked again at Blanca, his heart breaking at her silent pain.

Two uniformed policemen stood on his step. The short one had smiling eyes. "Hello, I'm Officer Castro." He gestured towards his partner, who was of average height and wore a stern expression. "This is Officer Souza. You reported a crime?"

Carlos nodded. "Yes, I'm Carlos Silva. Please come in." They followed Carlos into the living room. "This is Blanca Castellano."

Officer Castro took out a notepad while Officer Souza sat beside him. "Can you tell us exactly what happened." Blanca explained the incident with a flat tone while the officer took notes, making occasional eye contact.

Carlos still couldn't believe she had almost been raped. He shuddered to think what could have happened if he hadn't got to her in time.

Officer Souza spoke up. "So the threats started with notes and escalated to this physical attack?" He straightened his posture and looked at his partner.

Blanca nodded. "That's right, Officer. Ever since we've started asking questions about this missing girl, Antonia, and writing about the favelas as part of our job, we've had these threats."

Carlos handed him the threatening note in a plastic bag. "I don't know if you can get fingerprints from this note, but Blanca has more."

Officer Souza nodded. "We'll bring this to forensics and have it analysed." He faced Blanca. "Please bring in the other notes, too."

"You're sure you don't have any enemies to speak of?" Officer Castro asked. Blanca shook her head. "What about security cameras, Mr. Silva? Do you have any?"

"No, I don't, but I might consider getting them now."

Officer Castro asked her a few more questions, and routine things about her address and job. "Okay, we'll check upstairs while we wait for forensics to get here. If the attacker exited through the window, we might find something. Fibres or prints. A forensic examiner is on her way to check your wounds and take photos. We might get the attacker's DNA from his kiss or his hair. At this stage, it'll be hard to prove attempted rape without anything more tangible, like bruising. If you believe you were drugged, it will most likely still be in your system. We'll need a description of this woman, too."

The officers headed upstairs while Carlos and Blanca waited in the living room. He watched her as she crumbled on the couch and bowed her head.

Carlos sat beside her. "We'll get this bastard, don't worry. Surely they'll find something." Blanca shrugged. "I'll take you to the hospital and they can check you out."

"I'll be fine. I don't need to go to the hospital." She sighed. "I hope they find evidence so that whoever's stalking me doesn't get away with it."

Carlos hugged her tightly. She lay her head in the crook of his neck, reaching for her phone from her handbag. "I'll try Isabela again." She pressed the screen and listened. "Damn, still voicemail. Why isn't she answering, Carlos? She wouldn't leave without telling us, and she usually answers her phone. Do you think she's okay?"

Carlos didn't want to worry her. "I'm sure she's fine." As they sat in silence for the next ten minutes, a door slammed outside. Carlos went to the front door to see a van parked in the driveway behind the police car. What he assumed was the forensic team walked in. They introduced themselves and made their way upstairs.

A woman remained downstairs. She was tall and had bright blue eyes, and held a large bag from which she took a camera. "Hello, Blanca. I'm Beatriz, the forensic examiner. I am sorry to do this to you, but I will need to examine your wounds and take photos. I'll also need to take a blood sample to determine what kind of drug you were given." She turned to Carlos. "Are you her husband?"

He liked the sound of that, but it was a ridiculous thought. "I'm Carlos, a friend and her support person."

Officer Beatriz took photos of the bruises that were beginning to emerge on Blanca's face, arms and legs. "Is there somewhere private we can go to so I can examine you for any DNA?"

Blanca led her to the bathroom, looking over her shoulder at Carlos with a dark expression. He hated the idea of Blanca being prodded by a stranger, but if they could get the attacker's saliva or DNA, they'd be able to catch this bastard. He thanked god again she hadn't been raped, but her wounds would still cut deep. Her reaction in the bedroom, along with the way she had gone almost catatonic, suggested to Carlos that this had happened to her before. Or something very similar.

He froze at the thought she'd been attacked before. Who could have hurt her back then, and how? But then, he thought, he should not be surprised, given the ongoing exploitation of children. If Blanca got a note at the airport in Brazil, this group of thugs must have been connected to organised sex trafficking, and whoever it was must have known she was coming to Brazil on a mission.

CHAPTER 33
THE RETURN

The following Monday, Blanca arrived at the office, expecting to find Isabela at her desk.

It was empty. *She might be running late.* A part of her doubted it, as Isabela would not be late without notifying her. Worse, she hadn't heard anything from Isabela over the weekend. She and Carlos had told Officers Souza and Castro that Isabela may be missing, and the police promised to investigate, but so far, she hadn't heard anything.

Her parents were still unwilling to tell her the truth. She would have to find other ways to get information. But what if it got too dangerous to keep searching? What if her attacker was somehow connected to her past? She wondered if she knew things in the deep recesses of her mind, which she couldn't remember.

She turned on her computer and opened her notes for an article about business expansion in Sao Paulo. An hour later, she was satisfied with it, but her mind was no longer on her work. Isabela had still not arrived. What if she was hurt, or worse? No, she refused to go there. Not yet.

Carlos entered her office. He had stayed at her aunt's house over the weekend to show his support. She didn't know what she would have done without him. "I was checking in to see if Isabela showed up." He frowned at her empty seat. "Let's have a coffee break, Blanca."

She shook her head. "I'm not due for a break yet." Her hands fidgeted. "Please, Carlos. I need a distraction with work. I don't want to think the worst about Isabela." Her hands trembled but Carlos took them in his own.

Pedro walked into her office. "Blanca, have you heard anything from Isabela? I am worried about her."

She shook her head, fighting the onset of a headache. "I was hoping she'd be here today, but she is still missing. Where could she be? Have you spoken to her family?"

Pedro stood with a stiff posture, avoiding her eyes. "I have, but they haven't seen or heard from her. If you hear from her, let me know."

Her phone interrupted them. She picked it up, noticing Carlos's worried expression. "Hello, Blanca Castellano?" a male voice asked.

"Yes, who is this?"

"This is Officer Castro. Your friend, Isabela is in the Rio hospital with minor wounds." He gave her the details of Isabela's ward in the hospital.

She clutched her chest. "What happened?"

"We found her on the street close by, wandering as if she was lost. We took her to the hospital to get checked out, and the doctors have run tests to see what made her dazed and confused. They will notify us with the results. But we do have news about your blood test results."

Blanca's chest tightened. "What did you find?"

"An antipsychotic drug, Seroquel, was in your system. It must've been what gave you those symptoms. Because it appears you were drugged, we've handed the case over to detectives. They'll be in touch with you soon."

Blanca nodded. "Right. Is there anything else you can tell us, Officer?"

"An anonymous caller has given us a lead, which detectives will follow up."

"What kind of a lead? What do you mean?"

"Nothing we can say at this stage. I suggest you never walk anywhere alone. Call us immediately if anything else should occur. Please be careful, and let us do our job. The detectives will be in touch."

Blanca nodded. "Of course, Officer. We'll be careful." She turned to Pedro and Carlos, explaining the interchange.

Pedro gestured for her to leave. "Go to the hospital and I will visit her later tonight. Take the day, both of you."

"Thanks, Pedro," said Carlos.

***

Carlos and Blanca swept through the glass sliding doors of the Rio Hospital and headed straight to Isabela's room. The room was large with crème walls and a partially drawn Holland blind that emitted a ray of sunlight, opposite the bed.

Blanca rushed to Isabela and wrapped her arms around her, squeezing her tight. "How are you feeling, Isabela?"

She lifted her body upright in bed, wincing as if in pain. Her eye was black, her lips grazed, and one side of her face was bruised. Who could have done this to her? "In a little pain, but I will survive. Thanks for coming, guys."

Carlos leaned in and kissed her on the cheek. "You had us worried there, Isabela."

Blanca sat on the edge of the bed while Carlos sat on a chair beside her. "The police mentioned you were in the street. What happened?

Isabela had a sombre expression, unreadable. She put her hand against her forehead. "I met some guy at the party. I started to feel out of it, and he took me somewhere. I don't remember much after that. Sorry."

Carlos leaned forward. "Did you get his name?" Isabela shook her head. "So you don't remember where you've been for the past two days?"

"I can't remember. I've lost time. I think I was drugged. I only remember wandering the streets, but I don't know how I got there."

Blanca's lip trembled and a coldness settled over her body. She wondered whether whoever took Isabela was because of her. Was this her fault? "Did you know I was attacked?"

That seemed to wake Isabela. "What?"

Blanca explained the attack. "None of this makes sense. This has to be my fault, Isabela. What if this woman, Consuela, overheard us talking about my secrets. What if you were targeted because of me?" Her shoulders ached and she fought back tears. Carlos touched the small of her back and rubbed it tenderly."

Isabela reached for her hand. "This is not on you, Blanca. The police will find who did this. Don't worry, girl. As you can see, I am fine."

Blanca nodded. "I'm sorry, Isabela. If I can help, let me know. I'm your friend." She wrapped her arms around her again and stroked her back.

Carlos faced Isabela. "Hopefully you might remember more of the details."

Why was Isabela targeted this way, Blanca wondered. *Was she taken for a purpose related to my attack?*

CHAPTER 34
DISCOVERY

The next Sunday afternoon, Blanca sat in the living room between Maria and Julio. She had hidden her bruises with concealer as she didn't want to worry them. It wasn't fair to get them involved in her mess, whatever it was.

She had asked Julio to play old family videos in hopes they would trigger her memory. Julio happily obliged. He set a laptop on the coffee table in front of them. "My nephew is great with technology. He put our old videos of the family on the computer and showed me how to use it."

"That's nice of him," Blanca said.

"These videos might help you remember your past, Blanca," said Maria. She seemed more energetic over the last few days, but still refused to speak about the favelas.

Julio hit the keyboard and an image of Maria began moving on the screen. Blanca fought back tears over having missed her aunt for all these years. She was thankful for their time now, and hoped Maria and Julio could visit Spain soon.

In the first scene, Maria poured a bag of flour into a glass bowl, dropping some onto the floor. More flour smeared across her cheeks. She looked ghostly and smiled at the camera with a shake of the head. "You are a sight for sore eyes, my love," said Julio behind the camera. Blanca turned to Julio and beamed as he returned the smile. Maria's face flushed.

Julio chuckled. "Maria made the best cake in the world that day." He turned to Maria with light in his eyes while Blanca touched him gently on the shoulder. If only she could have love like her aunt and uncle's.

"Oh, stop it, Julio. I might be a great cook, but it was not the best cake in the world," said Maria, who caught Blanca's eye and shook her head.

Their eyes fixed on the next scene: Maria leaning over a two-tier cake, her cheeks puffed up to blow out candles for her fortieth birthday when Blanca was in Brazil at ten years of age.

She remembered the family gathering, but nothing unusual sprang to mind. In this scene she was content.

Another scene showed ten-year old Blanca, helping her mother and Maria in a messy kitchen. She recalled her uncle making this video during her childhood visit to Brazil. She wore a gorgeous gold locket with an inscription, but she couldn't make out what it said

She had forgotten about the locket over the intervening years. The one her mother had bought for her in Spain. Where did it end up?

Blanca turned to Julio. "Do you know what happened to my locket? I think I remember my mum buying it for me back in Spain, especially for the trip here. But then I didn't bring it back to Spain. Did I leave it here?"

Julio shrugged. "I don't know, Blanca. You'll have to ask your mother." He closed down the videos and put aside the laptop.

The locket her mother had bought her had meant the world to her, but she didn't recall bringing it back to Madrid, so she must have lost it in Brazil. Now that the video had reminded her of it, she also remembered her emotional attachment to it. Suddenly, she wanted to find it again.

Maria got up to stretch. "I remember you wearing the locket every day you were here. You refused to take it off, even when showering." Her eyes peered into the past. "But I'm sure on the day you left, you weren't wearing the locket. You must have dropped it somewhere."

Blanca rose, too. "Was I wearing the locket when we left to stay at my dad's friend's house?" She paced the carpeted flooring and turned her mind back to the past, but she could not recall the events from seventeen years earlier.

Maria nodded. "I'm certain you were wearing it, dear. You must've lost it at this friend's home. I wouldn't have a clue how to get in touch with them."

Blanca had to learn the fate of her mother's gift. "I've had dreams about this locket, but I can never remember what's going on in the dream." She paced the floor. "I'm calling Mum. She might know something about it." She took out her phone and waited for her mother to respond.

"Blanca. It's good to hear from you. How are you doing in Rio?" her mother asked.

Blanca explained the videos she'd watched. "Mum, what happened to the locket you bought for me in Spain just before we came to Brazil? I saw it in the video."

Her mother hesitated. "I think you lost it."

"In Brazil or Spain?"

Her father's voice came on the phone, sounding hollow, indicating he was on speaker. "It's only a locket, Blanca. Who remembers it all those years ago?"

"Mum? Where did I lose it?" The locket meant something, Blanca was sure.

Her mother cleared her throat. "I don't know, Blanca. As your father mentioned, who remembers all those years ago, darling. You forgot about it afterwards."

"What was the inscription on the locket?"

"It said 'Love between a mother and a child is forever.' It had a birth stone and a red heart charm at the bottom."

An image flashed in her memory: she and her mother standing in a jewellery store. Her mother was explaining to the salesman how she wanted Blanca's birthstone, blue sapphire, on the locket. Blanca had jumped up and down in excitement at the prospect of having such a pretty gift. How could she have lost it?

"Mum. Are you sure you don't know anything about this locket?"

"I really don't recall, darling. Can you please put Maria on." Was she telling the truth? After all these years, she could never get them to open up much about their trip to Brazil. It was as if it had never occurred.

Blanca turned the memory over in her mind, but no further images emerged. She didn't remember losing the locket and didn't remember ever taking it off in Spain, so maybe she had lost it on her trip here.

But Blanca knew the locket also had sentimental value for her mother. She didn't believe her mother knew nothing about the locket. It looked expensive. It was only a locket, but she had a sense it had an important connection to her past.

CHAPTER 35
HOSPITAL INTERVIEW

Carlos approached the reception desk, standing in a queue as he waited to speak to a receptionist in the Rio hospital.

He reached the front of the queue. "Yes, hello. I am here to see Dominique Calo."

The stocky hospital receptionist clicked on the computer and leaned over the counter. She looked suspicious with her squinting expression. "Does she know the reason for the visit?"

Carlos moved closer. "Yes, I called ahead and arranged an appointment for today about..." a health matter, he was going to say.

She shook her head and waved him away. "I don't need your life story. I asked if she is aware of your appointment today.

"Ah, yes she is."

She avoided his eyes, fixated on her screen. "Name?"

"Carlos Silva."

She picked up the phone. "Dominique Calo will be with you shortly, Mr. Silva. Go down the corridor and turn left to the other waiting room. Next."

She wouldn't win any awards for politeness, he thought as he made his way down the corridor, the smells of disinfectant and chemicals prominent. Health staff carried folders and clicked their pens on clipboards while scurrying down the shiny flooring, some of them staring at him with curiosity. He passed by muted conversations, and beeps and alarms in the wards until he reached the waiting area.

In the waiting area, Carlos sat with others who looked bored or browsed their mobile phones. He understood Dominique would be busy, but because they had been acquainted for years within his father's circle of friends, he knew she'd make time for him. She was an old nurse who had treated his mother when he was a teenager. He didn't understand how a healthy woman had experienced a heart attack and died suddenly. Given the information he garnered recently about his mother, his mind started wandering. Was there more to her story or was it an actual heart attack?

He wondered how Blanca was doing with the stalking and, worse, the attack. In spite of not wanting to aggravate whoever was hurting them, if he did nothing, things would most likely escalate anyway. He wanted justice for whoever hurt Blanca, and he had the feeling his mother and Blanca's past were somehow linked.

He wanted to keep Blanca safe and asked her to move in with him until the police found her attacker. Stubborn, she had put on a brave mask and refused, but he knew she wanted safety and security. He couldn't push her and hoped she'd come to him in her own time. The problem was that she'd be leaving soon. He had to tell her how he felt before then.

Isabela, too, had been recovering well after her kidnapping. Luckily, her physical wounds were minor, but her emotional wounds were a different matter. He had to stop whoever was hurting them.

A soft touch on his shoulder broke him out of his reverie and made him jump. "Carlos, hi."

He stood and smiled at the woman who bore a wrinkled forehead, grey hair, and a short but sturdy stature standing beside him, wearing scrubs. "Hello, Dominique."

"It's good to see you again." She gestured down the corridor. "Follow me." She led him past hospital wards and administrative areas, into her small, cramped office. "We'll have privacy here. The others are doing their rounds." She sat across from him. "Now from your telephone call, I got the impression you have unanswered questions about your mother?"

They sat on two low stools and he leaned forward. "Yes. I want to know how a healthy woman could have a heart attack all of a sudden?"

Dominique stared into her hands as if measuring a response. "Carlos, I spoke to your father about this at the time. Anyone can have a heart attack, even if healthy. A sudden emotional trigger, poor nutrition, general stress or lack of stress, poor exercise activity, and burn-out. Any number of circumstances could have caused it."

"But my mother was looking after herself as far as I knew, and she didn't have any stressors at the time. At least none I knew about."

Dominique stared at the ground as if measuring what more to say. "I probably shouldn't be telling you this, but you deserve the truth." Rolling her shoulders back, she continued. "She did have high potassium levels in her blood, but apparently it was ruled out as inconclusive. The doctors ruled it out as a heart attack with no known cause."

Carlos drew back. *Inconclusive!* Was it a cover-up? "What's your personal opinion, Dominique? Do you think it was a gross hospital error, murder, or simply a heart attack with no known cause?"

Dominique's eyes grew wide. "Murder? Now that's ludicrous. Your mother was loved by everyone. That's quite a stretch, Carlos. You have a great imagination."

"Okay, but I'd still like your opinion."

Dominique shrugged and cleared her throat. "I don't have an opinion, Carlos, because there was no real evidence to suggest otherwise." Her eyes softened. "I'm sorry it's not what you wanted to hear, but I don't know what else to tell you. She led an interesting life, and it was a shame she died so young, but the journal she kept might have explained what was going on inside her mind. The actual truth."

Carlos's head tilted. "What journal? My mother kept a journal?"

Dominique nodded. "When you injured your ankle not long before she died, your mother was waiting for you while you had tests and treatment. I saw her in the waiting room, writing in a journal. She said it kept her sane and gave her perspective on things. You didn't know?"

Carlos shook his head. "No, my father never mentioned it."

Dominique leaned forward. "Hmm." She paused. "Your parents had a huge argument the day you injured your ankle. I'm not sure what it was about, but I remember he knocked her journal over while you were sedated after your surgery. He didn't like her writing in it."

A sense of unease and tightness fell across his chest. "Did you hear any part of their conversation?"

"No, sorry, Carlos. But I'm sure it was nothing important." She got up. "Sorry to rush things like this, but I have a busy day. It was great seeing you, and I'll call you. We can have lunch one day soon. You take care."

"Thanks for your time, Dominique. I look forward to lunch." Carlos strolled towards the corridor with one thing on his mind. Why didn't his father tell him about his mother's journal, and what were they arguing about?

CHAPTER 36
A STERN WARNING

A week after visiting Isabela in the hospital, Blanca arrived at the office and went straight to Pedro's office. She found him speaking on the phone, talking fast and loud, nostrils flaring and head jerking. He nodded at Blanca once, remaining focused on his conversation.

She stood cross-armed and cleared her throat, playing with the sleeves of her top as she waited for Pedro. She knew he held the key to the mystery of her past.

He startled her when he slammed down the phone, then fixed his intense gaze on her. Blanca took a deep, calming breath, wanting to get to the point. "I know you and my father were friends, but something happened seventeen years ago, when we vacationed here. What came between you and my father?"

Pedro froze. Several seconds later, he swallowed and his fingers tapped on the table. "It was a matter of growing apart as friends. It happens to the best of us." He turned in his ergonomic chair so he had his back towards her. "Why do you ask?"

She didn't want to mention her nightmares, nor the stalker. "I'm curious. My parents won't tell me anything about what happened, but I know something made us leave earlier than scheduled. Did you and my father have a fight when we were here?"

He turned back around, his eyes piercing hers. "Your parents had lunch at my house, but my wife was away. Then you left to go to your father's friend's house, but I don't know what happened after that. It's all I know, Blanca."

"Right. But it doesn't explain why my father never contacted you afterwards. He's kept in touch with his other friends from Brazil. What really happened?"

Pedro turned again and looked out the window. "I don't know what to tell you, but as I mentioned, we grew apart. I'm sure you've lost touch with some of your old friends. It's part of life, and as sure as death and taxes."

He looked convincing and she was inclined to believe him. Friends did sometimes grow apart, and she'd had gained and lost friends in Spain. Was her vacation seventeen years earlier just normal and uneventful, in spite of her nightmares?

No, her intuition told her otherwise. "I had a locket when I vacationed here. I definitely had it on in Brazil. Did you ever see me wearing it? It had sentimental value, and was a gift from my mum. Do you know what happened to it?"

Footsteps sounded behind her. She looked over her shoulder at Jose who watched Blanca with curiosity. "Jose."

He nodded. "Father. My computer's crashed and I have to get it rebuilt, so I'll work from home today. Is that all right?"

"If you must. I'll get Martim from IT to check your computer."

Jose turned to Blanca. "Are you here about the agenda for tomorrow's meeting?"

She shook her head. "No. I'm here about a personal matter." She didn't want to talk about her personal life to Jose, but then again, he might recall her locket. She didn't remember much about their relationship back then, but he might've seen her wear it.

Pedro waved Jose away. "You go on home, son. Blanca and I have matters to discuss. I'll talk to you later."

Jose knit his brows. "What matters? Blanca has articles to write and needs to hand them over to me. She doesn't have time for personal discussions."

Blanca's chest thrust out as she glared at Jose. "Are you kidding me? Who nominated you as my patriarch? I am free to do what I like, Jose."

Jose frowned. "I apologise, Blanca. I didn't mean it that way."

Pedro's face flushed. "Go on. We'll talk later."

Jose leered at his father. With a last suspicious look at Blanca, he stormed out of the office.

What's with Jose? Why doesn't he want me to talk to Pedro? I wanted to ask him about the locket, but Pedro shut him down. Why?

Blanca locked her eyes on Pedro's. "The locket. Do you know if I lost it?"

He hesitated and turned his head. "I'm sorry, Blanca. I haven't any inkling of a locket. I don't even recall you wearing it. Why is it so important to you?"

She shrugged. "I told you: it was a present from my mother. Never mind." She turned. "I'll leave you to it." As she was about to step out of his office, a familiar-looking man entered. The tall man with the bald spot wore a grey suit over a black cotton shirt with an expensive-looking watch on his wrist. It was Fernando Paes, the Governor of Rio de Janeiro who had been at Pedro's party. What was he doing here?

He drew a hand through his white-grey hair on either side of his bald patch, and forced a smile. "Hello. You look familiar, dear."

She put out her hand. "I am Blanca." They shook hands. "We met at Pedro's party. It is good to see you again."

Pedro played with the collar of his shirt. "As Governor, Fernando Paes has been instrumental in providing funds for the favelas and reducing drug wars. Not to mention opening up new women's shelters. He is a man of importance in this city."

Fernando waved his hand away. "I am simply doing my job, Pedro." He turned back to Blanca, his eyes boring into hers. Her eyes wandered and her heart raced at the scrutiny.

She glanced his way again. "I am honoured to meet a man who has done a lot for the community." Clearing her throat, she shifted. "I had better get back to work. It's been a pleasure to see you again, Mr. Paes."

She rushed out before his response. The door closed behind her, and again wondered what the Governor was doing here.

CHAPTER 37
RESEARCH

Blanca crawled on a dusty floor; all she could see from the narrow gap below the grimy rag over her eyes. From not far away, she heard chuckles and muffled voices. A hand touched her thigh. She shoved it away and shook her head. Tears poured down her young cheeks. "No, please."

More sounds around her. "Leave her alone, man. He said not to touch her."

Blanca whimpered as she reached a corner and cowered in a futile attempt at security. The smells of vomit, cigarettes, and cologne filled her nostrils. She lifted up her hand to reach for her locket, but her chest was bare. It had always made her feel safe, and now she remembered losing the locket days ago.

Large hands lifted and carried her away. She screamed, her body writhing. "Nooooo."

Blanca jolted upright in her bed. A bead of sweat trickled down her neck and her heart pounded. She kept her eyes closed to try to remember the dream.

It wasn't a dream. It was a memory. A memory of the favela. She was sure of it. It had to have happened when she was ten years old. Had she been in the favela as a child, or was it the memory of someone else's experience, triggered by her research into the favelas?

It was morning. Blanca put on her robe and made her way to the kitchen, where Maria and Julio were sharing small baked cheese rolls and a plate of fruit. "Come and have a roll, Blanca. I baked them myself," Maria said.

Blanca slouched into a chair. She picked up a roll and bit off pieces, chewing mindfully. "This is amazing. You should open up a bakery and sell these."

"Thank you, dear." Maria gave Julio a look, then turned back to Blanca. "Are you okay? You look as if you've seen a ghost."

"I had a nightmare. I was in the favela and these men were laughing and trying to hurt me. Then I remember being carried outside." Maria's face paled and Julio flinched. "I wonder if either of you know if anything happened when I was here the last time. My mum and dad never mentioned anything, but I feel as if it's so real. It has to be a memory. It has to mean something."

Julio rose. "Blanca, your parents never told us anything, but Maria will explain something." He squeezed his wife's shoulder. "I have to see my friend, Mateus. He needs help with his garden."

Blanca nodded. "No worries, Uncle." She watched as he dashed through the door like lightning. "What's going on, Aunty? I know there's more."

Maria sipped some orange juice and put the glass down slowly. "I didn't mention this before as I didn't want to worry you, but Julio's right. We don't know exactly what happened as your mother and father shot out of here as if Brazil was about to explode. But I know something happened." She took a deep breath. "I wanted to tell you this before, and now that you're getting involved in the favelas, you have a right to know." She bowed her head briefly then looked up at Blanca. "You and your parents had lunch at Pedro's place, but straight afterwards, from what your parents mentioned, you all stayed with an old school friend of theirs. You were there for one week. Your mother called and said something about making new plans with your father's old friend. They had bought tickets for these particular Latin shows, and if they didn't go, they'd lose their money. But something wasn't right. Your mother didn't sound like herself. When you returned after one week, suddenly your father said he had to leave due to a work emergency."

What the hell! Something must've happened in that week. "Why would my parents lie? Do you think they were in some kind of trouble?"

Maria shrugged. "I don't know, but given you've been having these recurring nightmares, it has to mean something. There has to be a compelling reason why they'd be quiet about it. It might be about protecting you from something. I doubt they'd be doing it maliciously, but for your own good."

Blanca processed the news, but something else was bugging her. "So you're saying we had lunch at Pedro's house, then later travelled to my dad's friend's home?"

Maria leaned in. "Yes. That's what they told us. You and your parents were gone for a week, then when you returned to us, you were catching a plane back home. We didn't get to spend more time with you. It was all very sudden."

Weird! "Something had to have been going on, Maria."

"Talk to your parents again, Blanca."

"No, they're adamant that nothing happened. They're afraid of something, but I've got other ways of finding out." She straightened, feeling parched. Blanca got up and poured herself a glass of water and sat back down. "You know my mother never told me much about the favelas or her life growing up in Brazil. As if she had something to hide. What was it like growing up with my mum, Maria? I know you grew up poor, but that's all I know." Maria's face paled. "Please. I know my mother is haunted by the favelas as if it's personal. Did she get hurt as a child?"

Tears trickled down Maria's cheeks. She wiped them with the back of her hand. "Oh, Blanca. I didn't want to tell you. I'm still ashamed of it." Blanca waited. "My family was poor and we lived in the favelas, and even poorer after my father left us. We were so desperate for money that if one of us didn't work, we'd be starving and living on the streets. Your mother was only five then, but I was eleven and old enough to sell my body." She swallowed and sat up straight. "Without going into the details, I prostituted myself for five years until I saved up enough money and got my family out of there. Your mother was younger and didn't know what was going on until many years later. I was abused, made fun of, humiliated, and beaten almost to death. It still haunts me to this day, but in some ways, it made me tough, too. Ever since I was able to afford it, I've donated to help end the exploitation of young girls. We even fostered a few young children from the favelas. They stayed with us until they could finish school and get a job."

Blanca was speechless. She got up and wrapped her arms around her aunt. "I can't believe this." Tears streamed down her cheeks. "I am so sorry for what you went through, Aunty, and I appreciate you sharing that. It can't have been easy."

Maria swallowed, rubbing her tears. "No, it wasn't, but if something like that happened to you, you deserve to know the truth.

"How could your mother let you do such a horrible thing?"

Maria shrugged. "She had no choice after my father left. She knew the young girls was what the men liked, but I promised myself they would never hurt your mother. I protected her from that by sacrificing myself."

Tears poured down Blanca's face as she hugged her aunt again. "Is that why you keep getting sick? Because you've been triggered by those newspaper articles and my own writing about the favelas?"

Her aunt frowned. "It is possible. I don't know, dear Blanca."

Blanca clasped her aunt's hands. "Oh, Aunty. You need to get some treatment so you can get past it."

***

Later that evening, Blanca sat up on her bed, her laptop propped against her thighs, and searched for news stories from seventeen years earlier. She found a multitude about child exploitation, prostitution in the favelas, and the nation's big problem of sex among children. Some of these were written by the journalist who wrote those other articles she'd seen with Carlos. *Paola Almada.* She decided to track down the reporter.

CHAPTER 38
SEARCH FOR TRUTH

Blanca and Carlos sat across the kitchen table from the reporter, Paolo Almada, who had written the story about Antonia seventeen years earlier. They had invited him to meet them at Carlos's house.

Blanca had visited the newspaper that had published his article about Antonia, but no one there would tell her anything about him other than he had retired a few years earlier. But as she left the newspaper building, a young man stopped her on the footpath. He said he'd remained friends with Paolo and gave her his phone number. Blanca had called him immediately, and he had agreed to meet in private, on the condition his name would remain hidden.

The man was in his sixties and had wrinkles around his eyes and forehead. His black hair had grey highlights on the sides. He had a broad stature and dark eyes, and sipped on his Brazilian beer a little too quickly.

"What can you tell us about Antonia and other girls?" Blanca asked.

Paolo fixed his gaze on her. "Do you promise to keep my name out of this?" She nodded. "Antonia was happy to talk. I blame myself for her going missing. In fact, I don't think she's missing at all. She's most likely dead and they hid the body."

Carlos leaned in. "Who's 'they'?"

He shrugged. "I don't know. They didn't have the guts to tell it to my face. It was over the phone. This guy, whose voice was disguised, threatened me. He told me to retract my story about Antonia and threatened to kill my wife and kids. I couldn't pursue any related stories."

Blanca threaded her hands through her hair. "I found a reference to a few articles you wrote, but they were general in nature. What was this retracted story about?"

Paolo frowned. "I wrote about Antonia meeting her pimp in his fancy car. She told me he didn't want his name known, and that he'd asked her to recruit new girls. Not only were they prostituting themselves, but these girls were forced to video-record their encounters and hand over the footage to their leader. She did tell me a woman was involved, but she'd never met her. She only spoke to her over the phone." *A woman!* "These recordings were later used to extort more money out of these men."

Carlos shook his head. "What happened if these men refused to pay? Were they killed or threatened?"

Paolo pursed his lips and stared into the distance. He played with the rim of his empty glass. "These men were either killed, or they stalked their families until they paid. In the end, they had no choice but to pay. Antonia said a few men were killed because they thought the pimps were bluffing. She mentioned this before I submitted the article." A bead of sweat appeared on his forehead. "After my last article and the retraction, I refused to publish anything as I didn't want to get killed or have my family threatened."

Carlos sighed. "Has anyone else approached you about this?"

Paolo rested back against his chair. He gazed into his lap and took a deep breath. His hands clenched. "About eighteen years ago, a woman approached me, saying she knew my work. She wanted to write a newspaper article and asked me questions about child exploitation. She wanted to go to the police before publishing. I warned her to stay out of it for her own safety, and I hoped she listened."

Carlos's face turned white as he stared at Paolo. "What was her name?"

Paolo glanced upward as if the answer was hanging in the air. He scratched his temple. "What was her name?" He closed his eyes briefly while Blanca and Carlos watched him. "I honestly cannot recall. It was a long time ago. I'm an old man now and my memory's getting worse."

Blanca saw the disappointment in Carlos's eyes. "Is there anything else you can tell us?"

Paolo stood. "No, that's it. I don't know how much I helped, but I urge you not to get involved in this. No doubt, you have corrupt police and politicians being paid off by gangs and ringleaders." He faced Blanca. "Why the interest?"

Blanca stood as Paolo moved toward the door. "I have a feeling I might've been involved seventeen years ago when I was ten, but I don't remember much. I keep having these nightmares and I'm tired of not knowing the truth."

Paolo stopped by the front door, knitting his brows. "These guys sometimes drug these girls so they don't remember many details if the police question them. If something did happen to you, they might have drugged you, which is why your memory's hazy."

That had to be it. She had to have been drugged. "Thank you, Paolo. We appreciate your time and honesty."

Carlos opened the door. "You take care of yourself."

The old reporter nodded. "Bye, now." They watched him walk towards his car and open the driver's door. Before he entered, his body jerked. He rushed back to them. "I remember the name now."

Carlos's eyes widened. "The woman who sought you out?"

He nodded. "Yes, yes. It was Francisca. Francisca Silva."

Carlos wobbled on his legs and gasped. "What?"

Paolo touched Carlos on the shoulder. "Are you okay? You look like you've seen a ghost."

"Francisca Silva was my mother. She's dead."

Paolo turned to Blanca, flinching as he put his hand in front of his mouth.

CHAPTER 39
THE JOURNAL

"My god, Carlos. Your mother was involved in this all those years ago? Are you okay?"

Carlos ignored her question, ran into his bedroom and returned with a notebook. He prodded Blanca to the couch as he flipped the pages of what looked like a journal.

"What do you have there?"

Carlos took a moment to straighten a curl at the edge of the rug. His throat was parched and his stomach tight with disgust. As he had so many times, he wished his mother was still here to set things straight.

"I got this journal from my father after I confronted him. He had kept it hidden in the garage, and mentioned never reading it. I don't know if I believe that." He sighed. "It has details in here about Antonia and her involvement in sexual exploitation." He continued to flip pages. "It even mentions how the girls would be given antipsychotic drugs to make them hallucinate, and how Antonia recruited other young girls and threatened to hurt their families if they didn't join her. Not only about sex, but blackmail for money, too. It seems as if Antonia played along."

Blanca moved closer to Carlos. "Can I have a look?" She took the journal with a shaky hand. "You already knew about some of what Paolo said because of these entries. But you didn't know your mother planned on publishing an article, did you?"

"No. What if the reason her article wasn't published was because she was murdered to shut her up?"

"But I thought you said she died of a heart attack."

"Supposedly, but I recently found out something from an old friend who works at the hospital." He recounted what Dominique had mentioned.

"So high levels of potassium caused her heart attack?"

Carlos put his fingers under his chin. "It was inconclusive, so I believe someone might've hidden the results or paid someone to keep quiet about it. Brazil is known for bribes and corruption even in the medical field, Blanca. Oh, this is such a mess." He felt nauseated, and wondered if it had been his mother who had hidden the journal to protect him. What if his father knew more than he was letting on? He had a sudden insight. "You know, Pedro and my father stopped talking around the time of my mother's death. What if it's related to this situation with the young girls?"

Blanca winced. "Are you saying you think Pedro's involved in all this?" She shook her head. "He's your uncle and he encouraged me to write articles about the favelas, albeit more the business side."

Carlos hoped she was right. "Pedro's acted strange over the years. First the fall-out with my father, and then forbidding Jose to hang out with me. Not to mention, his divorce from Ana, which Jose mentioned was because of an affair." *Oh, Christ! No!* "What if Pedro and my mother were having an affair? It makes sense if both brothers had a falling out."

Blanca shifted forward. "You might be clutching at straws. I can help, Carlos. I can approach Pedro's ex-wife and see if she'll open up to me. She might not want to hurt your feelings if your mother was having an affair with Pedro. We had a good relationship years ago, and she might be more open with me than you. Plus, she might know something about my past."

"Let me come with you, Blanca. You're a stranger to her now." Blanca flipped the last page of the journal, and stopped, staring at something on the back cover. "What are you looking at?" Carlos looked down. "Oh my god! It looks like something was stuck to the back cover. Do you think it was a USB stick?"

Blanca nodded. "The mark is shaped like one. Maybe she put her article on there. Who would've taken it? Your father?"

"I don't know. I'll have to speak to him again." He breathed in her musky perfume. "Have you heard anything more about your attacker from that night?"

"No, nothing. I think the case has run cold. Besides, my stalker's been quiet lately, so he might have got tired of me."

Carlos squirmed, not wanting to let his guard down. "I hope you're right, Blanca. But I'm here for you day and night. If ever anything goes wrong, I want you to call me. Will you promise me that?" He pressed his lips together. "I don't want you to get involved in this. It's too dangerous. Please stay out of it."

She swallowed. "This is my life, too. There's no way I'll stay out of it." She looked away briefly. "I'll be in touch if something goes wrong, but nothing will, so don't worry. I'll hopefully get answers from Ana and we can be rest assured that Pedro has nothing to do with this." Blanca got up. "I have to get going, Carlos. I'll call you." She took a step, but her foot caught on a curl in the rug and she pitched forward. Carlos caught her in his arms, and ended up getting lost in her eyes. Her gaze lingered, too, desire evident in her eyes. He stroked her cheek and brushed his hand over her bottom lip. Leaning forward, he tenderly kissed her on the lips and slid in his tongue, circling it around her mouth as she moaned. He tasted mint and his arousal got hot, fast. With one arm around her waist and the other around her face, he kissed her with a hungry need as their tongues explored and the kiss deepened.

The ringing of the phone broke the spell. Carlos settled Blanca securely on her feet. "Sorry. I'd better get that."

Blanca nodded. "I have to go." She swept out of his living room like a tornado and he stared at the closed door until his phone trilled again, vibrating on the coffee table. It was his father.

CHAPTER 40
VISIT TO THE PAST

That evening, Blanca searched online for Ana Santos, Pedro's ex-wife. She now lived in the centre of Rio de Janeiro.

She parked outside an apartment surrounded by trees and bushes with newly painted window frames at the front of the house. A freshly paved pathway led past a water fountain, lush shrubbery, and a statue of Cupid. But Blanca could think only of Carlos's amazing kiss. His tender lips and the way he drew her into his beautiful body.

No. She took a deep breath. She knew she couldn't get attached. It wouldn't work between them, and she had to let it go.

Blanca pushed thoughts of Carlos away, braced herself for news about the past, and rang the doorbell.

A tall, lanky woman wearing jogging clothes answered the door. She had smiling hazel eyes and auburn hair with grey ends. "Can I help you?" The woman angled her head. "You look familiar. Do I know you?"

Blanca remembered this woman's kindness when she had been a child. "My name's Blanca. You met me when I was ten. I work for your ex-husband, Pedro. He was friends with my dad." She smiled. "I was wondering if I could speak with you."

Ana's eyes widened. "Oh, my goodness! Blanca. How you've grown. Come on in."

"Thank you," said Blanca as she entered a fashionably furnished home. The spacious living room held a grand piano, as well as a three-seater, crème couch surrounded by two padded chairs and a glass coffee table. Bare windows displayed a view of the city with its mountains in the distance. A large photo of a rocky river hung on the opposite all. This woman had taste. "You have a beautiful home."

"Thank you. Please have a seat." Ana knit her brows, her eyes boring into Blanca. "Would you like a drink?"

She rested her back against a sofa. "No, I'm fine. Thanks."

Ana sat across from her, crossing her legs. "What brings you by? I had no idea you were back here after all these years. It is great to see you again."

Blanca wondered whether Ana had spoken with her son, Jose. "You would remember my father, Miguel. As I said, he was friends with Pedro while growing up here, and they had a falling out. Though he won't admit it, I think he's heartbroken about their lost friendship, and I get the feeling something happened the day we left Brazil all those years ago." Ana flinched and turned away, sitting stiffly. "Anyway, being back in Brazil has brought up a lot of memories for me, but my father won't tell me what happened years ago." Blanca continued. "I thought you might know, seeing as you had separated from Pedro not long after we visited. Pedro might have mentioned something to you."

Ana nodded as she continued to peer into the distance. "I don't know exactly what happened, but I know it had something to do with my son."

"Jose? What about him?"

Ana closed her eyes momentarily, as if she was taking herself back to that time. "All I can recall was that Jose and Pedro stopped talking after you left. They were estranged for months, but neither of them would tell me what it was about. The day you and your family were at our house, I wasn't home because I was taking care of my sick mother for a few weeks. I didn't see you that day. Pedro mentioned you were staying with friends afterwards. I was surprised your family left without saying goodbye, when you were supposed to stay for another few weeks. I was close with your mother. I wanted to say goodbye to you, too. Pedro didn't know why you left early."

"I'm sorry if I'm stepping out of line here, but what happened between you and Pedro? If you don't mind telling me."

Ana looked into her hands, a deep frown etched in her face. "I loved Pedro, but he cheated on me. Something came in the mail from an unknown sender, and there was a video."

Blanca shifted in her seat. "A video?"

She nodded and took a deep breath. "They were having sex. I don't think Pedro knew he was being filmed. But the young girl did."

Blanca lost her breath. "How old do you think the girl was?"

Ana shrugged. "It's hard to know for sure, but she looked to be about sixteen or seventeen." She shook her head. "In my opinion, the law is crazy to have the age of consent at fourteen years in Brazil. Total madness. In my eyes, it's still a form of abuse when a girl is that young."

Blanca nodded. "I agree, and I'm so sorry for what you went through." A coldness spread throughout her body.

Ana shuffled her feet. "It is what it is, but Jose is like his father. He was sometimes inappropriate with girls. One time, at school, he touched a girl's breast and the school suspended him. Another time, he kissed a girl without her permission. He was always doing that. Breaking the boundaries, and nothing I did worked. Pedro was never around, always working, and by the time Jose was a teenager, he was out of control. One girlfriend to the next. It never stopped. He liked girls far too much. It was as if he needed the distraction from his anger."

"But Jose has changed over the years, hasn't he?"

Ana nodded. "Somewhat. But both father and son love their women, and I can never see them being monogamous." She took a breath. "If you want to know anything about your father, Pedro kept a lot of old photos in his attic. You might find old pictures of your father—or letters. I remember seeing a letter in the mail when I visited Jose at the house not long after our separation. It was from your father, but Pedro snatched it off me when I took it from the mailbox. He might have kept them, and if so, it'd be in the house. There is an attic, and we did store a lot of things in there. You didn't hear this from me, but you'll need to find a way to get in there without Pedro knowing. He won't tell you the truth."

Blanca nodded, grateful for the lead. "Thank you, Ana. It helps." She braced herself for the next question. "I'm sorry to ask you this, but did Pedro have an affair with any other women?"

Ana turned to the window again. She touched her neck. "Not as far as I know. But then again, he was good at keeping secrets."

She rose from the couch and smiled at Ana. "I'm sorry for invading your privacy, Ana, and I appreciate your help. I'll get going now. Thank you for your time."

The woman smiled back. "I hope you find what you're looking for, Blanca. Please come visit me before you leave. Take care of yourself."

Blanca showed herself out and blew out a deep breath. She had a job to do in Pedro's house.

CHAPTER 41
THE SEARCH

Several days later, Carlos parked a hundred metres down the street from Pedro's house at six o'clock that night. Blanca sat in the passenger seat. He turned off the motor and turned to Blanca, ignoring her rosy lips he yearned to kiss again. No, they were on a mission and he had to focus on getting into Pedro's house. Carlos had a key to the front door, so there would be no problem getting in.

Blanca's past was a mystery to them both. Carlos knew that, if he hadn't been so young, he would have known what happened to her family seventeen years earlier. Her recurring nightmares linked her to Brazil, and he was determined to help Blanca find the missing part of herself.

"What exactly do you think we'll find here?"

Blanca's eyes scanned the area. "I'm not sure, but there might be a clue with the letter or photos Ana mentioned. I could be wasting my time, but if I don't at least check it out, I'll never know." She sighed. "Let's check the other parts of the house before searching the attic."

He nodded. "Pedro would be irate if he knew we were searching his house without his consent, Blanca. This had better be worth it."

She shrugged. "We can only hope, Carlos. But thank you for doing this for me. I appreciate it, and if he finds out, I'll take the blame." She pointed towards Pedro's house. "They just drove out. Put your head down."

Although there was some distance from Pedro's house, he might still spot them as he drove past his car. At least once a week, Pedro dined with his son; more recently, Pedro had begun seeing a new woman, and it wasn't Elina.

Carlos was happy for the man who had long missed his wife and had a challenging son. Jose had changed over the years, and Carlos had lost the connection they had when they were children. People did grow apart, but Jose had become distant and liked to party too hard.

Carlos wondered what had happened to make Pedro and Jose hate each other at one stage. Ana mentioned they weren't talking for a while after Blanca left. What was that about? "All right. I won't drive into the driveway, in case Pedro gets home earlier than expected. We'll make a run for it, Blanca."

As Pedro's taillights disappeared, Blanca and Carlos rushed to the house. Carlos unlocked the door and led Blanca inside. "Where to first?"

"Jose's room."

"What? Why there?"

"I remember playing in his room as a young child. I know this is their new house, but possessions in his bedroom might help me remember." She followed Carlos towards Jose's room.

"Hurry. We don't have much time." Carlos sifted through drawers, but didn't know what he was looking for.

Blanca eyed the bookshelf filled with erotic thrillers bearing Jose's name as author. "What if I lost my locket on the day we had lunch with Pedro? I left Brazil without it and I don't remember the last time I wore it."

They looked inside more drawers, underneath the bed, in Jose's wardrobe, and inside a filing cabinet. Pornographic magazines lined his cupboards and a box of condoms in assorted colours lay on top of his dresser. "Classic Jose," said Carlos. "There doesn't appear to be a locket anywhere."

Her hands on her hips, Blanca announced, "We'll check the attic."

Carlos frowned. "I know you miss your locket, but I doubt Jose would've kept it. Unless he found it after you returned to Spain."

Blanca looked up at the ceiling. "The locket might help me remember.

"Fine, I'll go get a ladder from the garage." Leaving Blanca in the bedroom, Carlos rushed to the garage, returning with a long steel ladder. Blanca stood awkwardly beside him as he positioned it below a trapdoor in the ceiling in the hallway outside Jose's room. He climbed the ladder and swung his legs inside the attic. Blanca rushed up behind him. "Hurry, Carlos. We don't know how much time we have."

He briefly turned to her. "Don't stress. I'll say it was my idea. If he wants to fire me, it suits me fine." He entered the dimness, reaching through cobwebs and smelling dust and grime. Using the light from his Smartphone, he explored his surroundings.

Cardboard boxes lined one wall of the unfinished attic, construction tools the other. He ignored the insects and dug into hefty boxes filled with clothing, old school items, and all sorts of papers, weathered and dusty from the years.

"No, we're in this together," Blanca emphasised.

Rummaging deeper into the boxes, he watched Blanca from the corner of his eye. She scanned the attic, her whole body trembling, and elbows pressing into her sides. *What is going on with her?* "Are you okay? Blanca?"

She suddenly rushed down the ladder. "Blanca, wait." He followed her and moved close.

She struggled to breathe, holding her stomach as if in pain. "Blanca. Breathe. Breathe, in and out. Slowly. That's it. Look at me. You're safe. You're safe." He wrapped her in his arms and stroked the back of her head. "It's okay. We don't need to keep looking."

After regaining her breath, Blanca shook her head. "I'm sorry. For some reason, I couldn't breathe. I felt trapped in there, but would you mind looking, Carlos? I'll wait down here."

"Are you sure? We can go. You still look rattled."

She pressed the palms of her hands together as if praying, her eyes yearning for something. "Please, Carlos."

"Okay. You can keep watch." His heart ached, wishing he could take the pain away from her. If she didn't discover whether a secret existed, she'd return to Spain without closure. He wanted to help her find the missing pieces.

She nodded and gave him a fleeting smile. He turned and climbed back up to the attic, wondering what the hell happened. She was freaked out about something, which triggered her. Had she been there before, and why did she feel trapped?

He took a breath. The damp smells, dust and dirt made him sneeze. He found old newspapers, toys, tax documents, and clothing. He searched another box containing more children's clothing, photographs of Pedro's ex-wife, Ana, and photographs of Blanca as a child with her family. Blanca was cute at that age, and had smiled happily at the camera. A gold locket hung around her neck.

Another photo showed an image of Jose and a young girl with freckles and pigtails. She looked at least sixteen, older than Jose, and the date-stamp at the bottom was the year of Blanca's childhood visit to Brazil. The girl in the picture wore a stained dress. Despite the stain on her dress, she appeared to be attractive—although, with her face turned away from the camera, Carlos couldn't identify her.

The image disturbed him, but he didn't know why. He glanced away and returned to the photo. *Wait! Was this girl Antonia?* He put the photo aside. *Oh, Christ!* He wasn't completely sure, but it looked like her.

Digging deeper into the box, he felt something cold and hard. He pulled it out.

It was a gold locket, the one in the photo. It bore an inscription: "Love between a mother and a child is forever." A birth stone and a red heart charm were embedded into the bottom of the locket.

This had to be Blanca's locket, but why was it stored in this box? Why hadn't Pedro returned the locket to her? Shaking his head, he found a letter addressed to Pedro from Blanca's father, Miguel. He unfolded it and read its single, short paragraph: "I'll keep your damn secret as long as you keep mine. This makes us even, Pedro. You are dead to me."

Carlos swallowed, realising the secret had to relate to Blanca and the reason the family had cut their vacation short. He had to show Blanca.

He shoved the locket, photos and letter into his pocket and rushed down the ladder. Blanca was staring out the hall window. She turned as he came up.

"I found it, Blanca." He handed her the locket.

Her face turned white. "Why didn't they return it to me if they found it?" Blanca whispered. "They took away a precious gift from my mother." She shuddered again.

He held her. "There's more you'll want to see." He handed her the letter and the photo of Antonia.

Blanca's face paled. "Oh, my God, Carlos. It sounds like both Pedro and my father have secrets. What's going on here?" She bowed her head. "Does your family know where Antonia is? Are they involved in something we shouldn't know about, Carlos? We have to talk to Pedro and Jose."

He felt a chill. "I hope there's a damn explanation for all of this, Blanca, but it's obvious something more happened when you left Brazil. Holding the locket might trigger something."

She pressed her lips together. "I'm tired of secrets, but at least I know I'm not crazy. If only my parents had the guts to tell me the truth."

He held her tight again. "Listen, I'm here for you. Whatever this is, you have my support. We'll confront my family and ask them about this, but not tonight. I think you've had enough excitement for one night. Get some rest and we will tackle this another day."

"Thanks, Carlos." She pulled away. "We'd better go. They'll be back soon." She stood with hunched shoulders, her mind obviously drifting elsewhere until he took her hand again and led her towards the front door.

Carlos and Blanca rushed out of the house just as a vehicle drove into the driveway. Pedro and Jose were back.

CHAPTER 42
MEMORY LANE

Blanca took calming breaths. *Oh, no. We've been caught*. She turned to Carlos, who gave her a nervous smile.

Blanca's feet shuffled and her chest tightened. She would have to face her demons and confront Jose and Pedro. They had to divulge the truth about what had gone on all those years ago. Particularly about her father's secret. She didn't know whether she knew him anymore.

Pedro and Jose emerged from the car with strange expressions on their faces. The air was thick with tension as father and son stopped inches from Blanca.

Carlos stepped between them. "This was my idea. All mine. But you have a lot of explaining to do."

Pedro ignored Carlos and turned to Blanca. "This is a surprise. I never expected you to go snooping around my house without my knowing. What is this about?"

She pressed her lips together, her body squeezing tight. "We need to talk about the past. You're hiding something and I need to know the truth."

Jose's eyes widened, his head tilting. "What do you mean?" He looked over his shoulder and into the street. His feet shuffled along the ground.

Blanca pushed forward. "Can we come in?" Pedro ushered them inside. She couldn't read his eyes, but Jose's shot daggers.

Blanca and Carlos followed them into the living room and sat on the black leather couch. The only light came from the streetlamp shining through the skylight. Pedro and Jose sat on the opposite of them, in armchairs.

She looked around the home with a new perspective now that she was no longer on a mission. A television set on top of a mahogany cabinet looked bigger than her living room in Madrid. Books of all shapes and sizes lined the tall cast iron bookshelf, and a large striped rug lay beneath her feet.

Blanca crossed her legs, facing Pedro. "I need to know exactly what happened the day we had lunch at your house seventeen years ago. I know you and my father are hiding something. Long-held secrets."

His face reddened as his eyes turned away. "Blanca. This is ridiculous. I believe you know what happened. As I mentioned before, you had lunch at my old house and later left to stay with Miguel's friend."

Her gut instinct told her that Jose's glare meant something. "Who stole my locket, Jose? I can tell you're hiding something."

He ignored her question. "I hear you've been talking to my mother. She mentioned you were catching up, but I know you asked her personal questions. Why would you do that?"

She swallowed, closing her eyes briefly. "Why are you distracting me from my question?" Carlos gave her hand a reassuring squeeze and was grateful he'd let her control the conversation. "I found my locket in your attic."

Pedro's eyes dilated and his body shifted on the armchair. His head bowed and he averted his eyes. "You had no right to invade our home. Carlos, I thought I could trust you of all people."

Carlos squinted. "How dare you put this all on us when you won't tell us what really happened?"

Blanca explained what they'd found in the attic. A fragment of the past flashed before her. She closed her eyes briefly. The locket. A pair of hands reaching around her neck and pulling it off gently so as not to break it.

Carlos touched her knee. "Blanca, what's wrong?"

She turned to him, swallowing. In spite of needing hydration, she carried on. "I remember someone in Jose's bedroom stealing my locket that day. But the rest is blank." Jose's eyes raked over her, but he remained silent. "I assume it was Antonia in your room." She showed them the photo they found in the attic. "What happened that day?"

Pedro pressed his lips together, his hands clenching. "Why are you fishing for answers when there are none? Leave it alone. Get on with your life, Blanca."

Blanca cringed at the cold tone in his voice. She cleared her throat. "Antonia went missing, so I wonder if you were the last person to see her. Where is she?"

Jose wrung his hands, his face suddenly aging ten years. "Leave it alone, Blanca. The past is the past." Blanca remained silent, defeated in her posture. "Your father and my father had a fight about a trivial work issue. That's all it was, so leave it."

Carlos scoffed. "We found a letter from Miguel to you, Pedro. What secrets is he talking about? And why can't you explain why Antonia was in your old house? We're not leaving until you tell us the truth."

Pedro gave Jose a reassuring smile and nodded. "Antonia and Jose were friends and that's why she was here that day. However, she left after you and your family left."

"My dad had a bruised nose the day we left, so what happened?" She scoffed. "I'm tired of everyone lying to me."

Jose's shoulders sank, his eyes turning dark. "And the truth shall set you free." He rose. "You're not going to let this go, are you?"

"No, never," said Blanca.

Pedro's mouth turned into a grimace. "How in the hell should I know what happened to Miguel? You were at his friend's house and we didn't see you again after that. Ask your father."

Jose touched his father's shoulder, addressing him. "Father, they're not going anywhere until we tell them the truth."

Pedro stared at his son for a minute, weighing his statement. He got up from his seat and paced the floor while threading his hands through his hair. He paced up and down without saying anything, cursing under his breath.

Jose rose. "Father. It's the right thing to do. They won't say anything."

Pedro squared his shoulders. "I want you both to leave or I'm calling the police. Son, stay out of this."

Carlos fixed his gaze on Blanca. "Okay, we'll leave but this won't be the last you'll be hearing from us. We'll get to the truth eventually."

Blanca ignored the shiver down her back. Her curiosity overshadowed her fear—she'd seen something in Jose's eyes. A look passed between her and Carlos as if they were both thinking the same thing. Jose was vulnerable and if they could get to him alone, he'd break.

CHAPTER 43
THE COLONIAL HOUSE

Blanca and Carlos stepped out of the car after Jose parked in front of a colonial-style house the following Saturday. It looked familiar. After a piercing look into Blanca's eyes, Jose led them into the building.

She looked nervously around her. A part of her remembered this old house where they'd had lunch all those years ago.

Jose walked to the house and took a tiny red box from his shirt pocket. From the box, he produced a key and unlocked the front door. Blanca's breathing shallowed as she stood on the front step, staring through the open door.

"Are you sure Pedro's at work today?" she asked, finally meeting Jose's eyes, her stomach turning. Carlos held her hand tight.

Jose's eyes turned hard. "He'll have my head if he knows I'm bringing you here to trigger your memories. But you need the truth. Come inside." His posture hunched and he looked smaller. "My dad still owns it, and rents it out, but there aren't any tenants at the moment. The place has been empty for a few months. New tenants are supposed to move in shortly. Once it's had a proper cleaning."

Slowly, Blanca walked into an ample living room. Daylight seeped through drawn beige curtains to reveal two cotton, chequered sofas, a mahogany coffee table, and a plush floral rug.

Blanca took her time to follow Jose past a kitchen and down a corridor to a bedroom. Her legs felt frozen at the door, and her hands were shaking. There was a lingering smell of something rotten. The stench of blood? Cautiously, she entered the bedroom after taking a deep breath, with Jose silent beside her.

Carlos watched her closely. "Are you okay? Do you remember something else?"

"Blood," she whispered. Carlos tightened his arm around her back, and wished he could ease her pain.

Wallpaper peeled from the walls. There was a bed with a cast iron headboard. Tiny pieces of quartz lay on the wooden dresser. Cobwebs lined the corners of the room. This was Jose's room, and Blanca's legs felt like lead as fuzzy images emerged in her mind. She remembered playing games here with Jose, and reading his comic books. But there was more. She knew it.

Space closed in on Blanca as she stood by the bed, as if drowning in water. The smell was foul and pungent. Her whole body shook as she looked around the enclosed space. Newspapers covered the bedside table, and women's magazines lay on the carpeted floor. She gently allowed herself to remember. Nothing came. The fear was too strong. Blanca rushed out of the bedroom to the front of the house.

Carlos followed her. "We can leave if it's too much, Blanca."

She shook her head. "No, I have to do this."

Jose stood beside Carlos, knitting his brows. "What do you remember?"

"Did someone get injured? I remember blood. Lots of it."

"You have to promise me you won't do anything about it, and forget it even happened?"

Blanca shrugged. "I can't answer that without knowing what it is."

Unsuccessfully hiding his disappointment, Jose ushered them back to the bedroom. Her throat was dry. "Let me get you a glass of water. I think you'll need it." Jose fetched her a glass and handed it to her. She gulped it down. The water soothed her parched throat. Pain stabbed behind her eyes, but she pushed it into the recesses of her mind. She steeled herself for the truth and sat on the edge of the bed with her arms crossed. Carlos sat beside her. Jose grabbed a chair and sat opposite, his eyes focused on her.

"I want you to know I am not a bad person, Blanca. I'm not."

Blanca listened intently as he recounted that day seventeen years ago. His words opened her memory like a crumpled piece of paper slowly unfolding.

Blanca was ten years old, kneeling on the carpeted floor of Jose's bedroom to build a Lego tower. Jose played on his phone when someone tapped on his window. He opened the window to allow a teenage girl wearing a dirty floral dress and torn runners to climb through. She looked as if she hadn't had a shower in days, but Blanca smiled and stopped building her tower. The girl pushed Jose onto the bed.

He shook his head. "No, Antonia. Blanca's here. We can't do anything."

The girl turned to Blanca. "Have you had a boyfriend, little girl?" Blanca shook her head. "You got any money?" Blanca got scared and moved back, but Antonia neared her, staring at her locket. "Ooh, I love your locket. I could sell that."

Blanca covered her chest. "No, my mummy gave me this locket. It's not yours. It's mine."

Antonia shoved Blanca onto her back, reached around and carefully unclasped the locket from her neck. She chuckled as Jose closed the window. Blanca started crying and was about to leave the room, but Antonia pushed her down onto a beanbag. "No, you're going to have a lesson you'll never forget."

"Leave her alone, Antonia. She's done nothing to you."

"Don't worry about her. She has to learn that life is hard for everyone, and the sooner she learns that, the stronger she'll become."

Jose shook his head and watched as Blanca stared into her lap, tears streaming down her cheeks. He turned to Antonia. "What are you doing here, anyway?"

The girl shrugged. "I was bored, so I thought of you." She looked over at Blanca, who cowered. She leaned forward, set her phone on his dresser, and kissed Jose hungrily on the lips. She pushed him down on the bed, touching his crotch. Jose moaned and kissed her back while touching her breasts.

He stopped and lifted himself off the bed. "We can't do this here. Not in front of a child."

She sighed. "Oh, god. Who cares? She can get a good education. She's older than a few of the usual girls."

Jose moved away from the bed, glaring at Antonio. He faced Blanca with a sorry expression on his face.

"Come on, Jose," Antonia said. "I'm hungry for you, baby. Don't you want me?"

Jose spotted a red light on top of his chest of drawers. "What's this?" He picked up Antonia's phone from the chest. "What the hell, Antonia. Were you going to video us having sex?

And how in hell can you afford a mobile phone? I thought you were poor."

The teenager smirked. "Someone gave me the phone." She played with the tips of her nails as if she was in control.

"Who?"

She turned away. "I'm not telling you. None of your damn business, Jose."

He pursed his lips. "You need to get out of here and don't ever come back."

She shoved him. "Give me my phone back."

"No, I'm deleting this and you're not getting it back." He tapped the screen. "You don't deserve it, and you can't even talk nicely to Blanca."

The girl turned on him in fury and kicked him hard in the legs. "You prick."

Jose held her by the arms and pushed her towards the window. "Get the hell out of here or I'm calling my dad."

"Go ahead. You can't prove anything now, anyway. You deleted the bit I had."

He shook his head. "I'm sure you can get it back. Now get out."

She chuckled and crossed her arms then lay on the bed. "Why don't you make me?"

Blanca quivered and whimpered, "Please go."

Antonia stared at Blanca with rage. "Oh, shut up!" She stepped towards Blanca and pushed her hard, knocking her head against the bookshelf. Blanca cried, bowing down. "Oh, the cry baby. Listen to her cry." Antonia laughed and threw her head back when Jose grabbed her by the waist and pushed her towards the door.

"You're meeting my dad, now." Antonia gouged her thumb into his eye and kicked him between his legs. Jose groaned in pain. When he recovered, he slapped her hard across the face.

She fought back, scratching his cheek and slapping him.

Blanca rushed forward. "Go and get my dad, Blanca," Jose cried. She ran towards the door, but Antonia pushed her into a corner and Blanca bent down low, her whole body shaking. Jose fought back, but Antonio was strong and filled with rage as he pushed her hard towards the door. She picked up one of his model cars and smashed it into his face. He winced in pain. She wasn't done, and elbowed him in the stomach. He shoved her even harder, closer towards his bedside cabinet. One last shove slammed her head against the corner of his cabinet. Blood poured out of her skull. Jose gasped, his hands over his head. Everything went silent.

CHAPTER 44
HIDING THE TRUTH

Blanca rose from the bed and paced the floor, shaking her head. She had witnessed a death at ten years old. That explained why she was anxious and panicky with certain types of people—and in this room. Even Jorge's physical abuse explained why she didn't trust romantic or sexual partners. "She died?"

Jose's eyes fixed back on her. "Yes. It was an accident. I never meant for her to die. I tried to get rid of her, but she wouldn't leave. It was self-defence after her violence towards me."

The silence was unnerving. "What happened next?"

Jose shifted in his chair, peering into his lap. "My dad and your parents heard the noise and rushed into my room. Your dad wanted to call the police, but my dad stopped him. He threatened to destroy his career if he contacted the police. He said my life would be ruined as the police wouldn't believe it was an accident, and I might go to prison." He looked up at Blanca. "But I think the real truth was my dad couldn't have anything get in the way of his perfect world. His perfect house, perfect wife, perfect career, and his idea of a perfect son. His need for perfection in everything and his ambition to climb the ladder in publishing. This case would've destroyed everything, created a scandal. I knew that, and I didn't fight him on it." He took a breath. "I ran for the bathroom and vomited, but when I returned, my dad made a call and convinced your father to stay the night. You were in shock and my dad didn't think you were in a position to go back to your aunt's house that night."

Blanca stilled, gasping for breath. "I understand it was an accident, but not reporting it only made things worse." Jose averted his eyes. "You were only a kid back then. Only thirteen years old, Jose. Whatever happened wasn't your fault. Antonia was violent, vindictive, and her anger made her strong." She bowed her head. "I met her mother, Juliana at the favela and she wants to know where Antonia is." Her body froze as she thought about Juliana and how she'd never got closure. She wasn't missing. She was dead. "What happened to her?" Blanca took a breath. "We didn't go back to my aunt's place. Maria mentioned we went straight to my father's friend's house. Your dad must've driven us there."

Jose stood up from his chair, his expression blank. A door slammed. He faced the door to his old bedroom as Pedro swaggered inside. "Dad? What are you doing here?"

Pedro swallowed, turning to Blanca with curiosity. "I could ask you the same thing."

Jose shook his head. "I couldn't hide the truth from Blanca anymore. She had a right to know."

Blanca stepped close to Pedro. "All these years you tried to hide this from me. Even my parents. What happened to Antonia?"

Pedro turned to Jose. "Why don't you leave us. I'll take it from here, Jose. I'll set Blanca straight and give her the full story."

Jose hesitated, and turned to Blanca. "I'm sorry. I tried to protect you back then and never wanted to hide this from you." He stepped out of the bedroom and out of the house.

"You didn't answer my question, Pedro. I deserve to know the truth."

Carlos spoke under his breath. "Bastard." He glowered. "You need to tell us why you didn't drive Blanca back to Maria's house that night. Why did they go straight to her father's friend's place instead?"

Pedro stomped over the floor, a pulsing vein looking as if it would pop out. He clenched his fists. "I'll tell you, but then you need to let this go and forget about it."

She crossed her arms and wrung her hands. "Answer Carlos." Silence. "The girl's parents deserve to know the truth. They need closure."

Pedro's eyes glazed over. He shook his head, and his eyes darkened. "Your parents didn't want your aunt and uncle knowing anything about what happened, so they decided to stay with his friend, Abel for a while. Given we were all in shock, you and your family stayed here for the night and I decided to drive you there the next morning."

Blanca rested back on the bed, closing her eyes. Something had happened on the way to Abel's. An image flashed before her. A man with a gun. "Christ, Pedro. What happened when you drove us?"

His eyes twitched. "Nothing."

She moved within inches of his face and pointed a finger into his chest. "You're lying. Have the guts to tell me the whole truth or I'll splash what I know to the newspapers. Don't think I won't."

Pedro avoided her eyes and stood cross-armed, his eyes a shade darker. "Fine." He turned to Carlos. "We were carjacked on the way, and they took you. They mentioned how they'd give you back once they received ransom money. I told them I would pay but they had something against your father and wanted him to pay. I tried to fight the two men, but I was knocked out."

Carlos leaned forward. "Was it organised crime looking to exploit Blanca, or was it really about money?"

Pedro shrugged. "How the hell should I know?"

Blanca pushed away images of a gunman that rose in her memory. "Where's Antonia?"

"She was buried in the backyard here, but she was only a poor peasant girl."

Blanca's stomach churned. "She was a person, Pedro. Have a bit of humanity."

"She came from the favela and was a first-class bitch." He paced the floor. "Jose is my son and I had to protect him. I know what the Brazilian authorities are like, and things would've been much worse for him. I vowed to keep him out of prison, whatever it took."

Blanca could barely breathe, knowing Pedro and Jose had covered up a murder. Her own parents were complicit in this too. "What do you mean she was a bitch? How would you know?"

Pedro's eyes looked a million miles away as he leaned back against the wall. "She set me up. This bitch recorded us having sex and sent it to my wife. I swear, I only slept with her once while I was married. I vowed I wouldn't cheat on Ana again, but she didn't believe me. She left me."

"My god, Pedro. She was only a child. How could you?" Bile rose in her throat. "*You* had a motive for her murder. Was Jose telling me the truth, or did you kill her because of the scandal she'd create in your life with that video?"

He scoffed. "That's ludicrous. I paid her off so I could get the original video back, which I did. I had no idea she was so young. I thought she was eighteen. I didn't know she was seeing

Jose behind my back until that day. Her death was an accident, but I wouldn't let that ruin Jose's life."

"Her parents deserve to know what happened to her in the favela. You have to tell them and give them closure."

He clenched his hands, moving closer to her, inches within her face. "You are not going to breathe a word of this, young lady. We are not going to prison because of that bitch."

"But Pedro, how would you feel if you were in the same situation? They have a right to know. It's cruel not to lay her body to rest."

He held her hard by the shoulders. "The only one who needs closure is you. Now that you know the truth, you're going to keep your mouth shut and go back to Spain. I don't want to hear any more about this."

She shook her head. "No, this isn't right. I experienced trauma witnessing her death. I have had this anxiety for years. You have to tell the parents."

Carlos squeezed her shoulder. "Maybe he's right, Blanca. This would affect you, your parents and Jose. Whoever's been stalking you might escalate what they're doing. Let it rest after all these years."

Pedro pressed his lips together, straightening his posture. "It's okay, Carlos." He turned to Blanca. "I'll think about it, but keep this to yourself for now. Please, Blanca. I'll fix this."

"I remember parts of the kidnapping, Pedro. Do you know anything about that? Was my story in the papers then?"

He shook his head. "Your parents didn't want the media involved and I used my contacts to keep it from becoming public."

She glared at him. "Is that why you stopped being friends with my father?

He nodded. "He hated me after Antonia's death. I don't blame him. He wanted to go to the authorities and I convinced him not to."

She knit her brows. "What did this gunman have against my father?" Pedro shrugged. "And how did you convince my father not to go to the authorities?"

Pedro hesitated, staring past her. "I can be very convincing, and he didn't want to be in such a scandal, too."

Blanca wondered if he was lying, and hoped she could eventually remember more about her kidnapping.

***

Later that day, Blanca and Carlos took a walk along the Ipanema beach. Her bare feet sinking into the soft sand, Blanca said, "I'm going to need time to process this, but Antonia's parents need to know the truth about her death. They need closure after all these years. How could anyone live without knowing what happened to their missing child?"

He nodded. "I get that, but for now, leave it alone. Give yourself time to process and don't make any rash decisions."

Blanca walked past seagulls pecking the wet sand and tourists swimming or playing ball, until she reached the concrete walk. She put her shoes on and walked alongside the shore towards where she had parked her car under towering trees in the quieter part of the area. She kissed Carlos goodbye on the cheek. "I'd better go. Maria and Julio will be wondering where I've been."

"Let me walk you to your car," Carlos said. His eyes roamed their surroundings.

Blanca had plans to read a good book with a glass of sparkling red wine, and possibly even indulge in a bubble bath. Could the past finally be laid to rest so she could move forward in her hometown? Would Pedro inform Antonia's parents about her death? She shook her head. "It's fine. My car's not far."

He ignored her and put his arm over her shoulder as he walked alongside her to her car. "I will make sure you're okay then I'll leave."

"Fine." Her car was several metres away, but in spite of Carlos standing close, a prickle of unease ran up her spine. She shook it away.

As she entered her car, she waved goodbye to Carlos, and drove off.

Blanca arrived home and parked in the garage. She swung open the car door when a jangle of keys sounded beside her. Before she could face the noise, she felt the sting of a needle in her shoulder. She drooped forward. The last thing she remembered was a set of arms holding her upright as everything went black.

CHAPTER 45
A CONFINED SPACE

Blanca pulled at the chains fastened around both wrists, but they only cut deeper into her skin, and she winced at the pain. The chains were attached to a steel pole cemented into the floor of a dark basement.

Her bottom was numb from sitting so long on the concrete floor. She had been here for what she estimated was a few hours. She hadn't yet seen her kidnapper and was dehydrated and hungry.

What was this place? It looked like a basement. In a corner, she saw a dirty blanket and a tall pile of weathered wooden boxes. Cobwebs covered the walls and the piles of old newspapers, plastic chairs and bookshelves lay strewn. An old single bed sat on the opposite side, and she wondered who lived here.

Pedro might have been behind her kidnapping, not wanting her to report Antonia's death to the police. It would ruin his stellar reputation. That made her a threat to him, now that she knew about Antonia's death. Maybe he was keeping her prisoner until he could make his escape.

How long was he planning to keep her here? Or did Pedro plan to kill her so she'd take this secret to the grave? She had to figure out a way to get out of here.

She must have drifted off to sleep when a scraping sound got her attention. She jolted awake to see a mysterious person, probably a woman, climbing down the stairs, wearing glasses and a dark hoodie. There was something familiar about her as she put down a dinner plate with a tall steel cup and a jug of water. "No, wait. Please. Don't do this. I promise I won't say anything to anyone. I'll leave Brazil early and you won't need to hear from me again. Please. Let me go. Tell Pedro he can trust me."

The woman chuckled, gazed into her eyes and lifted a hand to stroke her cheek. "You know you are very beautiful. I can see why Carlos has fallen for you." She knew the voice. A familiar woman's voice.

The woman slowly took off her glasses and put down the hood of her coat. "Surprise, Blanca. It's me."

Blanca swallowed, her heart pounding, gasping for air. "Elina. Oh, my God!" Her throat constricted. "How can you do this to me?" She shifted on the floor, her shoulders and arms aching. "Carlos will find me. I'm sure of it."

The woman turned away from her and walked out of the basement with an air of arrogance. "Don't hold your breath, darling."

"Don't you dare leave. Why are you doing this to me, Elina? Let me out of here. Please. Please." She hung her head, tears streaming down her cheeks. She was going to die in this place.

CHAPTER 46
NIGGLING DOUBT

Carlos parked in Pedro's driveway on Monday evening. Before getting out, he dialed Blanca's number. For the fifth time in two days, his call went straight to her voicemail. Why wouldn't she call him back?

He called his father, only to learn his job had sent him to Sao Paolo for a number of days. Once again, his father denied knowing anything about the USB missing from the back of his mother's journal.

Finally, he rang his uncle's doorbell. Pedro opened the door, and shrank back at seeing him. "What are you doing here at this late hour, Carlos?"

He pushed his way inside. "I'm looking for Blanca. Did you hurt her because she knows the truth?"

Pedro winced. "I've been trying to call her, too. She didn't arrive at work today. I don't know where she is."

Carlos was nowhere near satisfied. Something was wrong, and his chest tightened at the thought she was unsafe. "Where's Jose?"

"He's out with another one of his conquests." He squared his shoulders. "He doesn't know anything, either.

Carlos scoffed. "Are you telling me the truth? You know she wasn't planning on telling anyone, didn't you?" He turned at the sound of footsteps behind him to see Jose walk in, looking as pale as a ghost.

A shiver ran up Carlos's back. Did Jose know something? "I'm looking for Blanca. She won't answer any of my calls. Do you know where she is?"

Jose gave his father a strange look. "I don't know where she is. The last time we saw her was at our old place."

Carlos felt nauseated. "She wouldn't leave all of a sudden unless something happened. Even then, she'd be answering her calls. Isabela and her colleagues at work called her, but no response either. She wouldn't leave without telling anyone, most of all her friend, Isabela. She's obviously missing."

He stormed out of the house and jumped back into his car. He bowed over the steering wheel and closed his eyes. He could have kicked himself for not keeping a closer eye on her. He had watched her drive off safely in her car. Did something happen on the way? Would his uncle or Jose hurt Blanca because of the truth?

He dialled Blanca's phone number, and again heard her voicemail message. He slammed his fist against the steering wheel and cursed. If anything happened to her, he would make whoever was responsible pay.

CHAPTER 47
A STEP CLOSER

The first thing the next morning, Carlos went to the police to report Blanca missing, only to learn her uncle Julio had already done so. The desk officer apologized, but had nothing else to tell him. Carlos didn't hold much hope that they would even bother to find Blanca.

After a day's work he performed almost unconsciously, Carlos ate leftovers without tasting anything. He decided to call on Blanca's aunt and uncle for any ideas they might have about how to find her.

As he hustled up the cracked concrete path to Julio and Maria's home, he could not help but picture Blanca's beautiful, sweet face. How he missed her. Each day she was absent made him worry more. He couldn't bear to never hear from her again.

Julio answered. His eyes appeared dull with black circles below. "Hello Carlos. Have you heard from Blanca?"

He shook his head. "No, I was hoping you had." He stood awkwardly by the door.

Julio ushered him inside. "Please come in."

"Thanks, Julio. I hope you don't mind me coming over unannounced."

"Not at all. Have a seat."

Carlos's eyes roamed. "Where's your lovely wife, Maria?"

"Oh, she's gone to see her doctor for her blood pressure. It's been high lately. She went with a friend, but plans to come straight back home in case Blanca returns. We've been worried sick about her."

Carlos sighed, hoping they'd heard from her. "I was hoping we'd find Blanca, but no one's heard from her. I've spoken to her friend, Isabela, but she hasn't heard anything. Even Pedro and Jose claim to have not seen her."

Julio tilted his head and sighed. "I reported her missing to the police, but I doubt they'll be much help. Maria's been praying for her. I haven't called her parents yet, as I'm hoping she'll turn up or the police will miraculously find her. I didn't want to worry them at this time. I think we should hold off until we know for sure that something's wrong." He took a breath. "Do you know what's been going on with Blanca? Maria mentioned something about her nightmares and the favelas."

Carlos braced himself. He knew Blanca's parents had a right to know what was going on. "I need to tell you something and let you be the judge of it."

Julio's eyes darkened. "What is it?"

Carlos took a calming breath. "It has something to do with her past. We found a few things in Pedro's attic, but I don't know what it means." He explained how they found the locket, the notes Blanca received, and the physical attack at his party.

Julio got up to pace. "Why didn't she tell us any of this? We could have protected her or done something."

Carlos sympathised with the man. "She's independent and didn't want to worry you, Julio. She was trying to protect you." He exhaled. "There's something else you need to know about Blanca."

Julio leaned forward, his eyes fixed on the young photographer. "Go on."

His hands fidgeted and his eyes turned down at the floor. "She was witness to a murder, and later kidnapped by an armed gunman seeking ransom." He explained the details and watched Julio's face age ten years.

Julio threaded his hands through his hair. "Christ! What poor Blanca has had to endure. I need to talk to her father and insist they tell us the whole truth. Why didn't they tell us any of this? There has to be a reason why Blanca was targeted."

Carlos's heart beat fast, his head aching. "Do you think Blanca was targeted all those years ago? But why?"

"That's what I'm about to find out." He grabbed his cordless phone and dialled a number. "Miguel. I know the truth about what happened to Blanca when you vacationed here. I need answers, and I need them now. Blanca is missing and might be in trouble. She's been gone for three days." Julio nodded, his eyes darkening, his hands gripping the phone with all his might. Carlos waited patiently, listening to half the conversation with his hands clasped across his abdomen.

Julio's eyes widened, his head shaking and his lips pressed hard together. His nostrils flared and his face reddened.

"You piece of shit, Miguel. I trusted you. And now you tell me this. The dirt under my shoe has more value than you. Do not come here ever again, you bastard." Pacing the floor, he ended the call.

Carlos moved forward. "Are you okay?"

"Give me a minute." He took a deep breath and squared his shoulders, standing awkwardly for a few minutes. He turned to Carlos. "That piece of filth confirmed what Pedro said about the gunman and ransom, but they didn't have the money. They stayed at a hotel as they didn't want to endanger us, and were trying to think of a way to get the ransom money. Blanca was gone for one week when Miguel got an anonymous call about her whereabouts. They called the police and narrowly saved her while one of the kidnappers was transporting her to another location to further groom her for sex with older men." He scoffed. "They lied to us about visiting his friend, Abel. It was a cover. Instead, they stayed in a hotel while Blanca was held captive for a week."

Carlos sat back on the couch, his chest tightening and his breath coming short as he listened to the terror she'd experienced. "Dear god! Do they think Pedro or Jose might have kidnapped her to keep her quiet?"

"He doesn't think he would hurt her as he knows she's returning to Spain. But he can't be sure."

Carlos got up from the couch and punched a pillow. "Damn that bastard. Both of them. I never once thought Pedro or Jose could hurt Blanca, but now I'm worried they have." He turned to Julio who looked pensive. Something was on his mind and he wasn't sharing. "You know I realised something."

Julio looked up. "Hmm."

He angled his head. "Why didn't her parents tell her about the kidnapping in the favela? She had a right to know about her past."

Julio rubbed his hands across his legs, taking a deep breath. "There is something else you should know about Miguel, which convinces me he's a piece of turd. I never knew about this until now. He has lied to us all these years, the bastard." Carlos waited. "Back when Miguel and Claudia lived in Brazil, they had no choice but to leave. You see, Miguel was having problems with money at the time. He was twenty-five years old, newly married, and had embezzled money in the investment firm he worked for. A colleague of his, named Carolina, checked their finances, and

172

realised Miguel was cheating the company. He panicked when she confronted him after work one evening, and he implored her not to say anything. She refused and was about to call the police when he tackled her and hit her over the head with a paperweight."

Carlos's spine went cold. "Did she die?"

Julio nodded. "She did, and in that moment, he didn't know what to do. He called Pedro, who came to his rescue. They buried the body in a deserted location. Miguel owed his friend, which was why he couldn't mention the kidnapping to Blanca. His story would've come out."

Carlos frowned. "How does that relate to her being targeted?"

"The gunman, Rodrigo was Carolina's sister and he wanted revenge. He'd heard about Miguel returning to Brazil and thought what better way to get back at him by turning his daughter into a prostitute." Julio grunted. "Miguel had the nerve to say he didn't mean to kill Carolina, but what did he expect with a paperweight smashed over her head?"

Carlos shook his head as his blood ran cold. How could her own father kill someone in such a cold manner? "Do you think the gunman's back? Has he taken her again?"

"I asked Miguel the same question, but the gunman died back then. He was shot by police when they apprehended Blanca, so it cannot be him."

Carlos pressed his lips together. "If it is Pedro, then we have to do something. Confront Pedro and Jose again. Do something."

Julio held up his hand. "Now, wait. As sickening as this story is, you need to have a clear head. You've already confronted them, so what more can you do? We do not have any evidence that Pedro has hurt her. This is all pure speculation." He paced the floor again. "We have to be smart about this. Gather evidence. I think what we need to do is to come up with a plan."

Carlos closed his eyes briefly and breathed in and out to clear his head. He had to pull himself together for the sake of Blanca. He had to save her from wherever she was.

"What if I park near his house tonight and see whether he goes anywhere? I can follow him. If he is holding her somewhere, he might not leave the house until late to avoid anyone seeing him."

"Okay, but I am happy to take over if you need to sleep."

Carlos shook his head. "No, you need to be here for Maria and in case Blanca returns. Don't move a muscle, Julio." He went to the door. "I'll keep watch tonight, but if you think of anything else, call me immediately." He rushed out and drove to Pedro's house.

CHAPTER 48
A LEAD

Carlos rolled out the kinks in his shoulder and stretched out his arms in a yawn. He peered at his phone. The screen displayed midnight, and the lights in Pedro's house were off. He rested his head back against the car seat, waiting for movement from his uncle's house. He thought about Blanca's past, his heart breaking. She had experienced multiple traumas, each one overwhelming for an adult let alone a ten-year-old child. Now, she'd have to find out her father was a murderer. Too many secrets.

He shook those thoughts away to focus. The minutes and hours passed by with no movement, no sound from his uncle's house. Carlos struggled to keep his eyes open in the stillness of the night, his eyes drooping and his head falling back against the headrest. His breathing shallowed.

He jerked awake at the noise of a car door and starting engine. Carlos sank down in his seat to avoid being seen, taking a slow breath as he waited for the black Mercedes to whizz past him. Then he started his engine and turned to follow Pedro's trail, remaining a healthy distance behind.

Where the hell is Pedro going at this time of night? It was two o'clock in the morning, so unless he had a booty call, Carlos didn't think this was innocent. He'd been hiding something all these years, but never once had it been relevant until Blanca came into his life. She was his world, and if anything happened to her, he'd kill his uncle with his own bare hands.

He drove along quiet streets under towering palm trees. Passing the beach, he saw only a few crazy people walking along the shore at this hour. He experienced a sense of déjà vu. He was driving to Pedro's old house again, where Blanca's trauma had begun.

Chills ran down his spine as Pedro turned down the familiar street and stopped his car by the kerb. Why would he come back here at this time of night? Carlos pulled back and stopped behind another car down the block and waited.

Pedro went into his old house. This was it: the moment of truth when he'd find out what was going on with his uncle. He drove ahead and parked behind Pedro's car. He ran to the front door, finding it locked. How was he going to get inside?

Carlos ran to the back of the house, peering through the windows, but they were all covered with heavy drapery. He tried to open the windows but found no way to get inside. The house was like a fortress. What if Blanca wasn't here? Was his imagination playing tricks on him?

He went to the front door and stood cross-armed to wait for Pedro to come out. His eyes roamed the quiet street with its dull lights. After a time, he leaned against a window and checked his phone for the time and messages. He scrolled through social media posts as the cold wind cut across his cheek. After twenty minutes, he had had enough of waiting. He put away his phone and banged hard on the door. A short time later, he heard footsteps and the door swung open. Pedro's eyes widened. He wore sneakers and brown sweatpants, and played with the zipper of his black jacket.

Carlos pushed the door in his face, running past him into the dark house.

"Where is she?" Carlos switched on the foyer light.

Pedro's chin dipped to his chest and he stepped back towards the front door. "What are you screaming about, Carlos? There is nobody here. I needed to fix a leaky tap for a prospective tenant. I had forgotten about it."

Carlos grimaced. "Right. At two-thirty in the morning?"

"I couldn't sleep. Can you leave, please. You are trespassing on private property." His shoulders drew up and he tucked his elbows into his sides.

"Go ahead. Call the police, Pedro. I dare you." Making no response, Pedro stood cross-armed, his stance unsteady.

Carlos ran into the bedrooms, switching on lights but finding the rooms empty. He rushed into the laundry, kitchen and living room, but they were deserted. He stepped into the back yard when he heard footsteps coming towards him. He turned towards Pedro.

Pedro's face blushed. "Let's talk about this at my house, Carlos. I have a tenant arriving in the morning and we can't be here." He dangled a set of keys in his hand.

Carlos's fury exploded through his chest. He slammed Pedro against the back door of the garage, grabbing his shirt as bile rose in his throat. "What the fuck's going on, Pedro? What did you do to Blanca? I swear I'll fuckin' kill you if you hurt Blanca. I'll..." He spotted a shovel by the side of the shed. "What the hell, Pedro." He refused to think the worst. Surely his uncle would never have to bury Blanca? He was letting his imagination get out of hand. Pedro remained silent. "Why the shovel?"

"It's none of your concern. Please leave."

Carlos had an epiphany. "Is this about Antonia's body? Are you moving the poor girl's body? Is that what this is?" Pedro pressed his lips together. "Answer me, dammit." He clenched his hands and stood within inches of Pedro.

The older man slowly nodded. "I honestly do not know where Blanca is, but she's not here, and I have to get rid of these remains."

Carlos shook his head. "I am not going to be a party to your crimes. If you do not help me find Blanca, I will go straight to the police about this."

Pedro looked away as he appeared to be pondering the ultimatum. "I honestly do not know how I can help you."

Carlos stepped back. "Think about anyone else who might've been involved in this. Would Jose try to stop her? Or someone else?"

Pedro shook his head. "Jose would never hurt her. Never." He paced up and down with his hands in his pockets, staring down as if in deep thought. He looked back at Carlos with a hint of recognition. "It occurred to me recently. I may know who's involved in this." He cleared his throat. "I know my ex-girlfriend hated me for leaving her. She might be hurting Blanca to get to me as she knows the truth about Antonia's death. I believe she was the one responsible for Antonia making that video recording of Jose in order to make money. She must have found out that Blanca knows the truth and thinks she'll get in trouble with the police."

Carlos nodded, not sure whether to believe him. He'd go along with it for now, as he had no other leads. "Okay. Where does this ex-girlfriend live?"

"I'll drive," said Pedro. "She's smart. When we get there, I'll make up a reason for the visit and you can look around. I'll keep her away from the front door. From memory, she has a basement. I'll distract her and you can enter without her seeing you."

"How do I know you're not lying, Pedro? You might have kidnapped Blanca yourself and have her hidden somewhere else. You might be trapping me." He had a thought. "Why didn't you tell me this the other day? How am I supposed to believe you after what you pulled?"

Pedro shook his head. "It only came to me. Besides, Blanca gave me her word she wouldn't tell anyone about this. I have no reason to hurt her. Now, let's go."

Carlos had no choice but to believe him for now. If it was his ex-girlfriend who had been Blanca's stalker and sent the threatening notes, he prayed they got to her in time.

CHAPTER 49
SAVED

Later that morning, Carlos sat in the passenger seat of Pedro's Mercedes, staring out of the window as they drove over the long bridge across the Guanabara Bay with the rising sun. They stopped in front of a house in Niteroi. "You walk towards the next house, as if we're going our separate ways," Pedro instructed. "I'll distract her. Give me five minutes. Come inside and take a look around. She won't lock the front door." He proceeded to describe how to find the basement door, near the bedrooms.

"Will I need keys for the basement? Do you think it's locked?"

Pedro shrugged. "It might be. She keeps her keys in the kitchen." He took a breath. "I'll park a few houses away, not directly in front of her house."

Carlos knit his brows. "Why are you doing this? What's in it for you?"

Pedro turned off the motor and faced him. "I won't be complicit in another scandal, and I believe Blanca wasn't going to say anything about Antonia."

They exited the car, and Pedro walked ahead of him towards his ex-girlfriend's house while Carlos hung back and waited a few minutes in front of another house.

The ex-girlfriend's house had brown-framed colonial windows, a pitched roof and a multitude of towering potted plants on either side of a heavy-set timber door. A lounge chair rested by the door. A well-kept lawn surrounded a paved concrete path.

What if this all went wrong? Carlos shuddered at the thought of Blanca being hurt or worse. Checking his watch, he headed to the mansion-like home. He put his ear against the door but couldn't hear any voices. Pedro must have moved his ex-girlfriend far enough away so he could come inside. Taking a deep breath, Carlos turned the doorknob and crept through a large foyer, leading up to several rooms straight ahead.

He slunk towards the bedrooms, finding each empty. He found an arched door that Pedro had described as leading to the basement. As he expected, it was locked.

Carlos crept into the kitchen, where he searched until he found a set of keys hanging near the fridge. He rushed back to the basement door, where he froze in his tracks in case the ex-girlfriend was close. "I'm coming, Blanca," he muttered as he fumbled with the keys. He had to try all four of them before he found the one that turned the lock.

He ran down the steps, struck by the darkness and cold of the basement. He felt a chill as his body absorbed his surroundings: stacks of boxes, a dusty tall vase, scattered old furniture, and a shadow of a figure lying on the concrete floor.

Blanca! Oh, my god. She was chained to a steel pole. Chained like a damn animal as she tossed and turned in her sleep under a thin blanket.

He gently nudged her. "Blanca, Blanca. Wake up! It's Carlos."

She jerked awake. "Carlos. Oh, Carlos. Thank god you're here." They embraced, his body warming as he felt her heart beating against him. "Where's Elina?" She shivered.

Carlos looked at her strangely. "What? Elina?"

Blanca nodded. "If she finds out you've come, she'll lock us both in here. I assume Pedro's probably in on this with her, and most likely paid her."

Carlos decided to work out Blanca's statement after he got her out of there. He sorted through the multitude of keys, inserting one after the other into the lock. None of them unchained her. He scoffed. Carlos wondered: had Pedro lured him here to lock him in the basement with Blanca? Was this part of his plan? No, that was silly. Pedro was the one who had taken him to this house and his ex-girlfriend, who turned out to be Elina. He couldn't be involved. "Pedro helped me out and brought me here, but he never mentioned Elina was his ex-girlfriend." He tried the keys again. "Damn, none of the keys work."

Blanca shook her head. "I can't believe she's in on this, Carlos." She swallowed. "You missed a key. The small, silver one." She looked past him, keeping an eye out for Elina.

Carlos smiled. "You're observant and clever. I didn't see that one." He inserted the final key into the lock and finally opened the handcuffs.

"Not so clever to let my guard down and get kidnapped." She rubbed her wrists, which were red raw and sighed.

He wrapped his arms around her again. "Are you okay?"

"I'm good. Thanks."

"We can now…" Carlos's body fell when something from behind knocked him against his back. The last thing he heard was Blanca's voice.

"Noooo," Blanca shouted.

***

Elina took her glasses off, glaring at Carlos and Blanca while gripping a baseball bat. "He is not releasing you."

Blanca's eyes turned cold and dark, a shiver running up her spine. "You bitch! Where's Pedro?" She wanted to call for help but with the bat in Elina's hand, she would have to find a way to get past her. If she could find something to incapacitate the receptionist, she'd be able to find her phone.

"Pedro's indisposed. He won't be bothering us for a while."

Is Pedro dead? "Please, Elina. Don't do this. Let us go." She shifted back, aware of her surroundings. "Why are you doing this? What have I done to deserve this?" Her spine chilled.

Elina's face hardened. "You got involved in my business, and I couldn't risk anyone finding out. Those bitches are my ticket to making money. Lots of it, and you were ruining that. I will not go to prison. I will kill all of you first. I have too much at stake." She looked to the ground and whispered, "I can only rely on myself."

Blanca dashed towards the stairs, but Elina grabbed her waist and pushed her to the ground, where she landed on her front. The woman was strong. Blanca groaned as her knee scraped against a box.

Elina put down the bat, and while holding Blanca down by leaning on her palm across Blanca's chest, picked up a length of rope.

"Let me go! Let me go!" Blanca twisted, remembering the vase close to the boxes near the staircase. She reached out, grasped the vase, twisted again and smashed the vase across Elina's face.

The older woman fell unconscious to the basement floor. Blanca dragged Elina's body to the steel pole and tied her hands with the rope as tight as she could.

Blanca scurried towards Carlos and leaned over him, stroking his face. "Carlos, wake up. Carlos, please wake up."

He moaned and jolted awake at the sight of her. "Elina?"

"I've tied her up until we get help. Do you have a phone?"

He nodded. "In my back pocket, but we won't get reception down here."

Blanca helped Carlos climb the stairs and picked up the keys on the way. She locked the basement door, and together, they walked into the living room.

He retrieved his phone and called the police. "Yes, hello. I'd like to report a kidnapping." He asked for an ambulance, and then pulled Blanca to towards the back of the house. "We have to find Pedro. He has to be outside, as I didn't see him in the house earlier." They limped outside into an expansive yard with towering trees, a range of gardens, a garage and a shed. They found Pedro curled up on the garage floor. "Pedro, wake up."

Blanca checked his pulse. "He's breathing, but barely." His head was bloody and his face a purplish bruise.

Carlos nodded. "Now, we wait."

CHAPTER 50
FREEDOM

Three weeks later, Blanca strolled with Carlos through the favela, dodging a cyclist as they made their way to a house. A woman with bright, blue eyes stood outside, grinding some kind of root into a pestle. She looked up with a warm smile, her eyes expressing sadness and fatigue. She wore a tattered t-shirt and long flowing skirt. Her unwashed, tangled hair was tied. This must be Juliana, whom Carlos told her about.

"Carlos, this is a surprise," Juliana said.

He walked towards her. "Hi Juliana." He turned. "This is Blanca. We work together at the magazine."

"Hi, Juliana. Nice to meet you." Blanca felt uneasy. She didn't enjoy giving bad news.

Juliana put down the mortar and pestle on a nearby table, and tilted her head. She rested her hands on the back of a rickety chair. "Hello, Blanca." She squinted at Carlos. "What is it? Is it about Antonia?" Juliana stood cross-armed, initially with suspicion in her eyes and later, hope that her daughter was alive and well.

Carlos stepped forward. "It is about Antonia."

A smile splashed across her face. "You found my Antonia? Where is she?" The poor woman's eyes searched the surrounding area with light in her eyes.

He cleared his throat, leaned in and took her hands. "Juliana. Your daughter had an accident seventeen years ago. I'm sorry, but she's dead."

The woman's legs wobbled. Carlos caught her frail body as she fell. He helped her to the chair and fetched a glass of water from the house. "Here, drink this." He handed her the glass and squeezed her shoulder.

Juliana sipped slowly. Blanca stood there awkwardly for a few minutes until the older woman swallowed. "It's okay. I've prepared for the worst news. A part of me knew she wouldn't be alive after all this time, but I hoped and prayed." Tears streamed down her face and she wiped them away. "I'll be okay. Please tell me what happened?"

As Blanca recounted the story, Juliana sat stock-still, her eyes distant. Then she faced her guests. "I had a sense my Antonia would do anything for money. She had always been a rebel, challenging me. Her father couldn't deal with such an angry child and he left us, but I loved her just the same. She didn't deserve to die that way." The woman bowed her head. "I couldn't discipline her. She made enemies wherever she went. She was always out and about, angry at the world, and I wonder if her father had stayed, whether she would've eventually changed her ways." She wiped away a tear. "I know my Antonia was a handful, but we were poor, and in her distorted way, she wanted to make life easier for us. Please know I never wanted Antonia to survive this way as we were doing okay, but she wanted more. If her father had stayed around, she might not have resorted to such things."

Blanca touched her hand. "I am so sorry for your loss. At least you have closure now, as hard as it is."

The woman nodded. "What happened to those responsible? You mentioned Antonia was paid off by this woman and no doubt she's exploited a lot of girls. She has to be stopped, before more families get destroyed by this." She stared into her quaking hands.

Carlos pursed his lips, as if he wanted to give Juliana time to process. He leaned in and took her hand. "Elina's been charged with many crimes, including blackmail and the murders of several men who got too close to the truth. Even her ex-husband died when he found out what she was doing with these young girls. Pedro's been charged for burying the body as he was protecting his son, Jose, but he has a good lawyer who might keep him out of jail."

Juliana nodded. "Thank you. And Antonia's remains?"

"The police will be in touch to talk to you about the legal aspects of the case," said Carlos." He knit his brows. "Stay strong."

Juliana shook her head. "That wretched woman ruined my Antonia all because of greed. May she pay her karmic debt." The poor woman shivered.

Blanca hugged Juliana. "I am so sorry for your loss, Juliana. She'll be in prison for a long time and won't hurt anyone else again." She gave her a reassuring smile. "I have written articles about the favelas, which will help the government to increase funds for your community. You will be able to survive well."

Juliana's eyes lit up. "God bless you, Blanca. Thank you so much." She wiped away her tears and peered into the distance. She appeared to be at peace, knowing the truth.

Carlos waved goodbye. "Take care, and be safe."

As they made their way out of the favela, Blanca asked Carlos, "Why do you think Pedro kept my parents out of the story?"

Carlos turned to her as they strolled down the cluttered, noisy street. "He did it to avoid the scandal of having threatened your father. He wants a certain appearance in front of his circle of friends. He didn't do it to spare your parents. He has a motive for everything he does. He knew what he did was wrong, but he did it anyway."

Blanca sighed. "If you didn't find me when you did, who knows how long I'd be down there. I would've probably died in that basement. At least Pedro helped you."

"It still doesn't excuse the fact he started all this. He could've been honest from the start, and Juliana wouldn't have suffered all these years. Not to mention lying to me about Elina being his ex-girlfriend."

Blanca shuddered to think about the chill of the basement. "He was protecting his son, Carlos. It has to mean something." She took a breath. "Do you think Elina was working with anyone else?"

Carlos shrugged. "I don't know, but the police are investigating. Pedro mentioned Elina was married but never had children. A single woman, playing with these men's lives but using these poor favela girls to sleep with them, and selling videos via the dark web to perverts. I'm sure she paid these girls a pittance, compared to what she was raking in."

She squeezed Carlos's hand. "Such a horrible woman, and she seemed so nice at work. Boy, did she fool all of us. Thanks again for saving me." She frowned. "I remember the basement now. I spoke to my father about it. He filled in a few blanks. I have a complete picture now." She slowed down her pace, her body shivering at the thought of her father. "He seemed to think I knew about his past too. Why didn't you tell me about the woman he killed? You knew, and you didn't tell me."

Carlos stopped in his tracks as they made their way back to the main road to his car. "I am sorry, Blanca. I thought you had enough on your mind. You'd been through enough. At least now you know the reason your father not only kept his secret about Antonia, but also how Miguel sent Pedro that letter, telling him they were even. They both knew about Carolina's death and had to hide it. How else would the brother know about her death, unless someone witnessed it and told Rodrigo? Your father implicated Pedro, but who knows? The bastard eventually got to you, and that's on your father."

Blanca swallowed. "I don't know if I'll ever forgive my father for all he's done. It was partly his fault I got kidnapped. Revenge against him. I don't know him anymore. Even my mother knew and didn't tell me."

Carlos nodded. "I know it's no excuse, but I'm sure they wanted to protect you. Once you get home, you can work it all out." He gave her a reassuring smile. "I am glad you're okay. Nothing like this will ever happen to you again, Blanca."

Blanca half-smiled. "I know, but the police want my statement again as I've remembered a lot more about the kidnapping."

"Can I come with you to the police station as your support person?"

"I'd like that, Carlos. Very much."

CHAPTER 51
STORY OF TERROR

The towering detective set the video to record, then sat with his hands clasped across the table from Blanca. Carlos sat beside her.

"Let's begin, shall we, Ms. Castellano."

She turned to Carlos, who squeezed her hand. "Okay."

After Blanca had witnessed Antonia's death, she stayed the night at Pedro's house. First thing in the morning, he told her he would take her to her father's friend's house. As she sat in the back seat with her mother, Pedro turned to her father. "Maria and Julio will want to know what happened and we have to keep this quiet. Say nothing to your friend either, Miguel."

As they drove down a deserted road, a man standing beside a white van waved. Pedro stopped the car, and the man pulled out a gun and pointed it to Pedro. He was bulky and his beard covered most of his chin. "Get out of the car."

"What's this about?" said Pedro.

Blanca held her mother's hand tight and her father turned to his wife and daughter in the back seat. He put a finger to his lips.

The gunman pointed to Blanca and her mother. "Get out. Now!" She followed her mother out of the car, her body trembling and her head hurting.

A car drove by, and the gunman hid his gun, smiling at Blanca and her mother. When the car was out of sight, he pushed Blanca's mother back inside the car. "Give me your wallet, old man." Pedro handed him his wallet. He stared at her father. "Yours, too." Miguel handed over his wallet. The gunman sneered. "This is for Carolina, you bastard." Blanca ran back to the car but he grabbed her by the arm. "You're not going anywhere."

Miguel's face turned white. "Who are you?"

He scoffed. "I'm Carolina's brother, Rodrigo, and I'm your worst nightmare." He squinted. "I will let you know what real pain feels like, old man."

Miguel looked to Pedro then faced the gunman again. "But how do you know?"

Her mother screamed. "No, please. No, take me. I'll come with you."

"You're of no use to me, lady, but she is. Besides, your husband knows what he's done."

Her father jumped out and struggled against the gunman. "You are not taking my daughter. You will have to kill me first."

The gunman smashed the butt of his gun into Miguel's face. He collapsed, and the assailant pointed his gun at Blanca's father. "For an extra bonus and for emotional distress, you have to give me 450,000 Brazilian Real. I will be in touch to collect it."

Pedro spoke up. "I have the money and can give it to you straight away."

"We'll see, but I'll be in contact about instructions for the money. Do not leave the country or you will never see your beautiful daughter. I will trade the money for your daughter as payback for Carolina."

Her father cried and pleaded. "No, please. I will find the money, but give me back my daughter. I am sorry. It was an accident. Please, for the love of God."

A younger man emerged from the van and pulled Blanca by the arm. He shoved her into the vehicle, slamming the door. She could no longer see her parents.

The gunman got into the driver's seat, and the van began moving. After a time that Blanca could not calculate, it stopped again, and the younger man pulled her out. "Get up!"

She shivered. "Why am I here?"

"None of my business. I'm just doing my job. But for Rodrigo, it's personal." He was tall, had a missing front tooth, oily hair, and cold eyes. He pushed her towards an old house, and Blanca realised she was in a part of the favela.

Inside, three men eyed her hungrily. The small room in a downstairs basement was dirty and dusty, with a blanket hanging over a window. A round table with scratched timber chairs stood around it, and a black leather jacket hung on the back of a rickety chair. Cigarettes lay on a tall fridge. The single bed against the wall was covered with a dirty quilt and had blood on a hanging sheet. She smelled cigarettes, vomit and aftershave. She turned towards the door, but the young man had locked it after leaving. She stood against the walls as the men closed in on her, particularly the gunman who mentioned his name was Rodrigo.

Her body shook and her eyes widened at the men who stared at her from head to toe. One by one, they disappeared through the door, from which she heard a muffled voice. Rodrigo stayed behind, watching her. She couldn't make out who else was in the house and banged hard on the door until her hands bled.

Blanca shivered when Rodrigo pushed her on the bed. He stood at the door and guarded it as if thinking she might escape. She cowered into a corner of the bed and struggled to breathe.

One of the shorter men returned and blindfolded her, leaving her hands free. He started touching her cheeks. "Such beautiful skin."

She heard more footsteps, certain that someone else came into the room. "Leave her. The boss said she needs to be groomed first. All in good time, man."

She heard a man's voice as something dropped onto her lap. Feeling around, she found a tray. "Eat or the boss will get mad with you." She wondered who the boss was as she found a bread roll and devoured it without thought. The food was bland and tepid. Then her hands found a bottle on the grimy bed. She coughed in the dusty air until she could drink it.

After eating, she lay on the bed. Someone arrived to tie her hands to the bed with a rope. She started to fall asleep when a ringtone jerked her awake. It had an unusual tone with the crashing sound of cymbals and beating drums combined with the screeching sound of a girl laughing. Muffled voices filled her ears as she heard a few words. "Okay, boss. Another night." Within minutes, she felt a man's loud breathing in her ears. He touched her shoulder and squeezed it tight. His hands trailed down to her arm, making her quiver in disgust. She moved her body back, but the man slapped her hard across the cheek. He proceeded to punch her abdomen and she lost all breath. Her legs kicked his arms without doing any damage. Large hands wrapped around her throat and he proceeded to squeeze tight. Blanca wriggled, struggling to breathe. She was going to die. The next thing she knew, the front door banged and the man kept squeezing until another man shoved him away from her. "Stop. Boss will be mad."

Blanca opened her mouth to suck in air. Her throat was raw with pain. She was sure she could not talk in that moment as she faced away from the men and wanted to forget about her nightmare.

After a long time, Blanca awoke to the sound of a slamming door and loud voices. Her wrists ached from the rope digging into her skin. "You touched the girl. Never again," someone said. She jolted at the sound of a gunshot. Did someone kill the man who had choked her?

She heard the door open and someone took off her blindfold. Her eyes went to the door, where blood seeped across the floor from the other side. "Don't worry. You will get a nice man." The tall man wore a black, fitted jacket with a grey shirt and brown pants. He had thin, black hair, a dimple on his chin, and wore tinted glasses. He handed her a glass of water and pushed a pill into her mouth, forcing her to swallow.

She wanted her mum and dad, not a strange man.

A short man entered. Another tall man turned to him and picked up his leather jacket from the chair. He looked familiar. "Clean up." The short man nodded and closed the door to the other room behind him. The tall man wearing dark glasses, waited until Blanca became drowsy and the room around her spun.

The next day, the gunman kept giving her more and more pills. Blanca began to feel sick and saw strange things in the room. The gunman looked like a monster with thick, scaly skin, long teeth and claws. Pink elephants danced around the room. Ghosts screamed in her face. Voices came out of nowhere. Even the TV spoke to her. She lost count of how many pills she was given. Blanca closed her eyes and put her hands against her ears.

The gunman untied her and grabbed her then swung her over his shoulder. She attempted to break free from his grip, but he held her tight. He carried her into a car, and she flinched at the noises around her. Her body appeared to float, and she couldn't remember where she was. The next thing she knew, a group of policemen hovered around her, and carried her out of the car. "Are you okay?" said a male officer. Blanca couldn't speak, hear or feel anything as her body looked like she was floating, the people around her becoming distant, and the silence around her made her see black.

The detective got up. "I will get you a glass of water. You don't look good." He left the room and closed the door behind him.

Carlos was quiet. He pulled her into his arms. "My god, Blanca. I'm sorry you went through that. They drugged you so you wouldn't be able to remember the men's faces. And the man who tried to kill you was killed as they needed you to be groomed for other men. Sick bastards!" Stroking the back of her head, he continued. "I wish I could've protected you. Those bastards cannot get away with that sort of thing."

"At least they didn't get a chance to touch me, Carlos. Other girls are not so lucky." She quaked at the thought.

"The police got to you in time. I thank the anonymous caller."

Blanca nodded, hugging her body to fight the chilly cold in the room. "I hope they can help other young girls as they did me, Carlos."

Carlos's eyes shone with admiration. "You're safe now, Blanca."

"I hope so." Blanca opened the door but turned back. "Thanks for being here." Something niggled in her brain, but she didn't know what it was.

He touched her on the arm. "Of course."

A few minutes later, the detective opened the door again. "You are free to go, Ms. Castellano. We will be in touch if needed. Thank you."

She took a breath and followed Carlos out towards the exit of the building. Stopping in her tracks, Blanca shivered. "I just realised something about that man who attacked me in the favela."

Carlos tilted his head. "What about him?"

Her heart raced. "I'm sure he was the same man who transported me when I was kidnapped all those years ago."

Carlos took her arm gently. "Oh, Christ, Blanca." He sighed. "Let's go back in and let the police know."

Blanca had never wanted to see the authorities ever again, but what choice did she have?

CHAPTER 52
LASTING MEMORIES

The next evening, Blanca dabbed on lipstick as she beamed into the bathroom mirror. She had agreed to a night out with Carlos at an old tavern, to relieve what she'd been through over the past few months. She reached for her clutch purse, grabbed her keys and drove towards the centre of Rio.

Fluttering in her stomach and tingles down her spine brought up an image of Carlos. The way his dimples enhanced his looks, the way his muscular lean body made her lose all breath, and how his piercing dark brown eyes made her shiver. She loved the way he moved fluidly as he took photographs, his muscles rippling and dominating the space around him. She loved his creative flair and ability to give life to his photos. She couldn't sleep without an image of him in her mind. Blanca yearned to be intimate with Carlos, and as they'd become much closer, she learned to trust him implicitly. He had been her rock through her ordeal, and she had begun to need him.

She realised that, now that her world was safe again, she could breathe and enjoy her last month with Carlos before leaving for Spain. Whatever happened, she'd savour the last moments with him.

Blanca parked near the tavern. With a quick look in the car's mirror to finger-brush her hair, she took a calming breath and ignored the pounding of her heart. Exiting the car, she turned to the thick, red-brown timber doors. The statue wore a broad smile, a chef's white hat and an apron, and held a menu encased under his left arm.

She had worn high wedged black shoes with a thin-strapped skin-tight black dress that showed her curves and offered a tad of cleavage. Over her dress was a short chiffon cardigan that fell down to her elbows. She wanted to make an impression.

As she met Carlos at the table, he rose and she held her breath. He looked amazing in his white pleated pants, and tight-fitting black shirt that pressed against his biceps. Stubble lined his chin and his eyes slightly drooped, showing he hadn't slept much.

He kissed her on the cheek and she blushed. Why couldn't her body stop trembling?

Blanca sat down across from him as she pressed down on her dress. "It's good to see you again."

Carlos fixed his gaze on her. "You too, and you look gorgeous, by the way." Their eyes lingered for a minute and she wanted to reach for him over the table.

Blanca swallowed and looked at an elderly waiter who brought them menus. She scanned it briefly, then looked around at the tavern. It had a cosy ambience with wooden seats, and each rectangular table set with white tablecloths and wine glasses. Pictures of soccer balls, soccer teams at award ceremonies, oil paintings of the natural landscape of Rio de Janeiro, and cherubs covered the walls. There was a display of old-fashioned clocks, too. The curved bar was glass, showing an array of liquors and drink dispensers.

The smiling waiter returned five minutes later and cleared his throat. "Can I take your order?"

Blanca took another brief peek at the menu. "I'll have the fish stew and a glass of champagne, thank you."

"I'll have the feijoado and the vermouth." Carlos explained that his dish was a rich stew consisting of pieces of pork and black beans.

The waiter nodded. "I'll be back shortly." He walked off with a curt nod.

Carlos frowned. "I handed in my mother's journal to the police. You don't need to worry. The criminal activity in the favelas is in the hands of the police now." He knit his brows and hesitated. "How are you doing?"

The waiter brought them their drinks. "I'll be back with the food shortly."

Once he left, Blanca hugged her body tight. She no longer wanted to talk about the trauma she'd been through, but she answered Carlos's question. "I've learned to become resilient."

Carlos threaded his hands through his fingers, staring into the distance. "I'm glad. You need to move forward rather than look back."

Blanca nodded. "I hear you. What about news of your mother? Any updates about her death? Do you still think she was murdered?"

He swallowed and put a finger on his temple as if fighting a headache. "My father is adamant she died of a heart attack and didn't mention anything else. I need to look forward, too, and live my life."

"Given that Elina confessed to stalking me and paying others to watch and attack me, like the men in the favela, I assume I'm safe. But my father obviously felt the need to lie when he said we'd stayed with his friend when in reality I was kidnapped." She breathed deeply, thinking about what the police had explained to her. "And to think that Elina confessed to paying men to watch or hurt us, like the guy in the favela who tried to steal my purse. Then there was the man who put that note in my bag when I was at the restaurant with Isabela. She paid all of them so they could report to her."

Carlos nodded. "I know. She's a piece of work. Pure greed." He leaned forward and stroked her hand. "You are safe now, and we can focus on the future."

Blanca's body tingled at the way his cheeky grin lit up his eyes. What did he have in mind? "Now that you've resigned from the magazine, what's your plan?"

Carlos leaned back against his chair as the waiter brought their dishes, with Blanca's meal sizzling in a clay pot. The smells of fish and spices made her mouth water. He picked up his fork. "As I said before, I'm looking at starting an online business in photography and graphic design. I'd like to teach it, too. Luiz wants to join me. I have to register the business, get financing, create a website and get business cards made. Not to mention a whole lot of other things."

Blanca took a bite of her stew. The tangy flavours suited her palate, and the vegetables were encased in rich spices, and garlic. "It sounds great. You could look at consulting with large media companies, too. You'd have a lot of options with students and special events."

He swallowed a bite and sipped on his drink. "I'll take it one step at a time and see whether it's viable. I won't know until I do this." He lifted his posture. "Are you going to return to the same magazine in Spain, or have you decided on a change of career?"

She leaned forward in her seat. "I'm looking at changing companies and plan to apply to some human-interest magazines. I need something which reflects more of my personal values."

They finished their meals when Carlos asked, "Would you like to order dessert?" She shook her head, thinking she'd rather have him for dessert. "Are you ready to leave?"

"Yes, I need to walk off all this food."

"Are you going straight home or...we can stop at my place for a coffee if you like?"

Blanca's body heated up. The sexual tension between them was strong. "Your place." If they didn't have a future, she wanted to at least enjoy the precious last moments they had together. But if she was falling in love with him, she was in deep trouble.

CHAPTER 53
INTIMACY

Blanca pulled open the door of the tavern and fought the cold against her bare forearms. The touch of Carlos's hands on the small of her back made her gasp. He prodded her towards the street to her rental car.

His eyes sparkled in the moonlight as he opened the driver's door for her. "Are you sure about this? I don't want to pressure you if you're not ready."

Blanca's arms tingled as she smiled. "Yes, very sure. I'll meet you at your place." He closed the car door, waved, and went to his car and waited.

As she followed Carlos, Blanca's heart raced in anticipation of having Carlos to herself. Would she have the courage to take their relationship to the next level? They had only kissed, and she wanted him more than anything. They could enjoy these last moments together.

Parking at the kerb while Carlos parked inside his garage, she went to the front door. He let her in, and then took her hand and pushed her gently against the closed front door. He caressed her cheek and stroked her back and shoulders. He moved in and kissed her passionately on the mouth. Her whole body went weak as she returned his kiss, her tongue exploring his. He caressed her back, neck and arms and rubbed himself against her. Blanca moaned in response. He worked his hands to her breasts, fondling them, and began unzipping her dress. He gently kissed her breasts through her bra. He returned to her wet lips and kissed her passionately, rotating his tongue inside her mouth and tenderly biting her lip.

Blanca felt her inner thighs burn with desire. Her heart floated in the clouds, her feet seemingly in mid-air.

Carlos pulled down her straps and her dress fell to the floor. His gaze wandered over her body from head to toe as he licked his lips and tantalised her breasts with his fingers. He unclipped her bra and pulled it off her, then sucked on her nipples as she pressed his head against her. He lifted his head briefly. "You're gorgeous, Blanca...and I care about you so much."

Her heart opened up to him. "I care about you too, Carlos." The smile on his face warmed her heart as their lips met again, hungrier than before.

He led her to his bed and pulled her on top of him. He teased her inner thighs over her short, lacy underwear as she pressed his hands into her in a tantalising motion. She massaged his penis gently and savoured the sound of his arousal as he nuzzled her neck and breasts. Pulling off her underwear, he probed further with his fingers and quickened his pace.

"I want all of you, Blanca." He stared into her eyes, caressing her bottom lip. She wasn't able to form words. "You are safe with me. I want you to know that." She yearned to be touched by him in every way and couldn't get close enough to him. He was her safety blanket, and she longed to have all of him.

He trailed kisses down her chest while caressing her arms, his head lifting to scan her eyes briefly. "I will protect you, Blanca." His lips moved down to her abdomen as he teased the groove. "I want you so much." Blanca moaned at his tender kisses and stroked his head, savouring his touch. Lying against the bed, he leaned in and spread her labia with his fingers to expose her clitoris while probing her with his tongue, exploring her deeply yet gently. He stopped, his breath soothing against her mound, as he looked up at her with tenderness. As if satisfied she was pleased, he proceeded as she moaned and pressed his head tighter against her. "I want you too, Carlos." His tongue circled her mound passionately, tantalising her until she came. Carlos lifted himself up, kissed her hard on the mouth and reached for her buttocks, pressing them gently. "You are so beautiful when you come, Blanca." She beamed as his fingers played with her wetness.

He took off his jeans and underwear and rested on top of her, teasing her wetness again with two fingers. He gently penetrated her mound with his fingers, moaned and kissed her hard on the mouth. Their tongues danced and they licked each other's lips while Blanca caressed his penis and gently guided it inside her. He stared into her eyes with his erection building. She savoured his body and lapped up her increasing desire. Carlos quickened his pace and caressed her breasts as he peered into her eyes with hunger and desire. She moved with his rhythm and pressed her hands against his lower back. She closed her eyes, listening to the sound of his climax. She climaxed a second time moments later, and together they rested on the bed in a blissful silence.

CHAPTER 54
CONNECTION

Sunlight streamed through the window when Carlos awoke early Sunday morning. Birds chirped, and light sounds of traffic filtered through. He rose from bed and peered through the bedroom window. A short drizzle had dampened the ground before the glaring sun appeared.

He yawned, recalling his amazing night with Blanca. He looked over at her with further desire, a heated rush permeating his body. He had had a taste of her, and he wanted more. He realised he was falling deeply in love with her.

He returned to bed and watched Blanca sleep for a few minutes before she stirred and opened her eyes, lighting up at the sight of him beside her. The sheet was wrapped around her toned leg and she moved her arm over to his side.

His eyes lingered on her. "Hey you."

She blushed. "Hey yourself."

Carlos pulled her shoulders towards him and caressed her cheek and lips. His intense gaze drank her in. He eyed her from head to toe seductively. He grabbed her hand, drawing it to his lips. Carlos kissed her cheek passionately. "I have never felt this way about anyone." He remembered his girlfriend, Sofia; as much as he had loved her, his love for Blanca was more intense. "You're an amazing woman, the way you've handled everything you've been through." He paused and gazed deeply into her eyes. "I love you, Blanca. Completely."

She stared into his eyes as if she felt the same way. "I love you too, Carlos." She stretched out her arms. "What's your plan this Sunday morning?"

He glazed over her body completely naked, his arousal yearning to take her once more today. "I'm having a shower."

She nodded. "I can have breakfast ready."

Carlos had other ideas, rose from bed and propped her up. He steered her towards the bathroom and slipped off her underwear and unclipped her bra. "Let's have a shower together. Breakfast can wait. Is that all right?" He was so in love with her, he couldn't put it into words.

She gave him a cheeky grin. "Better than all right."

Carlos turned on the water and she followed him into the shower. He began soaping her body from head to toe, lathering the soap gently down her chest, over her arms, her abdomen, and in between her thighs to rub her clitoris. "You're beautiful, and I love you like crazy." He put the soap aside and leaned in, his teeth grazing her nipples as Blanca stroked his manhood. "I can never get enough of you." Blanca held her head back and savoured his tongue teasing her breasts. He felt close to exploding as her hand brushed up and down his erection, but he held back.

Her guttural sounds aroused him further. He moved his mouth to hers and kissed her with hunger and deep-seated need as she bit his bottom lip and brushed her tongue across it. He pulled away from her mouth and went down to his knees, his tongue trailing her taut, sexy abdomen until he reached her inner thighs, gliding his tongue over towards her sweet spot and brushing his fingers over her mound then probing two fingers inside of her. Her moans aroused him further as she pressed his head tighter against her. His tongue circled her mound passionately, tantalising her until she came. Carlos lifted himself up, kissed her hard on the mouth and reached for her buttocks, pressing them tenderly.

"I love you so much, Carlos. You make me feel new things." Blanca bit his bottom lip and dug her nails into the small of his back as he pressed hard into her wetness. She trailed her hand down to caress his penis and guide him gently into her while her back rested against the shower glass. He couldn't get enough of her and wanted to be with her forever.

The explosion was surreal, and his energy was spent.

CHAPTER 55
PARTY EVENT

Blanca sat back in her chair, her hand warm in Carlos's own, with Isabela sitting opposite them. The smooth, samba sounds of the Latin bar let her body sink into the stool as they sat around the round table.

Blanca's eyes roamed the groups of people who dug into their savoury snacks and drinks, while others carried trays back to their table opposite a large counter. Displays of football players, trophies won, and awards for the best-serving bar were prominent on the wall. Voices carried as Blanca looked to Carlos who brought his hand up to hers and kissed it tenderly. When he put down her hand, he circled his fingers around her palm, arousing Blanca with his warm caresses.

"Get a room, guys," Isabela sighed. "I honestly feel like a third wheel. I should've stayed home. Why did you guys invite me here anyway? I thought the police explained everything to you."

Blanca measured her words and took a sip of her sweet martini. "I'm sorry, Isabela, but you're my friend, so why wouldn't I invite you? I have to go back to Spain soon." She ignored the constriction of her chest.

Isabela's eyes softened in the dim surroundings. She held a glass of strawberry wine. "I know. I'm sorry, but I still feel jittery after everything that happened." Shaking her head, she sighed. "That is so selfish of me, Blanca. I'm sorry. After everything you've been through, I have no right to say that."

Blanca reached for her hand. "Of course you do. We both suffered, and I am here for you now, Isabela."

Carlos gave her a reassuring smile. He let go of Blanca's hand and sipped on his beer. He ate some of the nuts from the bowl on the table, then leaned forward. "It can't have been easy Isabela, and you have our support." He took a breath. "The police spoke to us, but we wanted your version of events at my birthday party."

Isabela nodded. "Okay, but nothing much to tell. I do remember a bit more, now. I was walking in the back garden and sat on a chair near your outdoor table, when a man I didn't know started a conversation. I asked him how he knew you, Carlos, and he mentioned he was an old school friend. I had a sense of unease and thought he might've been lying." She hesitated and took a quick sip of her wine. "I set my drink on the table and his own drink was close to mine. He went to have a sip but he spilled some of it on my dress. He apologised. I went to fetch a cloth and told him I'd be back. I was stupid and shouldn't have left my drink with him because by the time I got back, he'd got another drink. I finished drinking mine. He obviously slipped the antipsychotic drug in my drink while I was gone, because not long after drinking it, I was out of it. All I remember is him prodding me towards the back of your house, rather than the front, and pushing me into his car even when I resisted.

"I wasn't fully conscious, but when I woke up, I was chained up in a small house and the man waltzed in as if it was any ordinary day. He mentioned I was a chess piece in their game and I had to keep quiet about what really happened with me. He thought I knew what was going on with Elina and their operation with the young girls. The woman we met, Consuela, must've overhead our conversation. A couple of days later, they drugged me again and dropped me off into an unfamiliar street, which was where the police found me."

Blanca shifted her posture. "Did you see anything in the house which could lead the police to a clue?"

Isabela shook her head. "The walls were bare. No photos or pictures."

Carlos intervened. "I imagine whoever kidnapped you was following orders. The police told us they seem to think there are a couple of ringleaders who would've organised Blanca's kidnapping recently. I'm sure they're on top of it."

Isabela froze in her seat. "I couldn't believe what you told me, Blanca. The scum of the earth exploiting you at ten years of age. And you were targeted because of your father?"

Blanca's hands clenched. "Yes, but what is weird is that in spite of Rodrigo wanting to avenge his sister's death, he was still part of the child exploitation ring. I wonder if his sister, Carolina knew about it."

Isabela rested back in her seat. "You should be safe now, Blanca, as you're not a threat. Besides, the police are investigating. But I do wonder who's pulling the strings."

Blanca had a niggle of doubt about her safety. Something didn't feel right. They were missing something, but what? If the police didn't get any leads, would she return to Spain without closure? What if those men followed her back home?

Carlos touched her thigh. "Penny for your thoughts, Blanca."

She turned to the man she loved deeply. He made her feel safe and she wanted to fall into his arms and have quiet time, but they were in a busy tavern. "I remember this tall man who looked important when I was in the favela. He could be the one in control, but I wish I knew who it was."

Carlos held her hand. "Don't worry. The police are chasing leads. Let them do their job."

Blanca's chest relaxed. Carlos was right. She was no longer a threat and the traffickers had no reason to hurt her when she didn't have any information about who they were. She was home free. "Maybe you're right."

When Isabela headed to the bathroom, Carlos wrapped his arms around her waist and brought her close. He stared into her eyes and brushed his lips over hers. "You are so beautiful, Blanca, and I love you. So much." Carlos caressed her cheek. "We'll talk about you and me later."

Blanca's heart raced. She loved Carlos, but how could they make this work? It was an impossible situation as she'd be leaving Brazil soon.

CHAPTER 56
THE USB

Carlos's body lifted as if it was as light as air. He hadn't heard right.

He was sharing a light lunch with Juan in a local cafe. "Are you saying you want to promote my mother's work in your gallery?" He remembered seeing more of his mother's photos of the favelas at his father's house.

Juan nodded. "Of course. She had a story to tell about the favelas, and after what Isabela told me about Blanca's kidnapping, we have to do this. It's time. Whatever photos you can find at your father's house, hand them over to me and I'll get them prepared for the displays. We'll need all her photos so I can have a selection to choose from."

"Why didn't you mention this before? I could've had her photos instead of mine showcased with the others. She had more to express in her photos."

Juan rotated his neck as if he was in pain. "She needs an entire showing on her own, of all her works. It will be a way to honour her. Besides, you deserved to have your own photos displayed."

"I don't know how to thank you, Juan."

He waved his hand and shook his head. "No thanks needed. Come by my house tonight and we'll get the paperwork organised."

Carlos nodded. "I'll be there."

After wolfing down their meat dishes, Juan looked up and wiped his mouth with a napkin. "How's Blanca doing? What a tragedy to endure not only the kidnapping but the assault at your party, too. At least she fought back and you got to her in time."

Carlos angled his head. "I didn't realise you knew about that."

Juan swallowed. "Oh, Isabela mentioned it."

***

Blanca got off the phone with Carlos and returned to proofreading the freelance articles on her computer. She noticed Isabela looking at her curiously.

"What's the great news, Blanca?"

"Juan's going to showcase Carlos's mother's photos in his gallery. Isn't it amazing?"

Isabela nodded. "Sure is. But how safe is it doing that, with everything going on?"

"Carlos seems to think they'll be selective with the photos. The photos will tell a story of business growth in Rio, rather than child exploitation."

"Sounds like a plan."

An hour later, Blanca sent off one of the magazine articles over to Isabela to check. Blanca was tired of looking at the screen. She needed a break after getting little sleep.

Her nightmares had become less frequent, but why was she still getting them? She was still dreaming of the man with large hands choking her. The tall man pushing pills down her throat. The leather jacket hanging over the chair. Wasn't it the same one as in Antonia's photo? Was the nightmare telling her this wasn't over, or had she not dealt fully with her past?

Isabela spoke up. "Pedro mentioned he's working from home today, but I need one of the purchase orders back as it needs to be adjusted. I need to check it, as it can't be this high. It's addressed to a stationery company for the amount of 100,000 Brazilian Reals. I have my hands full here with these proofs. Would you mind fetching it from his office? It should be in his in-tray."

Blanca rose. "Sure. I'll be back in a minute." She walked down the corridor, grateful to stretch her legs after hours of staring at her screen.

Pedro's office door was closed, but she went in and began rummaging through his in-tray. She couldn't find the purchase order that amounted to 100,000 Brazilian Reals from a stationery company. Why was it so high?

She noticed Pedro's black leather jacket hanging on his desk chair. Her eyes roamed to a drawer. She pulled at the handle, but it was locked.

The filing cabinet might have it, she thought, but found each drawer locked. Where would he keep the key?

On top of the filing cabinet, Blanca saw a dark ceramic cup with a crumpled piece of paper inside it. Pedro obviously didn't use his cup for coffee. Under the paper, she found several small keys. She tried each in the filing cabinet until the final one unlocked the cabinet. Scanning through the manila folders, Blanca finally found the purchase order. She took it out, and saw a yellow sticky note stuck to the order. She pulled it off, transfixed by what was scrawled on it: the name, Juan, with his phone number. Two words beside his name made her shiver. *Destroy photos!*

What the hell! What photos did Juan need to destroy and why?

Blanca then saw a plastic pocket along the side of the drawer. She dug her hand inside it and pulled out a USB stick. Curious, she palmed it and closed the cabinet. She gasped at the voice behind her.

"What are you doing here?"

Turning, she winced. "Pedro...I thought you were working from home."

He watched her closely. "I came to get something I forgot."

She cleared her throat, her face heating up. "Sorry to barge in, but Isabela needed to adjust this purchase order." She waved it in front of him. "Sorry, I'll leave you to it." She scurried out, but as she turned back towards him, she saw the yellow sticky note had fallen onto the floor.

CHAPTER 57
A PHYSICAL ATTACK

Carlos felt a prickle of fear down his spine as he left the meeting with Juan at the cafe. He couldn't explain it, but something didn't feel right. He pulled out his phone and was about to call Blanca when it rang. The call display showed Dominique's number.

"Hi, Dominique."

"Hello, Carlos. Are you sitting down?"

"What's wrong?"

After a slight pause, she said, "Your father's been in an accident."

He gasped and his legs wobbled. "What? What kind of accident?"

"You need to come to the Cardio Trauma Ipanema Hospital. He's in surgery now, but by the time you get here, I don't know where he'll be. Reception will advise you." She gave him the details. "I'm sorry, Carlos."

"I'm on my way."

He drove in a heated frenzy to the hospital. He refused to believe this sordid chaos wasn't over for him and Blanca, but his father being in an accident could only mean one thing.

No, he refused to consider the worst. People had accidents all the time, and his father was aging and could be clumsy at the best of times. He would find out what happened and not jump to conclusions.

But what if this situation wasn't over? What if Elina wasn't Blanca's stalker, and it was someone else entirely? He had to call her to make sure she was safe.

He finally reached the hospital, and as he rushed to the emergency entrance, he called Blanca. He got her voicemail. He ignored his fear as she'd most likely still be at work. He could call her later and make sure she was safe.

A long queue waited at the emergency reception. *Oh, hell! How long would it take to get service around here?* He fidgeted with his hands and took deep breaths until he finally reached the front. A heavy-set woman with stern, dark eyes stared.

"My father, Nicolas Silva was brought into emergency. Is he still in surgery?"

The woman clicked a few keys on the computer. "Yes, he's still in surgery. The neurosurgeon will speak to you afterwards."

He flinched. "Neurosurgeon? What happened?"

"They will give you that information in the department." She gave him instructions to the waiting area." She stared past him. "Next."

He nodded. "Is Dominique Calo available?"

"Yes, I will let her know you are here, but you will need to wait in the specified waiting area, Mr. Silva."

Thank you." He rushed over to the waiting area, wondering what happened to his father. He would soon find out.

At least twenty patients and families waited around him. He smelled strong disinfectant mixed with body odour and spicy cologne. He shivered as he prayed his father was all right. Neurology only meant one thing: he'd had a brain injury, but how? Was he injured or did he have a self-inflicted accident?

Ten minutes later, Dominique stepped into the waiting area with a dark, intense expression. "Carlos, come with me."

He struggled to keep up with her along the corridor. They rode an elevator, passed another waiting room and settled in a large, open-plan office. Nurses sat at their desks, concentrating on their own work.

She looked behind her. "Sorry, I couldn't get anything more private."

"What happened, Dominique?"

"Your father was attacked after a home invasion. He suffered a head injury. The surgeon had to stop the internal bleeding and reduce pressure on the brain. He's in recovery at the moment, and you should be able to see him shortly. The surgeon will come speak to you within the next hour."

Carlos swallowed, the room around him spinning. His heart raced as he gripped the phone. "Will he be okay? What happened exactly?"

"I don't know the details, Carlos. It's a wait and see situation. It was a random robbery, but the police will be in touch." She cleared her throat. "Oh, another thing. While your father was still conscious, he mentioned his brother, Pedro. I assume he wants to speak to him?"

Carlos sensed bile in his throat and needed to desperately talk to his father. Why would he mention Pedro? "They're estranged, but he might want to sort things out with him. I hope he doesn't think he's going to die."

Oh, hell, the times he was rude to his father. The times he never visited, and the times he'd forgotten his birthday. Would he ever have the chance to explain how he loved him in spite of growing distant over the years? They'd both been afraid to express their feelings, and now it could be too late.

"I have to go for a walk, Dominique. I'll be back." He strode along the corridor and headed downstairs to the exit. He needed a breath of fresh air. He found a bench and sat, watching birds flying overhead. Taking out his phone, he placed a call to Pedro but it went straight to voicemail. He left a message.

Carlos called Blanca again, but only reached her voicemail. His chest tightened. Where was she? She would normally answer her phone, especially after finishing work.

He again resolved not to jump to conclusions. He would try again shortly.

He called Isabela, who answered on the second ring.

"Hey, Carlos. What's up?"

"Is Blanca with you?"

"No, she went home about an hour ago. Why?"

He gasped. "I've been trying to ring her, but she's not answering. Was she going straight home?"

"As far as I know, she was. You sound panicked."

"My father's in the hospital and I wanted to let her know." He explained the incident and ended the call. He closed his eyes and took calming breaths. There had to be an explanation for this, but as his father had been attacked and Blanca wasn't answering her phone, he couldn't help but think the worst.

***

Carlos rotated his neck to get the kinks out as he walked to his car in the hospital car park underground. His father had been sleeping post-surgery and was currently stable. The surgeon mentioned he would recover well, and get home care once he left the hospital. He was grateful it wasn't much worse, but who could do this?

He headed to the spot where he thought he had left his car, but another car was in its place. His eyes roamed in the deserted car park until he found his car, ten metres away. Had he forgotten where he had left it? Shaking his head, thinking he was tired from lack of sleep, he entered his car and started the motor when he caught a flash behind him. Before he had a chance to do anything, he felt the prick of a needle in his shoulder. Everything stopped.

CHAPTER 58
EXPLOITATION

Blanca pushed open the front door, expecting her aunt and uncle to greet her as they usually did. It was too quiet. She called their names with no response. In the kitchen, she found a note in her aunt's scrawl, telling her they were meeting friends for dinner.

It was for the best, given she needed to view the contents of the USB drive from Pedro's filing cabinet. Sitting on the couch in the living room, she set the laptop on the coffee table and inserted the USB.

She saw a list of files that bore women's names. Opening one, named Catalina, she sat to watch a video. It was a footage of a strange man looking out at her for several seconds, until it shifted to a naked girl lying on a bed, appearing drowsy. Blanca guessed she was about fifteen years old.

The man turned and slapped her face a few times. "Wake up, bitch. Wake up! We're about to have us some fun."

Oh, God! What the hell is this? Blanca's hair stood on end and she felt chilled to the bone.

The remainder of the video showed the man having sex with the teenage girl, who was obviously drug-affected. She fought back nausea and dizziness as she steeled herself. She could do this.

Blanca opened other files. Sure enough, they were all videos of teenage girls having sex with much older men. But the next one shook her to the core, her body frozen as she stared at a tall man with a bald spot. He was having rough sex with a girl, moaning as he was ripping her apart physically and emotionally. The girl was clearly drug-affected. Her mind took her back to that room where she was kidnapped. The tall man giving her pills. The man with the dimple on his chin. The one grooming her for sex.

It was Fernando Paes, the Governor.

She took a calming breath and closed her eyes to ground herself. She was out of that room and no one could ever hurt her again. She focused on her current surroundings.

Steeling herself, she clicked on another file, which hardly surprised her, knowing Pedro had slept with a young girl. This one showed Pedro having sex with Antonia. She didn't appear to be drugged, and looked like she was enjoying herself.

Blanca wanted to vomit at the next video that popped up by itself. It depicted Pedro and Antonia discussing how she recruited other young girls to blackmail men. But they weren't only blackmailing men: the videos would be sold to the highest bidder.

Blanca's head ached, thinking how these immoral, stupid men wanted sex with these girls, but kept it hidden for obvious reasons. These videos were still sold, most likely on the dark web, out of the prying, public eyes or the police watchdogs.

She had to take this sensitive data to the police. She replayed the last video of Antonia and Pedro when a thought occurred to her. Pedro didn't appear to be aware he was being recorded, so did Antonia use the recording as leverage? Was the story about her accident even true? *Christ! The leather jacket.* Wasn't it the same one she spotted in the favela home all those years ago? The same jacket he wore in his office? It couldn't be. Many people wore leather jackets.

The doorbell jolted her. Through the window, she saw a car she didn't recognise. Before opening the door, she closed the videos and put the USB between two books on a high shelf in her wardrobe. She'd back up the files on her computer later.

With trepidation, she opened the door. *Jose.* An uneasy sense ran up her spine but she didn't know why. She stepped outside. "Why are you here, Jose?" Was Jose involved in all this with his father, or was he innocent?

He looked over his shoulder then faced her. "You need to go home, Blanca. It's not safe for you here."

She swallowed. Was he innocent, but knew what was going on, or was this a threat? "Why not?"

Jose's eyes darkened and his hands fidgeted. "Take my word for it and leave. Please."

Blanca shook her head. "Unless you tell me why, I'm not going anywhere." She couldn't tell him about the USB in case this was a trick.

Her phone rang, but she ignored it. Jose had to tell her why she wasn't safe. Did Pedro know she'd taken his USB? Should she leave earlier for Spain?

He pushed past her into the house. Blanca followed, panic rising in her chest. She looked at her phone to see it was Carlos who had called a few times. She decided to call him later, after she determined whether Jose could be trusted.

"I'm locking this door," Jose said, locking it and turning to her. "What do you know, Blanca?"

She shrugged. "About what?"

He leaned into her face. "You better damn well tell me what the fuck you know, or you're a dead woman."

She backed away towards her bedroom, but he pulled her by the arm and threw her roughly to the couch. "Are you threatening me?" He shook his head, his eyes darkening. "Why are you doing this, Jose?" Blanca stared at the phone in her hand. She could call Carlos and get help. What if her aunt and uncle returned? She couldn't subject them to this mess she got herself in.

Jose's face contorted. "You're in too fucking deep and you have to leave. I'll help you pack, and then I can take you to a safe house until you can get a flight home. It's not too far from here, so hurry." He joined her on the couch, where she saw him adjust a switchblade tucked into his sock.

Blanca cleared her throat. "How do I know I can trust you, Jose? For all I know, you're in on this with..."

He scoffed. "My father, right? You were going to say his name, weren't you?"

She ignored him and stood up. "I'm perfectly capable of doing things on my own."

His hands shook. "Listen, I was the anonymous caller to the police when you were kidnapped all those years ago. I knew what my father was doing and I was too scared to stop it. Now, I'm going to bring him down. I can't take it anymore. I've been scared for too long."

Was he telling the truth? The doorbell rang.

Jose looked through the window. "It's Juan. What is he doing here?"

Blanca clenched her fists and her heart raced. She remembered the sticky note, but could she play him? "Oh, Christ! I think he might be working with your father. He wanted help with a gallery showing for Carlos's mother's photography."

"Shit! He most likely wants to destroy evidence. Don't answer the door."

"If I don't answer it, he'll get suspicious and think we're on to him. My car's parked outside so he'll know I'm home." She paused. Again, Blanca doubted Jose. For all she knew, the safe house could be a lure to her death. But then again, what if Juan wanted to tie up loose ends? She had a feeling Juan was involved. She might be better off with Jose than Juan. "Do you know Juan?"

"I've met him a few times. I'll talk to him." Jose unlocked the door. "Hey, Juan. Blanca's not home at the moment. She's gone in to work today. I had to pick up an article she wrote here, so she gave me a key. I'll get her to ring you or you can go to her work."

Juan grinned. "Hey, Jose. I wanted to get Blanca's help on selecting the right photos for the gallery. The photos are at my rented home. I couldn't get in touch with Carlos. His phone is switched off. We have to get it done today, given the deadline." He looked past Jose, into the house.

Jose leaned back. "As I said, she's not home right now. I'll give her the message."

"But her car's here. I saw her driving it at the gallery."

"Isabela picked her up so she left her car here. Why don't you go to her office?"

"I'd be happy to wait with you," Juan answered.

How can I trust anything Juan says when he has instructions to destroy photos? Blanca fretted. *These might be Carlos's photos or his mother's photos. Did these photos contain visual evidence?*

Jose shook his head. "I don't think so. Goodbye, Juan." He began to close the door, but before he could lock it, Juan pushed the door, slamming it into Jose's face, and burst into the house.

Jose fell onto the floor, gasping. "Run, Blanca! Run!"

Her feet felt frozen to the ground as she thought about the USB. He would most likely look for it. She had to save the evidence for the sake of the girls.

Jose got to his feet and swung a fist at Juan, who ducked and swung his own punch in Jose's face. Blanca shoved him hard to the floor, where Juan pulled out a gun from his pocket and aimed it at them. "Stay away or I'll shoot." With his free hand, he punched Jose until he collapsed unconscious. Then he turned to Blanca. "Where's the USB?"

Blanca shrugged. "I have no idea what you're talking about."

"Get me the damn USB or we'll wait for your family to get home and I'll shoot them."

Blanca nodded. "Fine. I'll go get it." He followed her to the bedroom when his phone buzzed. He retrieved it from his back pocket. "Okay, boss. See you soon." He turned to Blanca. "You're going to write a note to your family and get your bag. Remember, I have the gun."

"What should I to say in the note?"

"Tell them you've decided to go on a trip to America before you head back to Spain, then let me read it. Get your suitcase and your purse and give me your mobile phone."

After he checked the note and her bag, he pointed the gun to her face. "I want you to drag Jose to the car and I will put him in the boot. But if you try to escape, I will shoot Jose and then come after you."

"Why are you doing this, Juan? Please, don't."

Juan scoffed, waving his gun. "I have the gun, so do as I say or I will shoot you and your family. Now, do it!" He opened the door, scanned the surrounding area and pushed open the door while keeping the gun pointed on Blanca.

Blanca put her arms underneath Jose's and dragged him to the back of Juan's car. She panted, watching Juan shove Jose into the boot, the gun loose in his hand.

He handed her duct tape. "Now, I want you to use this to tie up his legs and wrists together. I will help, but like I said, if you try to escape, I will shoot him."

Blanca nodded. "Fine." She had no way out of this, but could make the binds on his wrists loose.

***

Juan kept his gun trained on Blanca to force her to drive his car to a house that looked abandoned in a rough part of north Rio. As she stepped out of the car onto the cobbled path, bile rose in her throat. The house was in the middle of a deserted, grassy area and she had no idea exactly where they were. What was he going to do to her? Did he plan to kill her?

215

Juan opened up the boot and hefted Jose outside. "Drag him to the door." He swung open a creaking, broken gate, and Blanca dragged Jose down an uneven and cracked pathway towards a rickety screen door. Dead brush, a tall pile of dirt, loose stones and wilting plants lined the front yard as an uneasy sensation tingled in her lower back.

"You had to go ruin everything, didn't you? You could've returned to Spain and you'd be none the wiser," said Juan.

He pointed the gun on her as Blanca opened up the screen door with its broken mesh, then opened a scratched and cracked wooden door. She tightened the hold on her bag strap as Juan dragged Jose into a dingy kitchen.

"Move Jose to the living room."

She hugged her body tight as she watched Juan's eyes twitch, his body trembling as if he was cold. "Why are you doing this to me, Juan?" Her body chilled, her feet frozen in place.

"I have my orders, Blanca. Nothing personal."

She felt sick as she realised he was the one who had attacked her at Carlos's party. "You tried to rape me. It was you."

He nodded. "You needed to be taught a lesson, then Carlos had to smash open the door. I almost had you. You couldn't stay out of it, could you? I did enjoy our kiss, though." Juan again pointed the handgun at her face, but his hands were quivering. "Give me your bag. I'm sorry, but I have to do this. It's bigger than both of us now. I don't know if I can wait for Pedro anymore. I'll give him the USB as it only implicates Pedro, not me. But you're a threat to me and you have to go. I can't lose my privileges or go to prison."

"I won't say anything, Juan. Please." Her eyes blurred as she stared down the barrel of the gun. She was going to die.

CHAPTER 59
ON THE EDGE

Carlos touched the side of his head, and felt excruciating pain. Where was he? His head spun as he lurched forward, then back. He realized he was in the back of a car. Oh, Christ! He turned his mind back to the hospital, where he was in the underground car park. Someone jabbed him from behind. He was out, so he didn't see who had injected him with a tranquiliser. But he knew whose car he was lying in.

He wondered about Blanca, too, and hoped to god she was safe. The fact he wasn't able to reach her made him sick to the stomach.

He realised his hands were duct-taped behind him. As he rose to a sitting position, wincing at the dizziness and pain in his wrists, he confronted his attacker in the driver's seat. "Why are you involved in all this, Pedro? You're my uncle, for god's sake."

Pedro scoffed behind the wheel. "Blood doesn't stop me from getting what I want: revenge, my dear nephew."

Carlos struggled to move, but his body felt like lead. "Revenge for what?"

"I had to hurt your father because he confronted me about you wanting to know about your mother. He knew too much, and he had my bank records. I had to get them back. The information would have eventually led to me. It would have alerted the police." He glanced over his shoulder. "I loved your mother, and he took her away from me. She was mine to begin with and he stole the love of my life. I met her in school. She was my girlfriend until he stole her from me then, and again, when she went back to him."

Carlos flinched. "So you had an affair with my mother while she was married?"

"Yes, we did. We loved each other, but she had so much guilt. She felt she needed to stay with Nicolas. She broke my heart even when we were a couple before she left me for your father. He always had her, not me."

He had to play nice and might get out of this alive. "I am sure my father didn't mean to hurt you. They loved each other." A thought occurred to him and he wanted to wring his uncle's neck. "So you killed my mother because she returned to my father? That's not love, it's obsession."

Pedro shook his head as he overtook a car and made a left turn into a street of an abandoned home. Where was he taking him? "I would never kill her. What happened to her was an accident." Carlos waited. "I only wanted her to let her guard down after she broke it off with me a second time. She claimed to still love your father." He scoffed. "With me she got excitement and fun, but with your father, she got boredom and felt trapped. I could have given her the best life."

Carlos wanted to vomit. "What the hell did you do to my mother?"

"I drugged her, but I must've got the dosage wrong. She went into cardiac arrest and I called an ambulance, but it was too late. She had high potassium levels in her blood."

He couldn't believe his own uncle would kill his mother, even if it was accidental. "Did you at least try to revive her?" Pedro didn't respond, so he had his answer. He claimed it was an accident when he had the power to save her. How he'd like to get his hands around his neck and squeeze the damn life out of him. "You expect me to believe my mother's death was an accident when you've kidnapped me, and most likely will kill me. When does this end, Pedro?"

His uncle chuckled. "It never ends, because I have a few policemen in my pocket and I plan to be the richest man in Brazil. This business of mine has made me a large sum, but I crave more. I earned the right to live a life free of stress, and I have the ultimate power in this country. I am God to you."

Carlos felt sick. "You're doing this purely for money? Exploiting young women and recording them on video as leverage on the men who have to pay you. You're sick, and playing with people's lives. No amount of money is worth that."

"Oh, shut up! Once I have Blanca taken care of, you'll keep your mouth shut or I will make sure I kill your father this time. I am not concerned enough about family to prevent having someone killed. That includes you, too." He chuckled. "Do not think your father was innocent in all this. He participated in his sexual exploits with a young girl, and he was forced to pay me to keep it quiet. Otherwise, I would have told the world."

Carlos's blood ran cold, his vision blurred. He remembered the account his father paid, to the amount of 60,000 Brazilian Real in 2006. "Are you telling me he paid Possessao Valioso, which was a dummy corporation that you organised?"

He nodded. "Oh, yes. Clever to think we were a reputable publishing company's subsidiary when it helped us to fund the young girls' business."

"So you expect me to keep quiet about all this? Was Antonia's so-called accident a real accident, or did you kill her?"

Pedro nodded as he parked by the kerb. "I planned to kill her after she tried to double-cross me. She recorded our conversation about recruiting girls without my knowing, but when she tricked Jose and he killed her accidentally, that fixed it for me. I didn't need to kill her. The accident made my job easier."

Pedro got out and opened the car's back door. "Get up." He pushed Carlos through an overgrown garden to a weathered door.

Carlos noticed another car in the driveway, but didn't recognise it. What was Pedro planning if not to kill him?

With Pedro behind him, he entered the abandoned house as the sun was setting. In the failing light, they walked towards an empty, unfurnished room. Jose lay on the carpet, tied up, but one of his fingers moved. They passed another room until reaching the kitchen. He stopped breathing when he saw Blanca, head bowed, averting her eyes from the gun pointed in her face. "Noooo. No, please, Juan. Don't hurt her." The curator's eye twitched and the gun in his hand shook.

Pedro closed the door behind him. "Do you have the USB, Juan?"

Surely they would let them go after getting the USB? If he wasn't scared for his life, Carlos would have appreciated the kitchen's cosiness with its high-backed chairs around a round table and a small window overlooking the view of the grassland. A cabinet stood close to a tall fridge with bottles of empty beer cans.

Juan nodded. "I have it."

Pedro put up his hand. "Do not shoot yet. Where is the USB?"

Juan's eyes wandered. "It's in my side pocket."

Pedro pushed Carlos into Juan's view as he rummaged into Juan's side pocket and took out a USB stick. His eyes lit up. He nodded in Juan's direction. "Shoot her."

Carlos's breath stopped. "No, Juan. Let's talk about this. Please. You're not a killer."

Pedro glared at Juan. "Shoot the bitch or I will. Do it."

A crashing sound reverberated in his ears when someone shuffled towards Juan and knocked him off his feet. It was Jose, carrying a switchblade. Juan dropped his gun, which slid across the floor underneath the cabinet. Juan swung his fists into Jose's face over and over, making him drop the knife. It glided across the floor as Blanca pushed Juan into the fridge.

Carlos used his shoulder to shove Pedro into the cabinet. The older man fell to the floor but recovered quickly as he leapt back on to his feet, and punched Carlos in the face. He saw stars.

Blanca grabbed the switchblade and waved it around. "Let Carlos go, Pedro or I won't hesitate to use this."

"Two can play at that game, dear Blanca." Pedro drew a knife from his back pocket and raised it over Carlos, when Blanca rushed forward and stabbed him hard in the leg. He fell to the floor, holding his leg and moaning in pain as blood seeped through it.

"Where's the gun, Carlos?" Blanca asked.

He pointed. "I saw it go underneath the cabinet."

Blanca turned to look for the gun underneath the cabinet. Juan snaked his hand beneath the cabinet and snatched it away from her. Carlos fell on him and wrestled for it until the gun went off.

He froze at the sound. Had he been shot? Blood dripped onto the floor from Juan's leg. Jose's face was bruised and bloodied, and Pedro's eyes drooped.

Blanca found a tea towel and wrapped it tightly around Juan's leg to stop the bleeding. He whimpered with his head bowed. She grabbed another tea towel and did the same for Pedro's leg, most likely wanting him to suffer in jail rather than bleed out and die.

She moved over to Carlos and cut the duct tape to untie him. He rubbed his hands, watching over Juan who remained cowering in the corner. He pulled the USB stick and phone from

Pedro's pocket. "Why are you helping the bastards?" he asked. "They wanted to kill you."

"I don't think he would've killed me, Carlos. Juan's not the type." She sighed. "As for Pedro, he should rot in jail."

"We need to call the police, Blanca."

She found a towel in the bathroom and soaked it under the tap. As she tended to Jose's wounds, Carlos made the call and explained their situation.

"Thanks for saving me, Jose. For the second time," Blanca said.

Jose nodded as he sat on the floor, letting Blanca wipe blood from his wounds. "Thanks for making the binds on my wrist loose. I managed to get myself free and then reached for my knife to cut the rope." He smiled reassuringly. "I should've done more for you, Blanca, but my father's a dangerous man. He's had me living in fear for years. He threatened my mother to keep me from saying anything." He turned to Carlos. "I'm sorry, man."

Carlos got up from the ground. "I get it, Jose. He attacked my father, too. He meant those words. You had to protect your family. But what I don't get is why Juan here was involved." He turned to Juan. "Why?"

Juan averted his eyes. "I got greedy, but murder is not what I signed up for, Carlos. You have to believe I didn't want to kill Blanca."

Carlos glared. "No, you would have. And you exploit young girls and threaten their lives. You're sick and you deserve to go to jail, you bastard." Juan bowed his head and remained silent.

As they waited for the police to show up, Blanca turned to Pedro. "You're a bastard and a sociopath, Pedro, and I hope you rot in prison. The evidence will make sure you live out the rest of your life there."

"Bitch," Pedro said as his eyes opened and closed. His hand was pressed against his wound, but the bastard would survive.

She glared at Pedro. "You will not die from this wound. You deserve to stay alive so you can suffer in prison."

Carlos stared at the USB. "What's on this?" Blanca explained.

Jose leaned forward and watched his father whose eyes were closing. "I wish I could face up to him, Blanca. I didn't want you writing about the favelas because it would make you an easy target. But also because I didn't want the truth about Antonia's death to come out. I'm sorry if I scared you."

Blanca sighed. "You were young, Jose, and your father brainwashed you and threatened your mother's life. You have nothing to be ashamed of. I am so grateful you saved me twice. How can I ever repay you?"

Jose smiled. "Live your life, Blanca. We have enough evidence to implicate the bastard and the men who worked for him. We can stop this."

Carlos heard the sirens, and a minute later officers, detectives, and a forensics team burst into the house. It was finally over.

EPILOGUE—JULY
ONE MONTH LATER

The day before leaving for Madrid, Blanca rubbed her arms against the cooler weather when she rang Ana's doorbell. The least she could do was put this secret behind her and ensure Ana was aware of the situation—more than what was splashed across the newspapers and Internet.

Ana swung open the door, her eyes bloodshot. "Blanca, what a lovely surprise. I thought you'd already left for Spain. Come in."

Blanca smiled. In the living room, the TV played a news program. "I'm going back home tomorrow, and thought I'd say goodbye. How have you been after what happened with Pedro?"

Ana sat beside Blanca on the sofa side by side. "It's been difficult, but I'm not surprised. My ex-husband was always more concerned about money than his family and friends. That evil ex-girlfriend of his will go to prison, and Pedro will answer to justice, too. Even that ringleader, Governor Fernando Paes."

Blanca again shuddered at the idea that Fernando was the one shoving the pills into her mouth. He was the one in charge. "I imagine you'll be back for the trial?"

Blanca shrugged. "Most likely, but the judge will let me know. After the judge issued a warrant, the police found a lot of evidence in Pedro's home and office. He is going away for a long time."

"He'll pay for what he did to you, Blanca." She gave her a reassuring smile then scoffed. "The bastard!" They sat in silence for a few minutes. "Would you like a cup of tea?"

Blanca nodded. "I'd love one."

As Ana went to the kitchen, Blanca pondered everything she'd been through in the past six months. She'd been stalked, attacked, and kidnapped twice. She was keen to get back to Spain and be done with these videos and poverty-stricken people who would sell their souls for money. She'd be safer in her home country. But her heart tugged at the thought of missing Carlos. She loved him, but how could they make it work?

Ana returned with a tray bearing steaming mugs of tea and sweet biscuits on a plate. She set down the tray and picked up her own mug. "Please help yourself to sugar and milk."

Blanca added sugar and milk to her tea, then sipped it slowly, the heat burning her lips. "Have you seen Jose? He stayed quiet to protect you."

Ana tilted her head. "I have seen him, and we're closer than ever. He's apologised for what happened to you and how he covered it up, but I understand why. He wants to take more responsibility over his life." She clenched her hands. "I'm sorry, Blanca, for everything that happened to you, recently and when you were a child. I am glad you got out safely."

Blanca smiled. "Thanks, Ana. I'll be fine once I'm back home. I can leave the past behind and live my life."

Ana put down her tea. "The work you did for those girls was commendable, Blanca. You've made a huge contribution towards more government funding into the favelas and stopping some of these groups from exploiting young women. Thank you." She peered into the distance. "What I don't understand is why Pedro accepted you into the company if you were a threat to their business?"

Blanca cleared her throat. "Apparently, he was ordered to hire me by Governor Paes, so they could keep an eye on me here. Pedro wasn't happy about it, but he didn't have the final say."

"They are pure evil," said Ana.

Blanca straightened her shoulders. "They were watching me from the first time I set foot on Brazilian soil at the airport. Elina sent me a note warning me against the favelas, already seeing me as a threat to their business. No doubt on Pedro and Fernando's orders."

Ana trembled. "At least the federal and state police continue to follow leads and will investigate these cases for many years to come," Ana said.

Blanca nodded. "Those involved in my kidnapping have been arrested and I can go back to Spain."

After chatting about her family, friends, and work, Blanca rose. "I'd better get back and finish packing. I wish you well, Ana. Thank you for inviting me into your home again."

Ana pulled Blanca into an embrace. "You take care. I want you to enjoy your life after what you suffered."

She grinned. "You take care of yourself, Ana.

"You too, Blanca." Ana closed the door behind her.

***

Blanca raised a toast at her aunt and uncle's house as she lifted her wine glass later that day. "To friends and family." Her eyes scanned the loved ones gathered: her aunt and uncle, Carlos, and Isabela. They clinked glasses and drank.

"What's the latest with Pedro and his minions?" Aunt Maria asked.

Carlos replied, his eyes dark. "There'll be a trial in the next few months. The police have a lot of evidence against Pedro and those who worked for him. He had a few young girls and men killed after they threatened to report him. The bastard should hopefully get a lifetime in prison. They have witness statements by those who worked for him and they even arrested Fernando Paes, the Governor. Apparently, he was the one giving orders and helping Pedro get away with a lot of things, and vice versa."

Uncle Julio interrupted. "Did you find out about your mother, Carlos? Was she murdered or was it an accident?"

Blanca could see his effort to fight back tears. "Pedro drugged her and claimed to have given her too high a dose of a medication, which increased her potassium levels. He had an affair with her while my parents were separated, but she left him to go back to my father. They were even a couple in school before she left him to be with my father."

Blanca touched his shoulder. "I'm sorry, Carlos. It's still hard to process that."

Tears streamed down his cheek. "The bastard claimed to love her, but he killed her. I never would've thought he was so evil."

Isabela threaded a hand through her hair. "That's tough, Carlos, but he had all of us fooled. Who would've known?" She stared at Carlos curiously. "What I don't understand is how he implicated Elina and helped you to save Blanca when she was kidnapped. Why?"

Carlos fixed his gaze on her. "The police said that Pedro thought Blanca would back off on the stories of exploitation and Antonia's death. He didn't have plans to hurt her then, but Elina

225

wanted to get rid of her anyway. They fought and he had to get rid of Elina."

Blanca put down her fork. "What a twist, though. We thought the bastard was innocent when Elina almost killed him. I imagine it's an ongoing investigation, covering the child exploitation. At least our part in it is all over now, Carlos." She gasped. "Oh, my goodness! Why didn't I remember earlier?" She watched the blank faces. "I remember on my first trip here how Pedro was exchanging money with someone in a restaurant. It was Rodrigo, and they were arguing. My guess is that Pedro must've told him about his sister, Carolina who died."

Isabela shook her head. "I am so glad he's going away for a long time. You don't need to focus your energies on that bastard anymore, girl." She leaned back in her seat. "To think I trusted Juan and all this time he was using part of his gallery as a sex studio. Disgusting." She turned to Blanca. "I cannot believe he tried to hurt you twice, Blanca. I'm sorry for introducing you to him. So sorry." She bowed her head. "I have known him since college, and over the years, he had this greedy streak about him, but I chose to ignore it. He was always hungry for more. If he got more, he wanted even more. It was never enough." She shook her head. "I should've used my intuition when I had doubts about his morals, especially when a few times I caught him staring at young girls. Even when he got arrested for stealing an expensive car and showed no remorse. I should have known then he was bad news. At the time I was in love with him. We had a brief relationship back in college, but he cheated on me. I thought he would change his ways and be nicer to people. Then he got into the gallery business and I thought he'd changed and become responsible, but it was all a lie, a front. I am so sorry, guys."

Blanca cleared her throat. "It's not your fault, Isabela. He fooled all of us, and he was your friend. At least in the end, I knew he didn't want to kill me. He could have shot me, but he didn't. Even though Jose intervened, I still think Juan wouldn't have hurt me. But it's no excuse for his sordid actions." She faced, Carlos who squeezed her hand.

"I nearly lost you there, Blanca. Thank god Jose managed to get out of his binds and attack Juan," Carlos said. "It was clever to keep a switchblade in his sock."

Blanca beamed at him then turned towards her aunt. "Aunty, you look much better now. What's changed?"

She grinned from ear to ear. "Your advice about having therapy has helped me so much, Blanca. I feel so much lighter after talking about my childhood."

Her heart warmed. "You deserve it. At least now I feel ready to return home. Thank you both."

After the meal was done and dishes washed, Isabela hugged Blanca. "I have to go, but I'll see you at the airport tomorrow. We have to keep in touch, girl."

"Of course, Isabela. You can come visit me in Spain one day soon."

"I'll hold you to that." She kissed Carlos, and her aunt and uncle goodbye.

Carlos walked Isabela outside with Blanca. When Isabela drove off, Carlos leaned against his own car, staring at Blanca with deep hunger. He opened his arms for her. "Can we talk?"

"Of course." She entered his embrace. The scent of lemon and musk filled his senses, and she yearned for him.

His eyes pierced into her own and he took a deep breath. "Blanca, I love you and I understand you need to go back to Spain, but I can't bear to not see you ever again."

She tilted her head. "I feel the same, but how can this work?"

His eyes shone. "I've already developed business leads for my new business, and Luiz will be working with me." He took a breath.

"What are you saying?"

"Blanca, I love the way you open your heart to people. I love how you know the right things to say. I love how you bite your bottom lip when you're nervous, and I love the way your body feels against mine. I eat, sleep, and breathe you into my world all the time, and I cannot live without you. I love you so much, Blanca and I want us to be together forever."

Blanca's heart raced. Her body felt lighter. "We live in two different countries, Carlos. On two different continents. How are we supposed to have a long-distance relationship?"

He nodded. "I've re-established my old business contacts in Spain." He braced himself and played with the small of her back. "I'm coming to Spain with you. Only if you'll have me. What do you say?"

Blanca's heart warmed and her back tingled with joy. "Oh, Carlos. Are you sure? Won't you miss your friends and family here? It's a huge step."

"My father's recovering well and I can come back to visit with him, family, and friends. I've already started my own photography business and freelance work. Luiz will take care of the Brazil side of the business and I'll start up an office in Spain. I'll be offering photography training, consult with magazines, and get investors. I have options, Blanca, and I want us to eventually get married. What do you think?"

Her eyes became wet as she pressed her lips together. "I'd love that too, Carlos." Tears kept pouring down her face and he wiped them away with a delicate finger. "I love you too, Carlos. So much more than I can express."

"You are forever mine, Blanca." He leaned forward and kissed her tenderly on the lips and they held each other for a long time before going back inside the house.

Check out Book 2 in the Women Of Strength Series, *Shadows Of The Past* which features Blanca's friend, Daniela in Madrid, Spain: http://mybook.to/shadowsofthepast

ABOUT THE AUTHOR

Lucy Appadoo is a prolific reader and author of the Friends In Crisis Series. After a childhood spent reading and imagining escapist worlds, Lucy has put her imagination into stories. Her work as a rehabilitation counsellor, and former work as a counsellor in private practice, have led to an interest in writing inspirational stories about authentic, driven women who manage adversity with strength and heart. She writes in the genres of romantic suspense/thrillers with significant life themes and contemporary romance.

Lucy's interests include researching crime stories and news to inspire her work, watching crime thrillers and suspenseful movies, travel, exercising, reading for entertainment or knowledge, meditation, and spending time with friends and family. She also appreciates her Italian background and culture, which has inspired her to write imaginative stories about her parents' childhoods, leading to The Italian Family Series novels.

Reviews are gold to authors and allow Lucy to keep writing. If you enjoyed this book, please consider leaving a review on Amazon.

Check out Lucy's website and sign up for a FREE romantic suspense novel here: www.lucyappadooauthor.com.au

ALSO BY LUCY APPADOO

<u>FICTION</u>

Women Of Strength Series – Romantic Suspense/Thriller
Shadows Of The Past (Book 2) -
http://mybook.to/shadowsofthepast

The Friends In Crisis Series - Romantic Suspense/Thriller
Haunted By The Past (Book 1) -
http://mybook.to/HauntedbythePast
Twisted Obsession (Book 2) -
http://mybook.to/TwistedObsession
Web Of Lies (Book 3) - http://mybook.to/EbookWebOfLies

The Hearts Series - Romantic Suspense
Rising Hearts (Book 1) - http://mybook.to/RisingHearts
Forbidden Hearts (Book 2) -
http://mybook.to/ForbiddenHearts
Kindred Hearts - (Book 3) - http://mybook.to/kindredhearts
Broken Hearts (prequel to Forbidden Hearts) -
http://mybook.to/Bhearts

Short Story Thrillers
Evening Interrupted - http://mybook.to/Eveninginterrupted
The Dreamcatcher - http://viewbook.at/Thedreamcatcher
Red Flags - http://mybook.to/Redflags
Collection of Short Story Thrillers -
http://mybook.to/collectionofthrillers

The Italian Family Series - Coming of Age Family Drama/Romance
A New Life - http://mybook.to/ANewLife
The Beauty of Tears - http://mybook.to/TheBeautyofTears
Dancing in the Rain - http://mybook.to/dancingintheRain
A Life By Design - http://mybook.to/Alifebydesign

<u>NON-FICTION</u>

Grief & Loss
Moving Beyond Grief - How To Shift From Grief & Loss to
Joy & Peace - http://mybook.to/MovingBeyondGrief

Stress Management & Anxiety
Holistic Spiritual and Mental Health - Building Resilience and
Creativity by Conquering Anxiety and Managing Stress -
http://mybook.to/Holistichealth

Career Guidance
Your Holistic Career Path - Create Career Change, Satisfaction,
and Work/Life Balance -
http://mybook.to/YourHolisticCareerPath

Journal and Record Of Books You've Read (with Quotes)
Readers' Journal - http://mybook.to/ReadersJournal